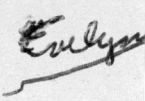

"Sexy." She grinned. "Every woman's idea of the perfect man."

Instead of smiling back at her teasing as he'd been slowly learning to do, Dylan frowned. "I have to tell you, honey, I'm anything but perfect."

She kissed his jaw where it had gone hard. "You're too modest," she murmured, and then would have kissed him again, but his hands were suddenly framing her face, holding her still.

"Arden, what if I told you there were things in my past, things I did that make my gut crawl just thinking about them? What would you say?"

It was a small thing that warned her, the tiniest flattening of a muscle, the flick of his blunt eyelashes, but Arden knew raw shame when she saw it.

Something to do with the death of his friend, she suspected. Something that had driven him into exile and his heart into hiding...

Dear Reader,

As always, it's difficult to know where to begin when talking about this month's Intimate Moments lineup. We've got so many wonderful books and authors that I guess the only place to start is at the beginning, with Kathleen Creighton's American Hero title, *A Wanted Man*. And I promise you'll want Mike Lanagan for yourself once you start reading this exciting story about reporter-on-the-run Mike and farmer Lucy Brown, the woman who thinks he's just a drifter but takes him in anyway. Like Lucy, you'll take him right into your heart and never let him go.

In *No Easy Way Out*, Paula Detmer Riggs gives us a hero with a dark secret and a heroine with a long memory. *Days Gone By* is the newest from Sally Tyler Hayes, a second-chance story with an irresistible six-year-old in the middle. Kim Cates makes her first appearance in the line with *Uncertain Angels*, the story of a right-side-of-the-tracks woman who finds herself challenged by a do-gooder in black leather. In *For the Love of a Child*, Catherine Palmer brings together a once-married couple and the voiceless boy whom heroine Lilia Eden hopes to adopt. When little Colin finally speaks, you'll have tears in your eyes. Finally, there's *Rancher's Choice*, by Kylie Brant, whom you met as our 1992 Premiere author. I think you'll agree that this book is a fitting follow-up to her smashing debut.

Enjoy!

Leslie Wainger
Senior Editor and Editorial Coordinator

Please address questions and book requests to:
Reader Service
U.S.: P.O. Box 1325, Buffalo, NY 14269
Canadian: P.O. Box 1050, Niagara Falls, Ont. L2E 7G7

NO EASY WAY OUT

Paula Detmer Riggs

Published by Silhouette Books New York
America's Publisher of Contemporary Romance

If you purchased this book without a cover you should be aware that this book is stolen property. It was reported as "unsold and destroyed" to the publisher, and neither the author nor the publisher has received any payment for this "stripped book."

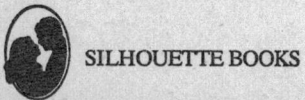 

SILHOUETTE BOOKS

ISBN 0-373-07548-0

NO EASY WAY OUT

Copyright © 1994 by Paula Detmer Riggs

All rights reserved. Except for use in any review, the reproduction or utilization of this work in whole or in part in any form by any electronic, mechanical or other means, now known or hereafter invented, including xerography, photocopying and recording, or in any information storage or retrieval system, is forbidden without the written permission of the editorial office, Silhouette Books, 300 East 42nd Street, New York, NY 10017 U.S.A.

All characters in this book have no existence outside the imagination of the author and have no relation whatsoever to anyone bearing the same name or names. They are not even distantly inspired by any individual known or unknown to the author, and all incidents are pure invention.

This edition published by arrangement with Harlequin Enterprises B. V.

® and TM are trademarks of Harlequin Enterprises B. V., used under license. Trademarks indicated with ® are registered in the United States Patent and Trademark Office, the Canadian Trade Marks Office and in other countries.

Printed in U.S.A.

Books by Paula Detmer Riggs

Silhouette Intimate Moments

Beautiful Dreamer #183
Fantasy Man #226
Suspicious Minds #250
Desperate Measures #283
Full Circle #303
Tender Offer #314
A Lasting Promise #344
Forgotten Dream #364
Paroled! #440
Firebrand #481
Once Upon a Wedding #524
No Easy Way Out #548

Silhouette Desire

Rough Passage #633
A Man of Honor #744

Silhouette Books

Silhouette Summer Sizzlers 1992
"Night of the Dark Moon"

PAULA DETMER RIGGS

discovers material for her writing in her varied life experiences. During her first five years of marriage to a naval officer, she lived in nineteen different locations on the West Coast, gaining familiarity with places as diverse as San Diego and Seattle. While working at a historical site in San Diego, she wrote, directed and narrated fashion shows and became fascinated with the early history of California.

She writes romances because "I think we all need an escape from the high-tech pressures that face us every day, and I believe in happy endings. Isn't that why we keep trying, in spite of all the roadblocks and disappointments along the way?"

Chapter 1

The problem was a woman.

This one had jerked Dr. Dylan Kincade from warm blankets into a cold February dawn and sent him careening down the slick mountain road toward town.

It was a brutal Oregon morning, with the wind from the north and a layer of ice frozen under the new snow. Overnight, visibility had lowered to mere feet instead of miles.

Studded tires helped his Bronco hold the road, and the hot coffee he kept ready twenty-four hours a day helped him stay awake, but the hard, fast jolt of caffeine did little to improve his foul mood.

He figured five, maybe six inches of snow had hit the valley floor since he'd fallen into bed around two, and he hated snow.

The hospital parking lot was nearly empty. The night staff was thinner than usual because of the flu epidemic racing through the county. Even his partner, Neil Christopher, was down with a particularly vicious case, which was why Dylan had been on call for the ER every night for a week and a half.

His body craved sleep, and his mind desperately needed to shut down for more than a few minutes at a time. Living like a monk was bad enough. Living like a monk without sleep was worse. Both had been forced on him. Neither seemed likely to change.

He parked in his space near the emergency-room entrance and left the key in the ignition. It was a habit he'd picked up a few months after he'd traded his old West Virginia license and his Boston driving habits for those of Oregon, mostly because it saved valuable minutes when he had to go out on a call.

There'd been a time when he'd worried about theft. Now he knew better. Just about everyone in Myrtle and a considerable number of county residents knew that the dusty blue wagon with the bashed-in right fender and the cracked windshield belonged to Doc Kincade.

After nine years, seven of which were spent as the only doctor within a forty-five-mile radius, he was as much a fixture in the valley as the towering trees that gave the town its name.

Folks even joked behind his back that he'd taken root the same as those trees. Never leaving the county, rarely taking more than a few hours off during any one week, never receiving a letter or even a phone call that wasn't related to a patient or the practice of medicine.

He'd heard all the gossip and ignored it. His reasons for staying in Myrtle were personal and none of anyone else's business, just like the reason he was still a bachelor at thirty-eight and destined to remain that way for the rest of his life.

As he paused to stamp the snow from his boots, he watched one of the town's two police cars cruising slowly through the lot. Myrtle had little crime. What it had was usually related to an overindulgence in alcohol or a lapse in good sense.

No Easy Way Out

The car stopped, and Dylan recognized the driver as Chief of Police Harvey Delacroix. Two weeks ago yesterday, the chief had severely wrenched his back while trying to break up a fight between two mill workers at the Proud Elk Saloon.

Dylan had been on call that night, too. Sometime between delivering a baby and patching up a trucker whose rig had hit black ice and slid like an out of control locomotive into a thicket of blackberries, he'd slapped Harvey in traction.

Spying him in front of the door, Harvey rolled down the window. "Hey, Doc, out early, ain't ya?"

"Thought I told you to stay off work until next week," Dylan called back over the idling engine.

"You sure did, that's a fact, but two of my guys called in sick this morning. Flu. 'Sides, I been goin' nuts cooped up in the house, just me 'n' the kids while AnnMay was workin' day shift at the mill."

"At least stay out of the Proud Elk for another few days."

"Gotcha! At least when I'm on duty."

Chuckling good-naturedly, Harvey drew his head inside the squad car again. Dylan didn't blame him. The temperature was hovering near zero, and the blowing snow made it seem colder.

As soon as he stepped into the building, his face began to burn from the instant fifty-degree temperature change. One of these days it had to stop snowing, he thought. Even in the Cascades.

Leoda Hooven was the nurse in charge of Myrtle General Hospital's three-cubicle emergency room. A fey, exceptionally competent woman in her late thirties, she worked nights in order to have time during the day for her five children and their mill-worker father.

"Lousy morning for a hot appendix," he called when she looked up from the chart she was annotating.

Greeting him with a grin, she seemed as chipper as usual, which only made his bad mood worse. No one should be able to smile at 5:00 a.m. He never bothered to try.

"From the looks of that white stuff in your hair, I'd say it was still snowing out there," she said with one of her unflappable looks.

She, like most of the old-timers, was used to Doc's black moods. Most put them down to overwork. A few wondered aloud if he had come to Myrtle to escape a painful past with memories that sometimes hurt.

Dylan knew about the curiosity and the speculation; he was even amused by the talk on the rare occasions when he was feeling mellow.

A doctor learned anatomy from textbooks and dissections. A knowledge of human nature came from on-the-job training, and he'd always been a fast learner. People would always be curious, and they would always gossip.

"Yep. Still snowing *and* blowing like a son of a gun." He shucked his heavy war-surplus jacket and fur-lined gloves, ran a careless hand through his dripping hair and checked the clock. Twenty-eight minutes door-to-door.

He'd made it in seventeen once, but the patient, a heart-attack victim, had been dead by the time he'd skidded into the lot. The dent in the fender was a bleak reminder that the town treasury couldn't be stretched far enough to support a full-time ER doctor.

"I had to shovel my way out of the driveway again, which is why I'm late."

Hooven was clearly unsympathetic. "It's good exercise. Keeps your heart healthy."

He stretched his aching back. "Gives me a pain in the rear, you mean."

Hooven took a starched white coat from a nearby closet and held it while he slipped into it. His name was stitched over the pocket that held his stethoscope. He had an identical setup in his office, and in the small state-funded prenatal clinic in a neighboring town where he spent one day each week.

Hooven brushed an imaginary speck of dirt from his lapel. A born mother, she loved to cluck over him whenever he'd stand still long enough. He pretended to be annoyed, but secretly he enjoyed the small gestures of caring from someone he respected.

"I didn't hear any heavy breathing over the phone, so I figured I didn't interrupt anything too hot at your place," she teased.

"Heck yes, you interrupted something!" he told her with an irritable growl that was rapidly becoming permanent. "The first good night's sleep I'd had in two weeks."

Hooven clucked her disapproval. A determined matchmaker, she never missed an opportunity to rag him for his monastic ways.

"You forgot to shave," she said, handing him a steaming mug of coffee with one hand and the patient's intake history with the other.

"Didn't forget," Dylan grumbled between sips. A quick check of Hooven's no-nonsense notes on the chart told him that he'd probably have a scalpel in his hand within an hour or so. "Been thinking of growing a beard."

Hooven eyed his stubbled chin dubiously, then slowly shook her head. "Forget it. You already look more like a lumberjack than a typical small town GP. A beard would make you too scary-looking, especially to someone who doesn't know you."

He'd never thought of himself as scary. Cowardly yes, but not scary. "Not too many people don't know me around here."

"This one doesn't." Hooven glanced toward cubicle one. "She's new in town."

He grunted his surprise. Poor as it was, and with the highest unemployment numbers in the state, Myrtle County rarely attracted new residents. The few who did come weren't likely to be a threat. Nevertheless, he knew all too well how easily his carefully reconstructed life could be blown apart by a chance meeting with the wrong person.

Knowing that kept him all but imprisoned in the valley and even more wary of any kind of publicity or notoriety. If the self-imposed exile sometimes chafed, no one knew it but him.

As casually as he could, he flipped to the admitting form. Arden Crawford, age thirty-four. Divorced. Owner and publisher of the Myrtle *Free Press*.

Surprise thudded low in his gut, followed by a moment of disgust. He'd known his share of reporters. He'd even respected one or two—until they'd turned their lust for blood on him.

From what he'd gathered from the snatches of gossip he'd overheard during the last few months, this one was the worst of the lot. More Hollywood bimbo than reporter. A starlet masquerading as a newswoman.

Anchorwoman, they'd called her in L.A. or whatever California city she'd hailed from.

Nice-looking and single, his office receptionist had mentioned more than once. Ripe as a virgin, some of the guys in the Proud Elk had said a time or two. But with the kind of look in her eye that warned a guy not to make a pass, unless he wanted to spend a couple days walking bent over.

According to Jack Fitz, the agent who'd sold her the *Press* after the former owner, Cliff Winston, had been killed in a hunting accident, she'd left L.A. because she wanted to raise her daughter in a small town.

More likely the kid had gotten herself into some kind of trouble in the city, Dylan thought to himself.

He hadn't met Ms. Crawford. In fact, he'd gone out of his way to keep from meeting her. Even arranged for Neil to take her and her daughter on as new patients when Ms. Crawford had called for a get-acquainted appointment.

So where was Neil now? he thought sourly. Probably curled up next to a nice cozy hot-water bottle, enjoying an X-rated dream, that's where. He nearly laughed aloud.

When fate decided to blindside a man, it damn near knocked off his head.

Glancing up, he saw Hooven watching him expectantly.

"Who's on call for the OR?"

Hooven consulted a clipboard. "Swanson, Crenshaw and McHenry."

"Hope they've had a good night's sleep. Looks like we're going to need them."

"Want me to make the calls?"

He hesitated. All three lived within the town limits, not more than five minutes away, even on a bad night. He was the only staff member who had chosen to isolate himself in a cabin on an undeveloped road.

"Not yet. Let's see how our famous patient is doing first." He tried to keep the cynicism in his head out of his voice. The look Hooven shot him told him that he'd failed.

"How long have you lived here now?" she asked impatiently. "Six, seven years?"

He was immediately on guard. Questions about his past made him edgy. "Nine. Why?"

"Because you've been here long enough to know that nobody stays famous in Myrtle for long. Folks here don't much care where you've been or what you've done as much as they care about the cut of your character while you're here."

He didn't believe that for a minute, but there was no use saying so. "Maybe folks here aren't impressed with Arden Crawford's fame, but I lay odds *she* is."

"She seemed real sweet to me," Hooven protested with her usual good humor. "Not at all hoity-toity."

"Yeah, but you like everyone."

"So do you. You just don't want anyone to know that there's a purring house cat under that tiger exterior."

He answered that with the silence it deserved.

Like or dislike had nothing to do with it. He knew Crawford's type all too well. He'd even loved a woman like that once, in another lifetime. Worse, he'd trusted her without reservation.

And then, when he'd needed her most, she'd lined up against him, just like everyone else he'd cared about in those days. Unlike everyone else, however, she'd been the one to deliver him bound and gagged and all but convicted to the lynch mob.

"Let's see how reasonable she is when I palpate her abdomen," he muttered, more to himself than Hooven.

"Cubicle one," Hooven reminded him, as though Myrtle General was as busy as Mass General, where he'd done his residency.

"Thanks," he said dryly.

Dylan tossed down the last of his coffee, straightened his shoulders and headed toward the first cubicle.

As soon as he pushed aside the drape and entered the crowded space, the petite woman curled into a miserable ball under the sheet, opened her eyes and managed a wan smile.

Even with her hair tumbled and her face pinched with pain, she was pretty enough to make a man suck in his gut and wonder if he should have taken time to scrape off his morning stubble.

"Dr. Kincade, I presume?" she murmured with an attempt at a smile.

"Yes, ma'am."

Her gaze found his face and held long enough for him to notice that she had liquid brown eyes and eyelashes so thick they seemed too heavy for the lids.

So this was the sophisticated newswoman he'd heard so much about. Only something was wrong. The hair he'd imagined to be blond and lacquered was a rich chocolate brown, with what appeared to be a mind of its own when it came to style. And her nose was decidedly crooked.

Her skin was white, and her eyes were rimmed with dark shadows, which didn't surprise him. She didn't appear to be wearing any makeup, which did.

"In case no one has told you the name of the rat who got you out of bed so early, I'm Arden Crawford."

"Yes, ma'am. And in case no one has told you why you get me, Dr. Christopher is down with the latest bug."

"So I understand, the poor baby. He works too hard."

Yeah, didn't they all? "I'll tell him you said so."

He drew the curtain behind him and stepped to the table. The space between partitions was close enough to be claustrophobic for a man of his size, but it had never seemed all that intimate—until now.

"You look very familiar," she murmured through what was obviously intense pain. "I... Have we met? Perhaps in L.A.?"

"Never been there."

He didn't ask her if she'd been to Boston—or Palm Beach or Newport or anywhere else where they might have crossed paths. He didn't have to, because he was dead certain they'd never met. He would have remembered a face like hers, even if he'd forgotten the name.

Her eyes stayed on his. Intelligent eyes, measuring him through the pain. His unease magnified.

"This is a lousy way to start the day, Doctor," she offered with another gallant attempt at a smile. "For both of us."

"I can think of better, yeah."

In spite of his deliberate reserve, she gave off subtle signals of friendliness that seemed genuine. And her manner was anything but haughty.

His guard rose higher. Snootiness he could handle in a woman, even welcome. Warmth tinged with humor gave him more trouble.

He took a moment to glance over her medical history, looking for potential complications in what was supposed to be an uncomplicated procedure.

"The last time you were in a hospital was to deliver your daughter?"

"Yes, in a town called Puebla in southern Mexico."

He noted that complications had left her with a limited chance of ever conceiving again without surgical intervention, something she'd apparently seen no need to undergo.

"Was May the last time you had a complete physical?"

"Yes. Dr. Christopher insisted on examining both my daughter and me before he would take us on as patients."

He made no comment. The policy had started with him when he'd discovered too many of his emergency patients had put routine care at the very bottom of a long list of things they couldn't afford. He'd also instigated a policy of bartering for those who had no money to pay for such care.

No doubt Ms. Crawford had simply written a check, he thought. With a suitably trendy monogrammed fountain pen, of course. He put aside the chart and let his gaze roam her pallid face.

"I understand you're worried about appendicitis."

"Not worried. Mad as hell!"

"Hurts, does it?"

"Like a dozen tiny men running around inside with spiked shoes. I tried to ignore the little monsters until I got the paper to bed last night, but I confess I had to give up when I found myself fighting a terrible urge to curl up under the press and suck my thumb."

Pain blurred her voice and tightened her jaw, but her eyes were laughing. At herself, mostly, he figured, wondering if that was her way of dealing with trouble.

He reached for her wrist and checked her pulse, which was galloping erratically beneath his fingertips. Her skin was far too warm to the touch, her bones so delicate he worried about hurting her.

"Try to relax, Ms. Crawford. It's easier that way."

"Arden, please," she murmured somewhat breathlessly. "And yes, I know I'm an idiot for ignoring all those nasty warning signs I've been having for a month now."

"Why don't you tell me what nasty signs you're talking about?" he suggested when he discovered her studying his face with a disturbing intensity in spite of her obvious discomfort.

"Uh, okay. Sure." Distracted, she frowned, furrowing the smooth brow beneath the disordered silk of her bangs.

"I guess I mean the pain, mostly," she admitted after a moment's thought. "It was just a twinge in the beginning, nothing to worry about, I thought, but lately it's been, umm, harder to ignore."

"Is it always a sharp pain?"

"Not always. In the beginning it was more of a dull thudding."

"No spiked shoes?"

She grinned. "No, more like leprechauns wearing sneakers. The last few days the little men and the leprechauns have been taking turns trying to kick their way out."

She licked her dry lips, her tongue darting in and out like that of a little girl searching for the last remnants of an ice-cream cone. She had a lovely mouth—sensuous, perfectly formed for kissing, the kind that didn't need paint to attract a man's attention.

Furious with himself for noticing something so trivial and unrelated to her present condition, he took refuge in routine.

"Let's see if we can isolate the worst of the discomfort, okay?" His smile was benign, his manner reassuring.

"If you say so, but try not to make those leprechauns madder than they already are."

"I'll do my best to sneak up on them."

Keeping his eyes on hers, he drew the sheet down to her thighs. As he'd expected, Hooven had outfitted the patient in a paper gown, open in the front. At the moment, the gown was securely closed.

Focusing on correct diagnostic procedure, he laid two fingers against the lower right quadrant of her abdomen and pressed gently. She gasped and closed her eyes.

"Right on target," she murmured with a wisp of apology in her tone.

"Sorry." He probed lower until he found the end of the rigidity. "Any nausea? Vomiting?"

"Some."

"Which?

"Both." She drew a shaky breath, then scowled. "I was right, wasn't I? Appendicitis."

"Looks that way, yes." He drew the sheet to her slender shoulders, his touch as impersonal as he could make it. At the moment he was a doctor, not a man who was finding himself drawn to a woman.

"Will you have to operate?"

He hesitated. Some patients needed bad news sugarcoated. He had a feeling Arden Crawford could take hers straight.

"In my opinion, yes. I could order some tests to make absolutely certain, but from the things you've told me, the delay could be risky."

"Damn! I was afraid of that." She tried to sit up, but instantly abandoned the idea when pain knifed deeper into her right side. "How risky?" she managed after regaining her composure.

"Extremely risky. Your appendix could burst, in which case peritonitis could develop."

"Like it did with Houdini and Valentino," she murmured. "And Jean Harlow, I think." She looked shaken, but game. "They all died, you know."

"Yeah, well, times were different then," he said as he retrieved his stethoscope from the pocket of his coat. "And I wasn't the attending physician for any of them."

She processed that with a small sigh tinged with amusement. Her eyes tipped up at the outer corners when she smiled, reminding him of a Siamese kitten he'd rescued from the knotted branches of his grandfather's favorite oak tree on the Cape.

Scarcely more than big, frightened eyes in a matted ball of fur, the tiny creature had grown into a sleek, elegant aristocrat who had hissed and scratched whenever he'd tried to show her affection.

"How long will I be in the hospital?"

"Depends." He stared at the wall opposite while he warmed the end of the stethoscope with his palm and fingers.

"Can you give me your best estimate?"

"Two days, if all goes well."

"Which it will, of course."

"That's the plan." He fitted the earpieces to his ears with one hand and drew back the sheet once more with the other.

"Positive thinking. I like that."

She kept her gaze fixed intently on his, as though she needed to know him better before entrusting him with her life. "In fact, I did a piece once on the effect of the mind on the body. It's amazing what power a thought has, isn't it? Even to changing a person's entire life."

"Perhaps."

He knew better than most that some things couldn't be changed, no matter how positive the thinking or how powerful the regret.

"Take a deep breath, please," he ordered as he slipped his hand between the flaps of the gown. Her skin was creamy and seemingly untouched by the sun, although he spied a small cluster of freckles just to the left of her sternum.

She cooperated by giving him two deep breaths, each one causing her small chest to rise and fall under the sheet. Her heart was strong, the beat accelerated beyond normal range, but regular.

"Cough, please."

This time cooperation hurt, causing her eyes to grow round and dark, and her mouth to tighten.

"Sorry," he muttered. "Almost done."

"Good," she murmured, closing her eyes. Her skin seemed to have paled even more, and the shadows now half-hidden by her lashes seemed translucent.

He had a hunch her fever had spiked higher than the 103 recorded on the chart earlier. As soon as he was finished, he would have Hooven run another temp while he drew blood for typing and cross-matching.

He slipped the stethoscope from his ears and replaced the sheet. "Anyone we can call for you?"

She frowned in concentration. "I guess you'd better call Ed Harkness, my press foreman. Someone should tell Stephanie, my daughter, and he's like a favorite uncle."

"How old is your daughter?"

"She's nearly ten, but very mature for her age—or so she's constantly reminding me."

"Where is she now?"

"At home, in bed." She winced at a sudden twinge only she could feel, then went on more slowly. "We live in an apartment above the paper. One of the pressmen stayed with her while Eddie brought me here, and Eddie promised to look in on her from time to time when he got back."

Twin lines formed between her eyebrows, and her eyes clouded. "Nettie MacGregor is the one I usually ask to sit with her. Steffie has just started piano lessons with her. I expect you know her."

His nod was curt. Impersonal. "I'll take care of it."

Her relief was nearly palpable. "I'd be very grateful, Doctor."

Nettie was also a retired librarian and the town's resident philosopher, known for her kindness to lost souls and worthy causes. She was also as close a friend as Dylan dared allow himself these days.

"Some folks think she's a bit too outspoken for these parts," he said.

"Not me. I like to see things riled up. Makes for a more interesting lead."

The smile in his mind vanished. For a moment he'd forgotten that she was a reporter. He wouldn't forget again.

"Do you have children, Dr. Kincade?"

"None I know about." He reached behind him for the tongue depressor Hooven had ready on the towel-draped tray. "Open, please, and say 'ah' for me."

She made a face. "Aargh."

When he'd finished examining her mouth and throat, she asked, "Would you like to have some someday?"

"At the moment it doesn't seem to be up to me." He tossed the depressor into the waste bin.

"You're not married, I take it?"

"No."

"Divorced?"

"No."

"Widowed?"

"No."

"Ah, so you're gay?"

The assumption didn't surprise him. He'd heard it before. A bachelor of thirty-eight who didn't chase women, or even pretend to, was always suspect.

"No, Ms. Crawford, I am not. What I am is your doctor, a doctor who's working against a time limit."

"Oops, sorry. I was prying, wasn't I?"

He shrugged. "You're a reporter. That's your job."

The lymph nodes felt normal. The thyroid appeared to be of acceptable size. Her skin was soft to the touch. Supple.

Glancing down, he found her studying him again, a pinched look of curiosity on her face. He visualized the dozens of muscles under her smooth skin, even catalogued them in his mind so that he wouldn't dwell on the provocative curve of her lips.

"Don't you like children?"

Ms. Crawford was not only nosy, but also tenacious, it seemed.

"I can take 'em or leave 'em." If he said that enough, he might just believe it, he thought cynically.

"And it's none of my business, right?"

He aborted a rude remark by reminding himself that she was a patient in his care at the moment and not a reporter.

At the same time, Hooven pulled aside the drape to ask, "Should I make those calls now?"

He nodded. "Alert the lab, also. We'll need her blood work stat."

"Will do." Hooven took time to shoot the patient a reassuring grin before withdrawing. "Don't worry, Ms. Crawford, you're in good hands with Doc Kincade."

"Nice lady," Arden murmured when the nurse had left. "Very sensitive to feelings." Her gaze came back to his face and held. "And so, I think, are you, Doc."

Dylan scowled. He wasn't, and he didn't pretend to be. What he was was a scientist. A mechanic who used a scalpel. And that was all he wanted to be.

"Hooven will have papers for you to sign," he said tonelessly. "In the meantime, I'll give Nettie MacGregor a call."

The OR was as icy as a meat locker and almost as cheerless. Everywhere Arden looked, she saw some kind of beeping, blinking appliance, most of which were hooked up to her in vastly uncomfortable places.

"I don't have time to be sick," she muttered, and then wondered if her mouth was really filled with cotton.

The OR technician in green surgical scrubs chuckled behind her disposable mask. Arden could only see the woman's brown eyes, and she noticed that they were more somber than smiling.

"Sorry, Ms. Crawford, but the folks down at the *Press* will just have to get the paper out without you for once."

"That's what they said," she murmured, "but I think they just wanted to get rid of me."

She struggled to clear her head from the first wisps of drug-induced stupor, but her eyelids were getting heavier by the second and her arms and legs seemed caught in cloying, clammy cement.

She closed her eyes, only for a second or two. Everything would be fine, she told herself slowly, distinctly. Steffie was safe and cared for; she even seemed excited at the prospect of playing hostess to Mrs. Mac.

Ed was dealing with things at the paper. "Don't worry about a thing," he'd boomed at her before he'd left. "Me 'n' the others will handle it."

A smile wavered in her mind. He knew very well that he was asking the impossible. Worry had become a way of life for her. About Steffie and her adjustment to small-town living after a lifetime in the city. About the paper's voracious appetite for money. About doors shut and doors opened. About a craggy-faced, sad-eyed doctor.

Dr. Kincade had often been the prime topic of conversation over coffee and bagels when she and four or five other women met on alternate Thursdays for breakfast.

She hadn't listened all that carefully, but a few things had stuck in her mind. Like the fact that he was a coal miner's son from West Virginia who'd gone to Harvard on loans and scholarships. And that he'd come to Myrtle to work off one of those loans.

Those were the facts.

The reason he had stayed after his five-year obligation had expired was wide open to conjecture. Love was ruled out. The man rarely dated a woman more than three or four times, and then only platonically.

Professional advancement wasn't even considered. Myrtle was a backwater town, with zero opportunities for the ambitious.

In essence, no one knew for sure.

They did know, however, that most folks forgave him for his reclusive, sometimes bad-tempered ways because he was an outstanding doctor.

And the only general surgeon in the county.

Something snapped next to her head, like a rubber band suddenly let go. Mildly curious, she forced open her eyes and slowly turned her gaze toward the sound. Not a rubber band, she realized after some serious thought. Rubber *gloves,* now held aloft by the same big hands that had examined her so gently less than an hour earlier.

Drifting on a blissful cloud, she was mildly surprised to find herself imagining those same big hands pressing her close to his roomy chest, and his mouth whispering soothing words between slow, moist kisses.

Prince Charming in surgical scrubs, she thought with a drowsy smile. A prince with an aura of melancholy about him and deep-set blue eyes touched with gray ice in the depths.

And a face that was far too aggressively molded to be considered more than marginally handsome in L.A., where gorgeous men were as plentiful as sunshine, and just about as monotonous.

Her ex-husband, Mike, had been one of those. A man temperamentally unable to pass up an opportunity to test his finely honed skill at seduction.

They'd met on the UCLA campus where she'd been majoring in journalism and he'd been a guest lecturer. Their marriage had lasted a little longer than four years. Four years of living out of suitcases while Mike's shadow grew longer and more smothering, and her own ambitions to follow her publisher father's footsteps began to shrivel and die.

And then, one night, Mike had walked into their cramped, sweltering apartment in the Yucatán, told her that he had accepted an offer to work in Europe and started packing. He didn't intend to take her or two-year-old Steffie with him.

It hadn't been an ugly divorce. Practically painless, in fact, when compared to some of the horror stories recounted by friends and colleagues. Or so she'd told everyone who'd asked.

They were still friends of a sort. He sent presents for all the major holidays and visited Steffie whenever he could squeeze in the time between assignments.

No Easy Way Out

Steffie understood. In L.A., all but one of her private-school friends had come from broken homes. More than a few had gone through multiple step-parents.

At least she had avoided that trap, she told herself as she watched everyone scurry to do Dr. Kincade's bidding, just as she'd once done Mike's.

"Ouch." Arden winced as the nurse-anesthesiologist inserted a needle into the back of her hand.

"This will ease some of the discomfort." The woman's tone was somewhat muffled, but Arden caught a note of sympathy.

"Thank you," she murmured, concentrating fiercely to keep her voice from slurring.

The last time she'd felt this awful she'd been in labor. Then, however, there had been the anticipation of seeing her baby for the first time to sustain her when the pain approached the unbearable stage.

Now she had little to cling to but the rich, calming cadence of Dr. Kincade's voice as he explained the surgery to her in slow, careful detail.

He was an interesting man, she decided when he'd finished. Not quite as friendly as his younger partner, nor as easy to like. But she found herself trusting him completely.

"Ready when you are, Dylan," a voice said crisply.

Shivering suddenly, she considered asking for a blanket, but the effort necessary to summon speech suddenly seemed beyond her.

"Ready, Ms. Crawford?"

Kincade's deep murmur accompanied a sudden feeling of warmth. Opening her eyes, she discovered that he had tucked a heated blanket around her shoulders. "Huh?" Eyelids fluttering, she dragged her gaze upward, past a wide male chest swathed in faded surgical scrubs and shoulders that seemed to spread forever, to a rugged masculine face partially hidden by a sparkling white mask and a snug-fitting cap.

She worked at summoning a grateful smile, but he turned away before she felt her mouth moving.

"How's she doing?" Muffled by his surgical mask, his voice carried the barest hint of hard Yankee vowels, leading her to think about the firm, unsmiling mouth beneath the white gauze.

Another voice answered, similarly muffled and also male. "Stable and prepped."

Prince Charming nodded. "Fine. Put her under."

Arden blinked, but the deep-set blue eyes looking down at hers didn't waver.

"Wait! I... Are you sure this is a good idea?"

His eyes crinkled, but they didn't smile. "I have to tell you, Ms. Crawford, this is a heck of a time to request a second opinion."

"Umm, where is it... exactly, that you went to medical school?" Her usually crisp tone and precise diction had been replaced by a wobbly whisper.

"Harvard. Did both my internship and residency at Mass General. The certificates to prove it are hanging on the wall in my office."

His voice reminded her of grit and smoke and a room full of hard men and cheap whiskey, and yet his manner was courtly, even refined, as though he'd been brought up surrounded by Chippendale and Renoirs and linen napkins tucked into heavy silver rings instead of dirty coal mines and austere poverty.

Her curiosity stirred, deepened. "Uh... did you get good grades?"

"I could show you my Phi Beta key, but I left it in my other set of scrubs."

That voice, those eyes... They *had* met. Somewhere.

Frowning, she struggled to bring the images to the surface. Sensations came and went, leaving her more and more certain, more and more excited.

No Easy Way Out

Yes, that was the feeling struggling to escape the drug-induced lethargy. Excitement—the kind that accompanied the smell of an important story.

"I'm going to put you under now, Arden," another voice murmured. It took her a moment to recognize the anesthesiologist. "You'll feel another little prick."

Arden tried to frame the words that would stop her, but found her numb lips refusing to cooperate.

"Count backward from one hundred for me, okay, Arden?"

She felt herself slipping away, her mind slowly, inexorably shutting down. With the last of her will, she forced her gaze to find those blue eyes that seemed so familiar.

"Just relax, Arden. I won't let anything happen to you." It was his voice. Oddly... familiar.

"Wait," she whispered through lips that all but refused to move. Before he had answered, the blackness closed in.

Chapter 2

Tired as he was, Dylan couldn't sleep.

Every time he'd closed his eyes, he'd seen the startled look on Arden Crawford's face an instant before she'd gone under. As though she'd suddenly recalled when or where she might have seen him before.

He put it down to pre-op paranoia. Or perhaps a dream. Tomorrow she wouldn't remember a thing. Anesthesia had that effect on the brain.

Dylan shifted restlessly, his cords rasping against the leather couch. The house was silent, except for the Mozart serenata coming from his CD. Even the wind had stopped howling.

He had gotten used to living alone. Sometimes he even liked it. Sometimes, like tonight, he didn't.

Bone tired, he lifted his glass to his lips, only to discover he'd drunk all but the melted water from the cubes. He wanted bourbon this time instead of the ginger ale that was his usual drink, but he was still on call.

No matter how much he needed the numbness alcohol could bring, he wouldn't touch a drop when there was a chance he might be called out to treat a patient. Alcohol, drugs, sometimes even exhaustion, took the necessary edge from a surgeon's concentration.

He didn't have many rules that couldn't be bent in a good cause. But that was one of them. Allowing himself the normal pleasures of a wife and a family was another.

Deciding to settle for ice cream instead, he heaved his tired body from the sagging cushion and made his way through the dimly lit living room to the kitchen.

The carton of triple chocolate delight was half-empty, not nearly enough to warrant dirtying a dish. Grabbing a spoon from the drawer, he dug in, letting the cold lump melt on his tongue. The taste was rich and silky, a rare turn-on for a man who rationed his pleasures in carefully thought-out ways.

Spooning another bite into his mouth, he wandered over to the double doors leading to the rear deck. Beyond the rough plank railing, his prized thicket of myrtle trees loomed dark against a slightly lighter sky.

The snow had diminished to an occasional flurry. Above the tree line, the stars twinkled like cold beacon lights.

Propping a shoulder against the jamb, he worked at relaxing the knots between his shoulders. Since a hotter-than-normal shower hadn't touched the tension, he gave a thought to trying Ms. Crawford's positive thinking.

Maybe it worked for her. Probably did.

Him, he believed in disciplining his mind. A man didn't want what his mind told him he couldn't have.

He moved restlessly, thinking of the years it had taken to turn himself into the unfeeling machine he knew he seemed to be to the majority of his patients.

A machine who wore the doctor's white coat and carried a stethoscope. A doctor. A man to be respected, if not liked.

Or loved.

From someplace far below him came the low keening wail of his nearest neighbor's elkhound. He felt for the poor creature, penned in a small, barren kennel for hours on end.

Suddenly aware of the carton in his hand, he glanced down at the half-melted ice cream. He bought gallons of the stuff. Even ate it for breakfast when the mood struck him.

It was a poor substitute for the pleasure of a woman's welcoming smile at the end of a brutal day or the warmth of a wife's soft fanny tucked against him in the night, but it was all he had.

Arden came to slowly, feeling her way. She was in the recovery room, still attached to an IV, and queasy from the anesthetic.

The pain in her side had shifted from piercing to dull, but it still hurt too much to move. Turning only her head, she saw two other beds, both of which were empty.

A thin, middle-aged woman she assumed was a nurse was sitting at a desk near the door, writing rapidly on a chart. Hers, Arden suspected, and then closed her eyes.

The room was spinning crazily, like the colored glass in a kaleidoscope, and her insides felt hollow. She had no inkling of time. Nor, she discovered, did she care.

Snuggling her cheek more deeply into her pillow, she let herself drift toward sleep. The worst was over. Her infected appendix was gone, and she was on the mend.

A day, two at the most, and she'd be back with Steffie and the gang at the paper. Back to work, where she belonged. Before she left, however, she must thank Dr. Kincade for his kindness.

A shadow passed over her mind. A wisp of urgent thought that she couldn't quite catch. Something to do with Dr. Dylan Kincade. Something terribly important, perhaps vital. Something she should know... but what?

Before she could put more pieces to the shadowy puzzle, she drifted back into sleep.

No Easy Way Out

* * *

It was light outside when she woke again, this time to find a warm, clearly masculine hand wrapped snugly around her wrist, testing her pulse. A quick readjustment of her line of sight had her gazing into Dr. Kincade's disconcerting blue eyes.

There was an instant connection, like a plug in a socket. She felt it. She knew he did, too. She'd felt it yesterday, in the small white cubicle of the emergency room.

It happened that way sometimes when she met someone for the first time, especially with a person she found particularly intriguing or newsworthy, or occasionally, in the case of a particularly virile stranger, attractive.

"Welcome back, Ms. Crawford. How do you feel?"

"Hello," she murmured, and then laughed aloud at the froglike croak she'd produced. At the same instant, she winced at the sudden sizzle of pain in her abdomen.

"Careful," he warned. "You have a selection of my best stitches under that bandage. I'd hate to see you bust 'em wide open."

A quick peek under the sheet revealed a clean hospital gown hiked high enough to reveal a heavy gauze pad neatly taped to her belly. Glancing up again, she found him watching her impassively.

His hair was slightly damp, and he smelled like soap, suggesting a recent shower. The white coat she'd come to expect hung open over a soft flannel shirt unbuttoned at the throat to reveal a V of soft, golden chest hair.

The tug came again, stronger this time, and undeniably sexual. She let it come, knowing that her mind had ultimate control over her choices, not her body.

"So... how am I?"

His eyebrows lifted, and she thought she detected an encouraging slant at one corner of his mouth, but the smile she expected never came.

Curiosity was a reporter's curse, or her greatest gift, depending upon a person's point of view. At the moment hers had her wondering what there was in the man that caused him to ration smiles so ruthlessly.

"So far, so good. Your vitals are fine, and other than a low-grade fever, you seem just about normal."

"That means I can go home today, right?"

"Tomorrow, if your temperature has returned to normal."

"How about a compromise?" she proposed in her most persuasive tone. "I'll split the difference with you and stay until tonight."

"Tomorrow morning—if there's no sign of fever."

She caught the faintest hint of hard steel encasing the genially voiced words. So Dr. Kincade had a stubborn side, she thought, amused and stimulated at the same time.

There was nothing she liked better than a good, clean battle of wits, especially when her opponent was so obviously used to getting his own way.

"But you just said I was practically back to normal," she protested with deliberate mildness, "and I feel fine. Terrific, in fact."

It wasn't a bald lie, just a slight stretching of the truth, she told herself firmly. Compared to yesterday, the few aches and pains she was feeling weren't even worth mentioning.

Instead of answering, he wrote something on her chart, the movements of his hand mechanical and swift. He had sturdy hands, she saw, perfect for reproduction by a sculptor's chisel, and meticulously clean, with very short, square nails and lean, capable fingers.

Yesterday his hands had moved over her skin with a doctor's skill and a doctor's detachment. All she'd felt then was a heightening of pain, followed by a ragged fear of the surgery she'd known was inevitable.

Now, however, with the threadbare cuffs of his faded shirt peeking out from the starched white coat and the signs of hard work showing on the tanned hands, she couldn't help seeing him as a man instead of a doctor. A man who was managing to raise her blood pressure without trying.

No Easy Way Out

Glancing up without notice, he caught the direction of her gaze and raised one eyebrow. Hastily she shifted focus to the plain metal stand by the bed.

"Does that phone work?" she asked brightly. "I want to call my daughter at Nettie's before she leaves for school."

"Stephanie won't be there. Nettie took her to the Coffee Cup for breakfast and then they were going to walk to school from there."

Dumbfounded, Arden started to sit up straighter, then changed her mind quickly. His best stitches or no, they pinched when she moved.

"How do you know that?" she asked, her voice revealing only a fraction of the discomfort she was feeling.

"She told me."

A good reporter never assumed; instead, she collated facts and drew logical, well-substantiated conclusions. After that, she checked her facts again.

"Who told you? Nettie?"

"Stephanie."

His mouth didn't seem so hard when he spoke of her daughter, she realized. Almost gentle, in fact. Or was that too a figment of drug-stimulated senses?

"You talked to my daughter?"

"I just said so, didn't I?"

He propped a foot on the lower railing of the bed and leaned the arm holding her chart on his thigh. As he did, she caught a whiff of woods and wind and found herself picturing him on a hiking trail with mud on his boots and sun in his hair. It was a tempting image, one she filed away for another time.

"You're enjoying this, aren't you?" she challenged.

He looked startled, then grunted. "Guess I am, at that."

She had it then, the faintest of smiles playing over that deliberate mouth of his, leading her to believe she'd done something remarkable.

"*When* did you talk to my daughter?"

He checked his strictly utilitarian watch, worn she noticed, with the face on the inside of his wide wrist in the traditional way of the Northwest woodsman.

"Oh, about an hour ago now. And yesterday, of course."

She blinked, giving him another good look at those thick silky eyelashes. "Yesterday? You spoke to my daughter last night?"

"Uh-huh. She and Nettie came about five. After Stephanie's piano lesson."

Deliberately hiding the eyes she seemed to find so interesting, he concentrated on brushing a wrinkle from the blanket with his fingers.

"Oh, and she said to tell you she finally got her recital piece just right. Chopin, I believe it is."

"Okay, let's back up. My daughter came to visit me?"

He found he was enjoying himself. Arden was easy to tease. "Yesterday. We had quite a talk."

"A talk? You and my daughter?:

"Yes."

"About me."

"Uh-huh, and other things, like Nettie's lemon meringue pie... and boys."

Her jaw dropped, and he had to work at keeping a grin from slipping through his usual mask. "Seems she likes one and not the other," he told her solemnly. "I imagine you can guess which is which."

Straightening, he dropped his foot and stretched. He'd been up since five, working on a total of four hours' sleep. He figured he could catch a couple of hours on his office couch before office hours started at noon.

"Did you talk to her before or after she came to my room?"

There it was again, a bulldog's tenacity under the classy elegance. He decided he wouldn't be on the wrong side of a debate with her. "Before."

"Aha."

No Easy Way Out

"And after. We had hot chocolate together in the cafeteria. She likes hers straight, like her mom, she told me. Me, I take mine with plenty of whipped cream."

"Lucky you," she exclaimed with a surreptitious glance at his belly.

Dylan realized he liked the appraisal of those warm brown eyes far too much. Worse than that, he was finding he liked the woman herself, even though he knew all too well that it was risky to let himself like anything about her. "Have the nurse in charge call me at the office if you have any problems. Otherwise, I'll see you tomorrow."

"Wait!" she called as he turned to leave. "What about our compromise?"

He raised both eyebrows and looked at her blankly. "What compromise?"

"You said I could leave tonight."

"Wrong. You said that. I said tomorrow morning—if the signs stay good, and that's what I meant."

Once again she was seeing steel beneath the genial bedside manner. Well, she had some of that herself, she thought as she frowned up at him.

"But, Doctor, you don't understand. Steffie has her first recital tonight—I *have* to be there. She'll be crushed if I'm not."

"No she won't, because she understands exactly what happened to you and why you have to take it easy. I told you we had a talk."

Her cheeks were suddenly flushed, and her eyes took on the fiery light of battle.

"I appreciate your interest, but she is my daughter, and I'm perfectly capable of explaining things to her myself."

"Never said you weren't."

He saluted her with a nod before heading for the door. Staying longer was dangerous. Ms. Crawford was far too easy, too much fun to be around when she got that huffy look on her face.

"Dr. Kincade, you come back here!" she called, then gasped. "Oh, fudge," she muttered in a breathless tone. "See what you made me do."

Dylan reversed course, took just enough time to make sure she hadn't done herself any damage, and then stood over her, his gaze boring into hers.

"*I* didn't make you do anything, Ms. Crawford. But I *am* the guy in charge here who's telling you not to get out of that bed until tomorrow morning for anything but the rest room and a short walk down the hall and back for exercise."

She opened her mouth, but he was on a roll, and it felt good to blow off some of the tension that had been riding him since this woman had come into his world uninvited, and definitely not welcomed. "Now, is that clear, or do you want me to go over it again?"

The flush was still there over her cheekbones, and temper had lit her eyes until they seemed gold.

"I am not a child," she enunciated clearly. "Please don't treat me that way." With each word, her mouth had taken on more of a rebellious, pouty look.

It moved him to answer the challenge of those soft, pouty lips with a hard, swift kiss. But she was his patient, thanks to Christopher's bout with the flu, and he was bound by an oath he considered more binding than any written contract.

Coward that he was, he gave her a quick nod, turned and fled.

"Good work, Ginny. Great! Come on now, give me one more push."

The baby slipped easily into Dylan's hands, full term and seemingly perfect. Red in the face and cute as a pink little bunny, she was already breathing, eager to get on with this brand-new life.

Exultation lifted the ache from his back, and he allowed himself a cocky grin behind the mask. Damn, but it felt good when he pulled off a long shot like this one.

"It's a little girl, just like the ultrasound said. A beauty, too, like her mom."

He glanced over Virginia Grossman's raised knees and gave her a wink. As soon as he was positive the baby was hearty and breathing normally, he placed her on the mother's tummy.

Ginny beamed through tears as she gently rubbed a forefinger over the baby's still-wet crown. Her other hand was tightly clutched in her husband's.

A rough-hewn logger of forty-nine, Ralph Grossman looked stunned, as though he couldn't believe that, after nearly five years of trial and error and a lot of prayer, he was finally a father.

"Ralph and me, we decided to name her Anita," the new mother said, exchanging loving looks with her now flushed and excited husband.

"Anita *Kincade*," he added, his Oregon twang softened by the mask he was wearing. "After the man who made this all possible."

Dylan had to swallow hard before he could thank them. "Believe me, you two are the ones who should take the credit."

The couple had come to him a few months after their wedding, unable to conceive and eager to have a large family. But Ginny had already passed thirty, with a history of miscarriages behind her.

Through the years, he—and they—had tried every method that appeared in the literature, with ultimately disappointing success. Twice Ginny had become pregnant, and twice she'd lost the baby in the first trimester. The couple had been about to give up when he'd come across a new and fairly complex type of surgery that would allow Ginny's malformed ovaries to function more normally.

Unfortunately, most of the doctors skilled in the new procedure were in Europe, although obstetricians in some of the larger medical centers in the States were reporting encouraging success, as well.

A bit of digging had revealed that the waiting lists for these doctors were understandably long. The Grossmans' best chance seemed to lie in Europe, but like virtually all of Dylan's patients, they had limited resources. Travel to Europe was simply out of the question.

After extensively reading up on the procedure to make sure it was within his ability, he sat the couple down and laid out the pros and cons, with special emphasis on the risks, given the fact he'd never handled that kind of surgery before.

Neither Ginny nor Ralph had hesitated. They trusted him, they'd said over and over again. More than anything in the world, they wanted a child. Whatever he thought best, they would do.

Best would have been someone more skilled at the procedure doing the surgery. Taking on that kind of responsibility had scared the hell out of him, but other than her reproductive problems, Ginny was hale and healthy, and he couldn't rationalize *not* giving it a try.

When it had worked and Ginny had conceived three months later, he'd been enormously relieved that he hadn't made a bad mistake. He'd also been almost as ecstatic as the Grossmans themselves.

"As soon as Marcie here gets Anita prettied up, you can have her in your room," he told the new mother, finishing up.

"She's already pretty," Ginny murmured. "The prettiest baby in the world."

"Now, honey, every mama thinks that," her husband chided gently, but his expression said that he absolutely agreed.

"But this one *is*," she maintained, her gaze flowing over her husband's weathered face. "Because you gave her to me."

Too overcome to speak, Ralph leaned forward and kissed his wife's trembling mouth through his mask.

No Easy Way Out

Averting his gaze, Dylan concentrated on his job and did his best to isolate himself from the love flowing between the happy couple. His joy was in his work. It had to be.

Seven returned phone calls and a long, steaming shower later, Dylan was heading toward the room at the end of A-Wing where he expected to find one Ms. Arden Crawford sticking pins in a doll dressed in surgical scrubs.

He planned to make a quick, impersonal examination, then head for the cafeteria and the meat-loaf plate Mrs. Deaver had put into the oven for him before she'd closed up at eight.

It was the third time in a week he'd missed dinner because of some emergency, and his jeans were beginning to bag. A man of his size and metabolism could exist only so long on ice cream and candy bars before it began to take a toll on him.

"Evening, Sal. Any problems tonight?"

Salita Moore had returned to Myrtle from Portland in order to care for her invalid mother. When Trude Moore had passed away last April, Salita had stayed on, practicing her considerable nursing skills at the hospital now, instead of in her mother's ramshackle farmhouse.

"Depends on your definition."

"Why do I think I'm not going to like this?"

He leaned over the counter of the nursing station and filched a chocolate-covered peanut cluster from the open sack he'd spied on the desk. Salita slapped at his hand, but it was too late. The chocolate was already melting in his mouth.

"You're impossible!" she exclaimed, glaring at him.

"Yeah, but lovable," he muttered, crunching on the nuts.

"A grumpy old grizzly is more like it." She snatched up the sack just in time to keep him from grabbing one more.

He swallowed the candy, savoring the last of the chocolate taste for a moment before he grew serious again. "Okay, what's going on that I should know about?"

"Your post-op in sixteen-A, Ms. Crawford..."

Before he could stop himself, he was picturing sparking gold flecks in deep brown eyes and a soft, pouting mouth.

"Giving you trouble, is she?"

Salita glanced over her shoulder, a disapproving look crossing her face. "Not now, she isn't. Checked herself out right after dinner."

He muttered a word Salita politely ignored. "I tried to call you, but you were in the middle of the Grossman delivery."

She grinned briefly. Ginny and Ralph were members of her church and were regarded as generous neighbors by most who knew them. Everyone had been rooting for them.

"Not that it would have done any good if you'd been here, however," she went on, her disapproval showing strongly, "because Ms. Crawford is a very determined lady."

"More like mule-headed obstinate," he muttered, already mapping out in his head the things he intended to say to the woman when he saw her again.

He moved to the rack that held the charts and extracted Crawford's. It was now flagged in red, indicating an unauthorized discharge.

"Can't help liking her, though, polite and nice like she is," Salita said grudgingly. "Especially when she smiles at a person the way she does."

"TV training," he muttered, scanning the last few notations. "Doesn't mean a thing."

"I expect not, although she doesn't come close to putting on airs the way folks thought she would."

He grunted something noncommittal. Crawford's personal attributes were none of his affair. Her physical well-being was.

"She asked me a lot of questions about you."

He froze. "Did she?"

"Uh-huh. Wanted to know when you'd come here to Myrtle County, and all about your background. Seemed to think it was unusual for a coal miner's kid from West Virginia to sound like such a Yankee highbrow."

"I see."

"'Course, I'd never noticed the way you talk all that much until she mentioned it, but come to think of it, she's right. You do talk sorta Eastern, especially when you get tired. Guess it's her TV training and all that gives her such a good ear."

"Guess so."

He closed the chart with a snap and shoved it back into the appropriate slot. He made sure nothing showed on his face, but his blood was pumping harder than it should, and his stomach was twisted into a painful knot.

"They'll be bringing Ginny up soon. Keep a close watch on her for me, okay? Make sure she doesn't walk out, too."

"Watch it, buster," Sal shot back, pretending to be affronted. "I'm not responsible if your patients take a powder on you. It's your lack of charm that does it, 'specially with the ladies."

"Charm doesn't cure patients." He was turning to leave when the pager on his belt buzzed.

"There goes dinner," he muttered as he took the phone Salita silently held out to him and punched out the number of the message center.

"What've you got, Gracie?" he asked when the familiar voice came on the line.

"Well, hello, Dylan. That was quick!"

"Lucky me, you got me between patients."

The elderly operator laughed. Over the years, the two of them had developed a bantering phone rapport that both enjoyed.

"Someone just called from the elementary school, you know, where Nettie is holding one of her recitals? One of your patients has fainted in the auditorium."

Alarmed, he glanced toward sixteen-A. Unless he missed his guess, one Ms. Crawford had managed to outsmart herself this time.

"Did you call the ambulance?" he asked, masking his worry with briskness.

"Yes, but Sam says the generator's on the fritz again."

He stifled a groan. Someday soon the town council was going to be forced to open that flea-bitten wallet of theirs and spring for a new, up-to-date emergency vehicle. Until then, the town of Myrtle had to make do with mortician Sam Thacker's refitted, hand-me-down hearse, which was in the shop more often than on the road.

"Call the school," he told Grace. "Tell whoever answers I'm on my way."

Chapter 3

Myrtle Elementary had been built in the thirties to accommodate grades one through twelve. It had been remodeled in the fifties when the new county high school had been built.

In the sixties it had been expanded when the population burgeoned, following the timber boom. Now, with a timber bust in full sway, it housed kindergarten through sixth, with ample room for the county's newest Head Start program and community events like Nettie's three-times-a-year recitals.

Dylan visited the school every August to inoculate entering students whose parents couldn't afford to pay for even the most basic pediatric care. It was something he did on his own, something for which he received no pay. It wasn't much of a penance for his sins, but it helped.

He parked in the fire zone and hit the door running, carrying his well-worn black bag in one hand and the foul-weather jacket he hadn't taken time to put on in the other.

In the foyer, he turned left, heading for the auditorium. Maxine Peavy, Myrtle Elementary's longtime principal, met him halfway.

"Thank God," she said, kindly eyes filling with relief when she saw him running toward her.

"What happened?"

"It's Nettie."

"Nettie? I thought... Never mind. Grace said she passed out?"

"Yes, right there on the stage, introducing little Steffie Crawford. According to Stephanie's mother, she complained of shortness of breath, but before Ms. Crawford could get her outside for some air, she just keeled over."

Maxine fixed him with a deeply worried gaze. "I hope it's not her heart again. She's been so much better since she had that bypass surgery a few years back."

Keeping his own worry to himself, he hurried ahead of the puffing principal.

The auditorium was hushed. Concerned parents and unnaturally subdued children, including he noted, Arden's daughter, were standing or sitting in groups, talking in funereal tones while casting anxious glances at the front of the auditorium where Nettie was lying motionless on the stage with her head in Arden's lap.

She was dressed in brown silk, making her look like a spirited but wounded little sparrow.

Making his way quickly down the crowded aisle, he heard his name repeated many times, along with several hushed greetings. He knew most of the bystanders by name, many others by sight.

By the time he reached the stage, Nettie's eyes were open, and she was trying to sit up. Head bent, Arden was doing her best to soothe the obviously impatient woman.

As soon as he knelt next to the two women, Arden's head came up, and her eyes came to his. Like Maxine's, they were filled with worry. Unlike Maxine's, meeting them had a definite physical impact on him.

"Thank goodness you got here so quickly," Arden whispered. "I'm hopeless at first aid."

His first impulse had him wanting to lay into her but good for walking out before it was medically prudent. His second, coming hard on the heels of the first, was to hug her hard for taking care of Nettie.

He did neither. Nettie was his concern now.

He noted the older woman's lack of color and the sheen of moisture on her skin. Her respiration was accelerated, each breath far too shallow.

"She said she couldn't breathe. I thought it was the heat in here."

"How long was she out?" he asked briskly.

"A few seconds. Not even a minute. She swears she's fine, but..."

"Of course, I'm fine," Nettie chimed in peevishly.

He wasn't so sure. "Not that I'd presume to disagree with a woman of your well-known wisdom and intellect, Mrs. MacGregor, not to mention *maturity*, but I only get paid for this call if I examine you."

Without giving her a chance to respond, he took her hand and counted her pulse. Her skin was clammy, her bones more suited to the sparrow she resembled. Her pulse was galloping almost too fast to track, and he didn't like the erratic rhythm pounding the pads of his fingers.

"Bah," Nettie muttered. "You're a lousy bookkeeper, Dylan Kincade. Half the time I have to remind you to send me a bill after one of our visits in your office."

"That's because I'd rather have the pecan brownies you bring me than the whopping fee I should be charging you."

As casually as he could, he opened his bag and pulled out his stethoscope. "Put that thing away," Nettie ordered the moment she realized his intent.

"Humor me, okay? I'm trying to recruit new patients."

Before she could answer, he had the business end of the stethoscope pressed to her chest. Her dress muted the sound somewhat but not enough to mask the telltale sounds of a chronically ailing heart.

Eyes unfocused, he concentrated on the rhythm he knew almost as well as his own, listening for signs of further damage. As far as his ear could detect, she hadn't done herself any harm this time. Just to make sure, however, he wanted her in the hospital for more tests.

"All done," he said when Nettie showed signs of fussing again.

"About time," she muttered. "Darn waste of time."

Still holding her hand, he glanced up and skimmed his gaze over the now attentive faces, looking for the seamed features of Harvey Delacroix. He spotted him near the rear where Harvey was subtly but skillfully keeping an eagle eye on the crowd.

Dylan meshed his gaze with the chief's and nodded. Without hesitation, Harvey made his way forward. "What do you need, Doc?" he called when he neared.

"Are you driving the squad car or your van?"

"The van. Why?"

"Sam says the ambulance is down again, and my Bronco's crammed with junk. How about giving Nettie a ride to the hospital? Let her ride in style for once instead of in that old rattletrap of hers."

Nettie's 1948 Cadillac, given to her on her thirty-eighth birthday by her doting husband, Arthur, was her pride and joy. She swore she was going to leave it to Dylan in her will. He swore just as hard that she'd wear it out before then.

"It'd be my pleasure," Harvey said, winking at Nettie's outraged expression.

"He'll do no such thing," Nettie exclaimed, but her voice was far too wispy to be as fierce as she'd obviously intended.

Dylan squeezed the old woman's hand gently. "Humor me, darlin'. Just this once, okay?"

He gave her his best smile, the one he'd inherited from his Irish great-grandfather. Nettie worked hard at resisting, but finally gave in, just as he'd known she would. Who said he didn't have charm? he thought smugly.

"I don't have time to waste lolling in a hospital bed," she warned, glaring at him.

"Lord spare me from women who think they know better than their doctor," he muttered, then glanced up swiftly to find Arden trying valiantly to banish the guilty look from her face.

Now that he knew Nettie wasn't in any real danger, at least not for the moment, he allowed himself a few minutes to set his newest patient straight about the way things were done in Myrtle.

"Is it my bedside manner you hate?" he asked in a tone pitched for her ears only. "Or do you women have some kind of campaign going against overworked doctors this season?"

Arden struggled to produce an innocent look, but the heated blue of his eyes had her giving it up as a lost cause.

Worry about Nettie had dampened some of the pleasure she'd expected to feel at sparring with him again. But the small shiver she'd felt when he'd fixed those memorable blue eyes on hers had been purely physical and out of her control.

"No campaign," she said loftily, fully aware that Nettie was taking in the conversation with avid interest. "A compromise, remember?"

"According to my ninth-grade English teacher, a compromise means both parties give up something, not just one."

"I stayed until after dinner. Ask Eddie. He picked me at 6:30 on the dot."

His mouth slanted. As Arden had anticipated, just that hint of a smile changed his face for the better. Made it even more masculine. More stirring to a woman's libido. If a woman were to notice such things, that is.

"You were supposed to stay until breakfast." He returned his attention to Nettie, bending closer to say sternly,

"And don't you be giving me any trouble, Mrs. Antoinette MacGregor, you hear?"

Nettie's black eyes sparkled, restoring a bit of her usual ginger to her expression and settling some of Arden's concern.

"Or what?" the old woman challenged pertly.

Arden noted the quick look the doctor exchanged with the police chief, and her worry returned.

"Or I'll put you over my knee and spank you like the naughty girl you are," he said gruffly.

"*Woman*, you chauvinist," Nettie groused, but her color was better. "And don't you be forgetting it."

"No, ma'am."

"That's puttin' him in his place, Nettie," called a hearty male voice from the second row of bunched well-wishers.

"Yeah, Doc. She's got you cowed, just like the rest of us country boys."

Amidst the flurry of relieved laughter, Arden watched him acknowledge the comments with a slow, friendly grin that looked completely natural. Only she was close enough to notice that the deeply ingrained melancholy in his eyes remained undisturbed.

Or, she thought as she watched the doctor lift the small, blustering woman into the chief's burly arms and then tuck the blanket carefully around her, perhaps she was the only one who'd thought to look that closely.

"Tell Hooven I'll be there in twenty minutes," he called after the chief who nodded as he kept on going. Like the prow of a ship, Delacroix parted the crowd with ease, only to have it close in behind him again.

The noise level rose immediately, flowing easily again and salted generously with laughter that sounded far more natural this time.

Arden listened to the calls of encouragement directed Nettie's way from parents and students alike, and envied the old lady her knack for making friends.

No Easy Way Out

She herself had to work at it, and even then, had trouble being herself after so many years of having to watch her every word and every gesture.

"Is it serious?" she asked Dylan who was now regarding her with a dangerously stern frown.

"Hard to tell until I get her to sit still for some tests."

"She was so white, and when she grabbed her chest, I was sure it was a heart attack." She needed reassurance. Instead, she got a steely look.

"Could have been, but it wasn't." He dropped his stethoscope into the bag and snapped it shut.

"The pills she took...the nitroglycerin, she said they were for angina."

"She should know."

This wasn't the first fainting spell Nettie had had in the last few months, although he was fairly sure very few of her friends knew about the others. He'd known because he made it his business to know.

Nettie had been living on borrowed time for years. Six months, a year at the most, if she didn't slow down the way he'd all but begged her to do.

To his own personal dismay, however, Nettie had a mind of her own. So, it seemed, did Arden Crawford. "Now, let's talk about you, Ms. Crawford. Why did you disobey doctor's orders?"

"I didn't—"

"Yeah, yeah, I know. Compromise." He held out his hand to help her up.

"Thanks," she murmured, accepting the physical connection with a reluctance she didn't want to explore.

Standing slowly, she found herself suddenly light-headed and wobbly. Teetering on three-inch heels she shouldn't have worn, she grabbed a couple of quick breaths. His eyes narrowed, and his grip tightened until she was steady again.

He had a powerful hand with the callused palms and hard fingers of a day laborer, something she didn't expect in a man whose touch was deft enough for microsurgery.

"Stubborn woman," he muttered. "You should be in bed, and we both know it."

He kept her hand in his until the dizziness she was trying to hide passed. Even when he released her, he remained close, just in case.

"Look, I'm sorry I caused you any anxiety," she murmured earnestly. "Truly."

Arden found she had to angle her neck to look up at him. Not that he was all that tall. Definitely an inch or two under six feet, but so solid through the chest and shoulders that he seemed much bigger.

"How are you feeling?"

"I'm fine, really."

Fine wasn't the word he would have used. Sexy, yes. Appealing, definitely. And she smelled like a woman more used to silk sheets and champagne than Myrtle's serviceable cotton and draft beer.

"Any light-headedness? Sharp pains in the area of the incision?"

She wasn't as tall as he'd expected. Nor as skinny. Dressed in a boxy shirt and wool slacks, she was anything but glamorous. But the look and the smell and the feel of her was all woman.

Arden shook her head. "I admit I'm a little tired, but—"

She halted abruptly when a small, brown-haired whirlwind in pink came barreling into her, nearly knocking her flat.

"Mommy! Is Mrs. Mac going to be okay?"

Arden sought Dylan's gaze with hers. That same small but definite sense of connection was still there and still disturbing.

"I... Ask Dr. Kincade," she told her daughter with a reassuring smile. "He knows better than I do."

Stephanie Crawford arched her neck and looked up until she and Dylan were more or less eye to eye. "Dr. Kincade, is Mrs. Mac going to be all right?" she asked dutifully.

"I hope so."

Steffie considered that for a moment, then poked him in the belly with a small, definite finger. "But do you *know* so?"

He hid a smile. Arden's daughter was showing every sign of being just as much trouble to handle as her mother. "I know I'm going to do everything I can to make sure she's as fine as she can be."

He felt Arden's gaze on his face. It disturbed him to have her so near. It disturbed him more that he had noticed the sheen of her hair and the scent of her perfume almost as quickly as he'd noticed the tiredness around her eyes and the still too-pale complexion.

A doctor's sole concern should be the well-being of his patient. How she looked and smelled and made his blood sizzle had no place in the doctor-patient relationship.

Disgusted with himself and annoyed with her, he concentrated on her daughter. "And now, Miss Stephanie, I'm going to do something for your mom, who is also my patient, whether she likes it or not."

The little girl's eyes shone with sudden interest, eyes that were the exact shade of her mother's, framed by lashes that showed a promise of the same lushness.

"What's that?" she cried, looking from one to the other.

"I'm going to order her to go home and go to bed. And I'm going to appoint you the boss to make sure she does just that."

Stephanie giggled. "I've never been the boss of a grown-up before. What do I have to do?"

He'd always been a sucker for dimples, and Arden's daughter had two of them. He wouldn't let himself wonder if she'd gotten them from her mother.

"First you have to tuck your mom into her bed nice and warm and cozy, and then you have to take her temperature. Do you know how to do that?"

Stephanie's nose wrinkled as she thought. "I think so— if Mommy tells me where to find the thermometer."

Dylan shifted his gaze to Arden's. It was a mistake. She was smiling. Sure enough, she had dimples. On her, however, they seemed more provocative than adorable.

"How about it, Mommy?" he asked when he realized her smile had turned to a quizzical frown. "The thermometer?"

"In the medicine chest," she told her daughter, "but I think Dr. Kincade is just teasing us."

Her gaze came back to his, and he saw a hint of purely feminine speculation he didn't want to acknowledge. "Isn't that right, Doctor?"

"Nope, I'm dead serious," he assured both of them, before flicking Arden a quick glance. "And this is between your nurse and your doctor, lady, so butt out."

Stephanie giggled again. She didn't notice the curious looks now coming their way, but he did.

Tomorrow it would be all over town that he was trying to make time with Myrtle's newest and by far most celebrated resident. By noon, the grapevine would have them in bed together. By evening, folks would be asking him about the wedding.

Speculation like that was something he'd avoided for a lot of years. Talk about a man's future tended to lead to talk about his past.

"Look, we're wasting time," he said, glancing around. "Where's your coat?"

"In the cloak room at the far end of the hall, but—"

"I'll get it," Stephanie cried, spinning away swiftly, more like a wide receiver than a ballerina.

"Don't run," Arden called after her, but Steffie was already halfway to the wings. She watched to make sure she didn't slip in her new shoes, then breathed a sigh of relief when she disappeared into the backstage throng.

"Excuse me, everyone." Maxine Peavy was standing at the edge of the stage, clapping her hands. "Parents, children, can I have your attention, please?"

The immediate hush was almost comical. At one time or another, Maxine had taught most of those in the small auditorium, parent and child alike, and her knack for instilling discipline was legendary.

"Since Mrs. Mac is unable to be here for the remainder of the recital, I think it only best that we cancel tonight's festivities until she is fully recovered, at which time we will convene here again at a time of her choosing."

A faint buzz arose, quashed immediately by the principal's raised hands. "I know all of you wish Mrs. Mac well, as I do. Drive carefully on your way home and have a pleasant evening. Good night."

Like a benediction, her words produced a sudden silence, followed by an equally sudden burst of conversation.

Coats were collected, children gathered, and people began to file out. In a matter of seconds Arden realized that she and Dylan were alone on the stage. Without the proximity of others, the auditorium had taken on a definite chill, causing a small, swift shiver to pass over her.

His eyebrows drew together immediately. "Cold?"

"A little," she admitted, because the small tremors shaking her were impossible to hide.

Muttering something she suspected she should be glad she didn't catch, he scooped his own jacket from the floor where he'd stashed it and draped it almost angrily over her shaking shoulders. Strong scents of wood smoke and musky aftershave enveloped her, along with an immediate sense of weight and warmth.

"I...thank you," she murmured stiffly. "You're being very kind to me when I know you'd rather throttle me."

His quick scowl surprised her. "Kind has nothing to do with it, Ms. Crawford. I take my responsibility toward my patients very seriously—even the ones who don't deserve it."

"Well, excuse me," she shot back, then gasped at the sudden pain clawing her belly. Her skin turned clammy, and her knees went watery.

"Darn—" she bit off, ashamed to have cried out in public. Cold inside and out now, she was very much afraid she was going to be sick right there on the stage.

Things happened quickly after that. In spite of her mumbled protests, he somehow managed to retrieve his bag, swing her into his arms and head for the wings just as Stephanie appeared with the coats.

"Mommy?"

"I'm fine, sweetie," she managed to get out between shivers.

Dylan stopped long enough to order the child to put on her coat and cap and follow him. "Where're we going?" Steffie asked, skipping to keep up with his long strides.

"You and I are taking your mom home where she belongs."

"I can walk," Arden insisted while at the same time struggling to keep her head from banging his chin.

"Shut up," he ordered, anger abrading his voice to a low growl. "You've already upset your daughter enough. How do you think she'd feel if *you* keeled over in a dead faint at her feet?"

He was right, she thought as she fought the sickening dizziness. All day long while she'd fidgeted and fumed in her hospital room, feeling sorry for herself and cursing his tyrannical stubbornness, she'd been working at convincing herself that Steffie desperately needed her there in the auditorium that night.

But the truth was, she had needed to be there for herself more. Ever since she and Mike had divorced, she'd worked at being the perfect mother, the perfect news anchor, the perfect modern woman.

What she *hadn't* been was the perfect patient, and now the stark fear she'd seen on her daughter's face told her better than any words just how thoughtless she'd been.

"Looks like you got yourself another patient there, Doc," someone called out as he carried her through the wide, echoing hallway toward the front exit.

"Prettier than Nettie, anyway," another added. "Got good legs, too."

Someone else held the door while he carried her through, trailed closely by Steffie, who was still clutching the ratty old muskrat coat Arden had bought at a thrift shop a few days after the first snow of the season.

He didn't carry her far. She had a sense of cold on her face, blinked at the sudden transition from bright to dark, and then he had stopped next to some kind of dark-colored four-wheel drive vehicle with enough dings and dents in the fenders to raise a decent crop of strawberries.

"Get the door, Stephanie," he ordered, his breath puffing around his head in the frigid air.

Arden lifted her head, only to see a ring of curious faces. So much for her vow to keep a low profile in her new hometown, she thought as she buried her face against his neck again.

His skin was cold, reminding her that his coat was now keeping her warm instead of him. "Doctor—"

"Dylan—and I told you shut up."

He deposited her in the passenger's seat with what seemed to be the greatest of care, but when she sought his gaze in order to thank him, the bad-tempered scowl on his face had her biting her tongue.

Maybe she'd been out of line, but she *had* apologized, and quite nicely, too. He had no reason to treat her like she was no older than her own daughter.

"I'm not helpless," she said when he leaned past her to fasten her shoulder belt. He grunted something indistinct, but the meaning was as clear as any news item she'd ever read—*Sit still and shut up. You've already caused me enough trouble.*

"Just shove that stuff aside and make yourself some room," he told Stephanie, who was busy trying to find a place to sit in the back seat. "Make sure you use that seat belt. I have enough stubborn females on my hands already."

Arden heard Steffie giggle—right before she heard the click of another safety belt.

The passenger door was slammed shut, harder than necessary in her opinion. She wanted to unbuckle the stupid belt he'd fastened, open the stupid door he'd just slammed, take the daughter who seemed to enjoy his bullying and drive her own car home.

Instead, she sat stiffly, eyes straight ahead, trying to ignore the queasy weakness that made anything more than that impossible.

Dumb, dumb, dumb, she thought. For a supposedly bright woman, she'd pulled a real boner this time. Thinking she knew better than the expert again.

The last time she'd done that, she'd quit a well-paying, much-coveted job in a major media market, sunk all of her savings into a nearly dead-and-buried country newspaper, sold the only permanent home Steffie had ever known and dragged them both to the wilds of central Oregon to start a new life that wasn't coming close to working out the way it should.

"Which way?"

Arden realized that he had stopped at the street fronting the school. Light from the dash gave his face a diabolical harshness, and his hard-knuckled grip on the wheel had her thinking fleetingly of the fragile bones of her throat.

"Uh, to the right. We live above the paper, remember?"

She caught a look of surprise, quickly gone. "Right."

"In a dinky little apartment with only one bathroom," Steffie offered from the back. "It stinks."

"Stephanie Michele," Arden warned sternly, then wished she hadn't when the soup she'd forced down in the hospital threatened to reappear.

"Well, it does," her daughter muttered. "I hate it."

Nothing more was said during the two-minute ride, for which Arden was devoutly grateful. At the moment, she wasn't sure she could handle one more problem, one more doubt, one more decision. All she wanted right now was sleep.

"There's Eddie!" Steffie called. "He's sneaking a cigarette."

"So I see."

Dylan bounced the Bronco over the icy curb and pulled close to the rear door. As soon as the security light caught the truck full on, Arden's rawhide-and-crust press foreman crushed the butt under his heel, frantically waving the smoke away at the same time.

Steffie giggled. "He's trying to quit. Nobody's supposed to know he can't, but me. He said it was our special secret."

"Not anymore it isn't." Dylan shut off the engine and got out.

"Thought that was you, Doc," Arden heard Eddie call over the slamming of the driver's door. "Got the boss with you?"

"I've got her."

Eddie wheezed a laugh. "Got me a call from Ed Jr. who was over to the school. Heard she had her some trouble, pert near fell off the stage Eddie said."

Arden closed her eyes and wished for oblivion. Tomorrow, her aborted swan dive into the first row of seats at Steffie's recital would be all over town. So much for winning friends and attracting new subscribers.

The door opened, and Dr. Kincade had her seat belt unbuckled before she had her eyes fully open. Not fully prepared, she launched into the speech she'd rehearsed, anyway.

"Thank you very much for your help, and I'm sorry I... Hey, wait a minute!"

He scooped her into his arms, as easily as she'd lifted Steffie when she'd been younger.

"Hang on and be still," he ordered, ignoring her protests. "It's slippery out here. If I go down, so do you."

At least he hadn't told her to shut up this time, she thought as she hastily curled her arm around his neck. Over his shoulder she saw Eddie helping Steffie navigate the icy walk, dragging the muskrat coat behind her.

The back stairs were narrow and steep. Managing them without banging her head had Dylan cursing under his breath. The door at the top was unlocked and opened into an old-fashioned country kitchen, the kind that was more practical than pretty.

"Bedroom?" he asked after a quick look around.

"You can put me down here," she insisted, determined to regain control now that she was in her own home. To that end she put extra starch in her tone when she added, "I'm perfectly steady now."

He seemed to have a different idea. "Don't argue. Just point."

"Now listen here, Kincade—"

"Dylan," he repeated, his tone dangerously soft. "Left or right?"

She gave up. It seemed to be the only way she was going to get out of this mess with even a semblance of her tattered dignity intact.

"Right. First door."

He put her on the bed and turned on the light. The room was smaller than he expected, hardly larger than a big closet. Her bed was pushed into one corner, with a dresser, bookcase and rocking chair sharing the far wall.

He knew next to nothing about decorating, but the furniture seemed scaled to bigger rooms and more elaborate decor. The colors he saw were warm, reminding him of the roses in a country garden, and the air smelled pretty and sexy, like her.

Reminding himself that he was her doctor, not her lover, he concentrated on the shadows under her eyes instead of the soft curves presently covered by his bulky coat.

"Take off your clothes and get under the covers. I'll be right back." Retracing his steps, he found Stephanie and Eddie in the kitchen.

"...and then a policeman carried Mrs. Mac out to his car and Dr. Kincade told Mommy to shut up and I went to get her coat."

Eddie looked up as Dylan entered. His grin split his face like a watermelon slice. "Did you really tell the boss to shut up?"

"Sorry, Eddie. That's privileged information." He turned his attention to the little girl. "Steffie, get the thermometer from the medicine chest and take it into your mom's room, okay?"

Stephanie blinked solemnly. "I get to be the boss of Mommy tonight, don't I? Like you said?"

"That's what I said."

"Goody!" She tossed Eddie a triumphant look before speeding down the hall, the tassel on her bright pink cap bobbing wildly.

The press foreman's eyes sparkled. "Would've given a big chunk of my pension to see you 'n' Arden goin' at it. Yessir, that had to be a sight, all right. Two of the stubbornest folks I know, head-to-head."

Dylan didn't want to be reminded. At the moment, he was thinking dark thoughts about Neil Christopher and the bout of flu that had brought her into his life.

"Is Geneva home?" he asked. Eddie's wife was an ex-navy nurse and often filled in at the hospital whenever she was needed, as well as doing most of the private-duty nursing in the community.

"Yep. S'posed to be, anyway. Why?"

"Because I want you to call her and ask if she can special Ms. Crawford tonight."

Eddie's grin faded. "Well, sure, I'll call right now."

He cleared his throat and looked contrite all of a sudden. "It ain't serious, is it? I mean, Arden, she said there weren't no complications, and she seemed okay when she and Stef left for the recital and all. Otherwise, I swear, Doc, I never would've let her go."

Dylan laid a hand on the other man's shoulder. "Don't get yourself in a knot about this, okay? Something tells me she's tougher than both of us."

Eddie didn't seem one bit convinced, and Dylan wondered if his bedside manner needed fine-tuning.

"Yeah, but Doc, she's got this idea she has to outwork every blasted one of us on her payroll, and then some. I mean, I was the one who made her go to the emergency room in the first place. Never seen a woman argue like that one can. No sir, kept insistin' it was just a plain old bellyache—till she damn near turned herself into a pretzel from the pain."

"Don't blame yourself." Dylan dropped his hand. "You did what you could."

So did he, and look what it got him. An unexpected house call and a load of complications he didn't need.

"I'll use the office phone to call 'Neva. It's on a separate line," Eddie said before he clattered down the stairs.

Left alone, Dylan took a quick visual tour of the kitchen until he found the phone. With his back to the chipped counter, he punched out the number of the nurse's station in the ER and was relieved to hear Hooven's calm voice answer on the first ring.

"How's Nettie?"

"Stable, good color, steady respiration, pulse rate ninety-two when I took it three minutes ago. She's also mad as a hornet and threatening to call Pete's Taxi to take her home."

He stifled a sigh. "Send her up to a room and keep her there. Take her clothes if you have to, and then ask Manny if he'll run over to my office and get her file so I can look it over tonight."

Nettie's file was a thick one. Too thick.

"Okay. He'll be happy to get out of here for a few minutes."

"Hectic?"

"Not really. Cuts and bruises mostly, from a fender bender out on the pike. Nothing that needs your immediate attention."

He glanced at his watch. He was nineteen minutes and counting. "I'll be a little late getting there. I have a small chore to take care of first."

"Yes, I heard about that little chore. How is Ms. Crawford feeling now?"

Closing his eyes, he called on the last of his rapidly unraveling patience. "She's fine. I'm the one who needs three weeks alone on a desert island, preferably one that's off-limits to women of any age."

Hooven was still laughing when he hung up.

Consequently, his mood was edging toward testy when he returned to the bedroom. Stephanie was already there, without her coat and hat now, hovering over her mother, who was sitting on the edge of the bed, still fully clothed, a thermometer sticking out of her mouth.

His jacket was folded neatly next to her thigh, and she'd kicked off her shoes, apparently her version of getting undressed and ready for bed.

As soon as Arden saw him, her face screwed into a frown and her dark eyes promised revenge. A curiosity he couldn't quash had him wondering if a kiss would turn the anger in those eyes to passion.

Because he was too tired to exercise his usual control, he let his mind linger for a long moment on the forbidden fantasy of a woman—this woman—looking at him with soft yearning.

Fool, he told himself savagely. He was her surgeon, nothing more. He was concerned with her recovery, not the shape of her mouth or the softness of her hair.

Noting that her color was better, he set about ignoring her and concentrated on her daughter. "Looks like you have things under control, kiddo."

The little girl beamed. "Mommy had to tell me to put it under her tongue, but I put it in by myself. Just like a doctor."

"Sounds good to me." He crouched by the bed so that he and Stephanie were eye to eye. "Perhaps it might be a good idea for me to show you how I read a thermometer so that you can see if our methods are the same."

She considered that with a pensive frown before nodding. "Okay."

Arden scowled, but let him remove the thermometer without protest. Holding it close to the light, he took a quick reading.

"What's it say?" Stephanie asked eagerly.

"One-hundred-one point six."

He showed her the tiny numbers and how to find the silver mercury. "Does that mean Mommy has a temperature?" she asked, head still bending over the circle of light.

"Everyone has a body temperature. When it gets higher than ninety-eight point six, it's called a fever, which means the body's busy fighting off something bad."

Stephanie studied him intently with her mother's big brown eyes. "If Mommy's, umm, temperature is one hundred and one that means she has a fever, right?"

"Right." He ruffled her thick brown hair, then drew his hand back quickly. It wouldn't do to let himself become fond of this little imp. "And you're one very smart cookie."

"I am, aren't I?" she said, showing those big dimples again.

He rinsed it off and replaced the thermometer in the case before handing it over. "Better put that back where you found it so Mrs. Harkness can find it when she needs it."

"Mrs. Harkness? You mean 'Neva? Eddie's wife?"

He nodded. "She's going to stay with you and Mommy tonight."

That's it, Arden thought. Enough is enough. "She is not!" she declared.

Stephanie glanced inquiringly toward her mother, who was now scowling at both of them. "Why not, Mommy? I like 'Neva. She tells neat stories."

"Because, sweetheart, Mommy doesn't need a nurse. A good night's sleep will fix me up just fine."

"Tell me, Ms. Crawford," Dylan drawled, folding his arms and cocking his head to one side for a better look. "Just when did you graduate from medical school?"

"I don't need a degree to know what I want, which is to be left alone."

"No problem." He turned to Stephanie and held out his hand. "C'mon, let's let Mommy sulk while we have a consultation."

"I'm not sulking!" Arden called after them to no avail.

Stephanie lead him to the bathroom, where he replaced the thermometer and collected a bottle of aspirin. It wasn't as strong as the medication he would have prescribed from the hospital pharmacy, but it would do for now.

"What time do you go to bed?" he asked the now sleepy-eyed little girl while he filled a glass with water.

"Eight-thirty on a school night," she admitted with clear reluctance. "But tonight is special, 'cause of the recital and Mommy being sick and all."

"Maybe you'd better hit the hay, anyway. That way you'll be well rested tomorrow morning if Mommy needs you to help with something."

"Maybe she needs help now."

The kid bargained like a pro, he thought. But then, she'd been taught by an expert. Fortunately, he was on to them now. Both of them.

"Don't worry, I'll be here until Mrs. Harkness arrives."

"Promise?"

Some of her earlier worry about her mama was creeping back into her voice again, touching him deeply. There had been a time when he'd been part of a family that took care of one another like this one seemed to do.

"Promise," he said, ruffling her hair. "Now scoot. I want you in bed by the time Mrs. Harkness gets here, okay?"

"But I want to help."

"If you're tucked in for the night, your mom doesn't have to worry about you, which will be the best help you can give her right now."

Stephanie didn't concede gracefully, nor did he expect she would, given her mother's stubborn nature. But finally, reluctantly, she *did* concede, taking herself off to her own room slowly. He followed her into the hall, making sure she was okay.

The house was quiet, settling in for the night, and strangely peaceful, tempting him to drop his defenses and absorb some of that peace to hoard for later, when he was alone again.

"Pssst, Doc."

He glanced up to find Eddie beckoning him from the end of the hall. He shoved the aspirin into the back pocket of his cords and, still carrying the water, made his way to the kitchen where Eddie was now standing by the window, staring out at the falling snow.

"'Neva's over to the hospital, fillin' in for someone on the night shift," he whispered as soon as Dylan was within range. "She's trying to find someone else to stay with the boss, but she doesn't hold out much hope, especially on a night like this."

"Damn."

"Yeah, well I can stay if you think I should. Soon as me and the boys get the paper off the presses, that is."

Dylan glanced over his shoulder. Light shone under the door of one bedroom—Arden's. The other was dark. It hadn't taken Stephanie long to get into bed once she'd bowed to the inevitable. Perhaps she was already asleep. He hoped so.

"No, I'll arrange something. Don't worry about it."

"Sure? Arden's been good to me 'n' the others. I don't mind repaying the best way I can."

"I'm sure. Besides, getting the paper out on time is probably the one thing she wants most right now."

"That's true enough." Eddie shot one last worried look toward the back of the apartment, then nodded goodbye and left.

Dylan's gaze shifted to the slit of light under her door. Walking into a woman's bedroom late at night wasn't something he'd done often in recent years, but when he had, it had been to treat a patient, no other reason.

He would give her the aspirins and make sure she took them, even if he had to shove them down her throat himself. And then, when she was asleep, he would make some calls, find a private-duty nurse willing to do him a favor on such short notice.

Right now, however, he had a patient to treat. And if there was any mercy left to him, she would be bundled into something flannel and frumpy, with the covers pulled to her chin, already fast asleep.

Chapter 4

The covers were thrown back, but she was still sitting on the side of the bed, fumbling with the last button of her nightgown.

Sure enough, he thought, it was flannel. Something white with little red roses and a high collar. It was just plain bad luck that, on her, common flannel seemed even more sexy than French silk.

"You're still here," she accused the moment she spied him. Some of the life had come back into her eyes, but he noticed the telltale signs of pain around her mouth.

"Obviously."

He put the glass by the bed and yanked the aspirin bottle from his back pocket. He shook out two and made it clear she was to take them. For once, she did as she was told. He didn't know whether to be pleased or worried.

"Where's Stef?" she asked, glancing past him. He kept his gaze on her face, away from the soft curves under the soft material.

"In bed."

No Easy Way Out

"Is she okay?"

Her gaze traveled to his face, reluctantly it seemed to him. Her throat was shadowed, its slimness so tempting beneath the clinging flannel he had to work to keep from groaning.

"Seems to be."

"Good." She glanced down at the water glass she was still clutching. "I, uh, apologize for being such a bad patient. I see now the trouble I've caused because I didn't listen to you, and I'm ashamed of myself."

Apologies came hard for him. For her, too, he suspected, although she had made hers with a graciousness he couldn't manage on his best day.

"Apology accepted, but stow the shame. Last I checked there weren't too many perfect people walking this earth."

"True, but I dislike stupid mistakes. Mine, most of all."

"Mistakes happen. The trick is not to make the same one twice."

"Ah, a philosopher as well as a surgeon."

He felt heat climb his neck. "No, Ms. Crawford. Just a guy trying to do his best."

She finished the water, then put the glass on the table and moved backward cautiously until she was pillowed against the headboard and her bare painted-pink toes were tucked beneath the folds of his coat to keep them toasty.

Since he seemed in no hurry to leave, Arden thought about asking him to pull up the rocking chair and "sit a spell," as Nettie invariably ordered her to do when she visited.

It hadn't taken her long to realize that Myrtle was a town that invited first names and long friendly chats between neighbors, none of whom remained strangers for long.

In his case, however, the wariness in his stance and the subtle stiffness of those tree-sized shoulders had her deciding against such familiarity.

"Are you always as generous to your patients as you were tonight?" she asked instead.

"Always. Keeps 'em coming back."

Arden recognized the attempt of a man with a soft heart to deny it, even to himself, and wondered what in his past made him discount himself so much.

"Living in the city for so long, having to be suspicious of just about everyone and everything these days, well, I'm not used to that kind of caring."

He moved his shoulders. "Comes with the office I inherited when I came here. Belonged to old Doc Sennett, the country doctor I replaced. He practiced for almost sixty years out of that office, and never once locked the door or turned away a patient. Guess his spirit is still hanging around, keeping me on the straight and narrow."

She cocked her head, her mouth pursing ever so slightly as she thought that over. Lamplight was reflected in her eyes, giving the illusion of an inviting smile in the depths. An illusion, he repeated with emphasis. Nothing personal in that look. Nothing a man could build into anything more than a purely professional relationship.

"Somehow I can't see you being intimidated by a ghost." Or anything else, she thought. Not with a chin as solid as mica and eyes that could cool to the same glittering flint.

His mouth twisted, and the warmth she'd managed to kindle in his eyes cooled. "You'd be surprised at the things that can intimidate me, Ms. Crawford."

"Perhaps, and I thought we'd gotten past the Ms. Crawford/Dr. Kincade stage?"

He found himself watching the way her lips formed his name. It was amazing how easily a man could get tangled in a woman's net when he let himself look no deeper than surface beauty. And how easily that same woman could rip his heart out and shred it to pieces right in front of his eyes.

Not this time, however.

And definitely not this woman.

He made a show of looking at his watch, although he knew within a few minutes how late it was becoming.

"I'd better be getting out of here before the roads close up again." He kept his tone brisk, his expression neutral,

No Easy Way Out 69

strictly doctor-to-patient. Something flashed in her eyes. He refused to see it as hurt.

"I heard you phoning the hospital about Nettie. Since you don't seem nearly as worried as you did at the school, I take it she's recovering?"

"Recovering is a relative term, Ms. Crawford," he said carefully. "Especially in heart patients."

"Arden," she emphasized softly. "Please."

He acknowledged her gentle rebuke with a nod. "Arden."

She grinned, her eyes sparking satisfaction. "I *knew* I'd heard a few broad Yankee vowels sprinkled through that West Virginia twang."

His fist clenched instinctively. Discipline had him relaxing the tense muscles before she had a chance to notice.

"Must be the Harvard influence. I was there eight years." He glanced at his watch again, more to keep from meeting her eyes than a need to check the time again.

"Sorry, I didn't mean to make this into an interview, although, actually that's not such a bad idea. For the Sunday features section, maybe." She slanted him a questioning look which he answered with a frown.

"I doubt there's anything about country medicine that would be remotely interesting to your readers on a Sunday morning."

"You'd be surprised."

She studied his face, thinking that a profile shot would have the most impact. All those solid planes and intriguing character lines begged for the stark contrast of black and white.

"Don't mind me," she said when she realized he was scowling again. "I get the strangest notions in the recesses of my mind sometimes, sort of like a toothache that just won't go away. In your case, I keep thinking we've met before." She shook her head. "Guess it's the reporter in me, you know? I can't rest until I know why I keep feeling that way."

He knew, all right. A reporter with a hunch was like a dog wrestling with a juicy hunk of meat, trying to keep it from everyone else, even though it was more than enough to satisfy even the most ravenous of appetites.

"Well, Arden," he said, consciously keeping his vowels shorter this time, "the *doctor* in me says I need to take a look at your sutures before I go."

"I expect you to bill me for a house call," she murmured as she gingerly lowered herself to a reclining position.

"Yes, ma'am."

Careful not to let his fingers slide over her skin, he eased her nightgown above her hips until it pooled out of his way at her waist.

He was relieved to see that she was wearing panties under the flannel, pink bits of lace and silk that weren't quite transparent, but might as well have been.

The skin beneath looked even silkier in the lamplight, all cream-colored sheen and inviting softness. He was a man accustomed to self-discipline and self-denial, but it took him a few seconds to remember that.

He concentrated on the large adhesive pad that she must have used to replace the one he'd applied early that morning after examining her.

"Did you notice any bleeding when you changed the dressing?"

She was lying stiffly, staring at the ceiling intently. "Just a little. Hardly any."

Easing his fingers beneath the edging of her lace panties, he removed the large adhesive pad as gently as he could. The suture line had already started to close. There was little swelling and no sign of infection.

He quickly draped the gown back over her thighs and pulled up the covers. Her eyes were open now, watching him.

"I think we can dispense with the bandage," he said, tossing it into the wastebasket by the dresser. "Be careful when you bathe, and avoid tight clothing for a couple of weeks."

She cleared her throat. "When will I have to come in to have the stitches out?"

"Friday will do. Call my office for an appointment, or stop by and take your chances. Your choice."

"I'll call."

"Fine."

He shoved both hands in his pockets and nodded at the bedside phone. "If you need anything, call Eddie downstairs."

She smiled stiffly. "I'm sure I won't need a thing but a good night's sleep."

A gust of wind rattled the panes in the windows fronting the street, and both glanced in that direction.

"It's a nasty night," she murmured. "Dangerous."

More than she knew, he thought. Grabbing his coat, he swung one arm into it, then the other. "If you hear someone rattling around in the night up here, don't worry. It'll be your nurse."

"But I called Geneva—" She stopped in midsentence, her teeth snapping together hard. "Okay, so I didn't want to put her out. But she was already committed to the hospital, so it doesn't matter."

He flipped up his jacket collar and discovered that the material was now impregnated with her scent. One more thing to put a finely honed edge on his already razored mood.

"You didn't happen to tell her not to try too hard to find a replacement, did you?"

"What if I did?" She tossed back her head and met his accusing look head-on. "This is my stitched-up body you're fussing over, not yours. I have rights, you know. Isn't that what the Hippocratic oath says?"

"Not exactly, but close enough."

He slipped one hand from his pocket and brought it up to knead the tightness from the base of his neck. As soon as he realized what he was doing, he stopped. It had been a mistake to linger long enough to allow tiredness to loosen his guard.

"Then why don't we consider ourselves partners in the recovery of Arden Crawford instead of adversaries?" she suggested with a smile that had probably started breaking hearts about the time she'd been Steffie's age.

"Sure, why not?" he said as he walked to the bedroom door and kept on going. "As long as I get to be the partner with the controlling vote."

"No way!" she called after him. "Fifty-fifty, or no deal."

"We'll talk about it tomorrow."

The clipped-off syllables were back, giving his voice a hard edge. Arden scowled at the empty doorway. "Kincade, you come back here! We need to settle this."

The doorway remained empty. "Name's Dylan, remember?" she heard from the vicinity of the kitchen.

"Dylan, don't you dare leave!"

"Get some sleep, Arden. Doctor's orders."

The door closed with an audible thump, and then she was alone in the silence—with the faint sound of rusty male laughter still lingering in the air.

By the time he'd reached the hospital, Nettie was fast asleep and showing few adverse signs from the incident at the school. Nevertheless, he decided to keep her for a day and run some tests as planned.

Since it was only a little past ten, he dropped in on several other patients, passing a few minutes of conversation with those who were still awake.

Satisfied that nothing serious was pending, he returned to the nurse's station to order Nettie's tests and pick up her file.

Geneva Harkness was still on duty. She was a raw-boned woman of fifty-some with an innate serenity he envied. Eddie was a lucky man.

No Easy Way Out

"Anything else I need to see before I get out of here?" He scrawled his signature on Nettie's lab order and returned his pen to his shirt pocket.

"Nope. That does it."

"Good. It's been a long day."

"Interesting, too."

He shot her a warning look that stung so hard she grinned as she added, "From a medical standpoint, I mean."

"Uh-huh."

He collected the bulging manila folder tagged with Nettie's name and tucked it under his arm. At the same time, he scanned the counter, looking for something edible to filch. Other than the charts and papers, it was clean as a whistle.

"How come you never bring any goodies into work with you?" he groused.

"I do."

Geneva reached into a tote bag tucked under the desk and came out with a large sack of raw sunflower seeds. "Here, have a handful. They're good for frazzled nerves."

He declined with a disgusted shake of his head. "It's my empty belly I'm thinking about, not my nerves."

"Missed dinner, did you?"

He took a moment to think back over the last few hours. In that time he'd treated two patients, both of whom gave him more trouble than any one doctor deserved.

One he was trying to keep alive in spite of herself. The other wore pink panties to bed and had him sweating in subfreezing temperature.

His tired body thrummed a warning that he'd do well to heed. Thinking about Arden in anything but professional terms was just plain dumb.

"Come to think of it, I guess I haven't eaten since lunch."

"Arden didn't feed you after you drove her home, I take it."

He shot her a look. "*Ms. Crawford* is a patient. I drove her home because she was in no shape to drive herself. I gave her two aspirins and told her to call me in the morning."

Geneva chuckled. "Tell me something, Dylan. By any chance, were you studying for the priesthood before you went to med school?"

Anything but, he thought. "Now, that's a dumb question."

"How old are you now? Forty-four, forty-five?"

He frowned. "Thirty-eight. Nine years in this town just makes me look older than I am."

"Thirty-eight and still a bachelor," she went on in a thoughtful tone he didn't like one bit.

Speculation about his private life was something he worked hard to avoid. He should have seen this coming, but he'd been too tired. Or maybe too preoccupied. Whatever the reason, he was trapped. Walking out now would only raise questions he knew he didn't dare answer.

"It happens."

"You're not gay, so—"

"How do you know that?"

"Because I lived and worked with men for a lot of years. After a while a woman gets a sixth sense when it comes to a guy's sexuality." She fixed him with a knowing look. "You're one sexy guy, doctor. A big hunk of hot-wired sex appeal, only you do your best to keep that side of your personality hidden."

He cursed the heated flood of blood to his face. "You know what, Geneva? All that so-called health food you shove into your body has scrambled your brains."

"Maybe, but I've got eyes. You're blushing."

"What man wouldn't when a cheeky woman like you starts mouthing off about his sex life?"

"Not sex *life*. Sex *appeal*. There's a difference. One you have, one you don't."

He shook his head. "You're certifiable, Harkness."

Her soft laughter followed him all the way to the elevator.

No Easy Way Out

* * *

Arden woke to find her bedroom lit by the gray of false dawn. Outside, the wind was howling ferociously, rattling the old windowpanes like castanets.

A muffled thud had her sitting up far too quickly. Pressing a hand against her sore flesh, she threw back the covers and had one foot on the floor when she heard another alien sound. Someone was moving around her house.

"Who's there?" she called, her voice stained with fear.

"It's me, Mommy." Steffie's voice came from someplace nearby, followed by the distinct click of a door closing.

"Stef? What's wrong? Are you sick?"

A small white ghost in pajamas appeared in her doorway. "No, I was just getting a blanket out of the closet."

Climbing carefully from the warm covers, Arden realized that the house had grown colder than usual and wondered if the creaky old furnace had gone out again.

The floor was ice-cold. So, she discovered, were the insides of her slippers. Her robe was only marginally warmer, even belted as tightly as comfort would allow.

"Come on, sweetie, I'll tuck you in, and then I'll check the thermostat." She held out her hand for the blanket, but Steffie shook her head.

"It's not for me, it's for Dr. Kincade."

Arden blinked, certain that her mind was still half-numbed by sleep. "For... Did you say Dr. Kincade?"

"Uh-huh. He's sleeping in your chair, and he looks really cold."

"In my chair?" Her hand crept to her throat, instinctively drawing the robe closer.

"Uh huh. In the family room. I got up to go to the bathroom, and I saw the light and I thought it was you and maybe you were sick, so I checked."

Steffie ran out of breath and stopped to draw a couple of quick ones before adding, "See, that's why I need the blanket. Because he looks real cold and awful tired."

Arden stepped into the hall and craned her neck. A slit of light was lining the carpet under the closed door between the hall and the family room.

"You go on to bed, sweetheart. I'll see to Doctor Kincade."

Steffie wrinkled her forehead and pouted. "I want to do it. I'm the one who thought of the blanket."

"And it was a wonderful idea, Stef. Very, very thoughtful. But you have school tomorrow and you need a couple more hours of sleep in order to be bright-eyed and bushytailed."

"Oh, *Mother*," her daughter said with preadolescent disgust. "I'm not a baby anymore, you know."

Arden stifled a sigh. "I know, sweetie. But just humor me, okay?"

"Oh, okay, but be sure you tell Dr. Kincade I saw him first."

"Cross my heart," she said, reaching for the folded blanket still clutched to her daughter's chest. Steffie let it go, but her pout deepened. Setting her jaw, she flounced back to bed.

Slippers silent on the carpeting, Arden walked down the hall and opened the door to the living room a crack. Sure enough, Dylan was stretched out in her ratty old recliner, one knee hooked over the arm, the other supporting a thick file folder.

His head rested against the back where hers had made a comfortable hollow, and his eyes were closed. He looked exhausted. No, *spent* was the proper word, she decided after a moment's reflection. As though he'd put everything he had into his day and had nothing left for himself.

Her conscience stung her into admitting she'd taken up a big chunk of that day and given him nothing in return but a lot of grief. No wonder he'd walked out with frustration stamped on his face and something akin to disgust in his eyes.

No Easy Way Out

Feeling too much like an intruder in her own home, she crept forward until she was only a few feet away. He didn't stir.

His hair, usually severely brushed away from his wide, square forehead, had flopped forward, showing a rebel's tendency to wave, and his jaw was prickly with thick stubble the color of long-weathered straw.

Asleep and defenseless, his stern features softened by the glow from her reading lamp, he looked like a different man. More approachable, even lovable in a sleepy-bear way.

But far too worn, she realized with a thoughtful frown. Especially around the eyes, where permanent lines etched the corners. Laugh lines imprinted on the face of a man who rarely laughed.

Shivering suddenly, she hastily unfolded the blanket and moved closer. As gently as she could, she draped the soft wool over his still body and watched as it settled almost caressingly against the length of him, softening only slightly the line of hard muscle and sinew.

But it was the sudden frown on his face and the mumbled protest that had her reaching out a hand to smooth his hair in an instinctive gesture of comfort.

Warm, electric with good health, his hair feathered her fingers, charming her with the unexpected softness. The only soft thing about the man, she suspected, letting her hand rest lightly where it had stilled. Other than his heart, she corrected.

Sleep well, she thought. And thank you.

Turning to go, she found herself caught by the wrist. Startled, she turned back with a small murmur of protest.

His eyes were only half-open and drowsy. A quizzical look had his lips parted in lazy half smile, the likes of which she'd never seen on him before.

"Hmm, an angel in white," he murmured, pulling her toward him until she was all but lying across his chest.

"I'm hardly an angel," she whispered, tugging uselessly against his iron grip. "And what are you doing in my house, anyway?"

His forehead furrowed, and one side of his mouth twitched. "What do you know, an angel who talks back." His gaze dropped to her lips, his sleepy lashes shining gold in the light. "Has to be named Arden."

His other hand fought free of the blanket and came up to touch her face. His fingertips were pleasantly rough, sending an involuntary shiver through her.

"Dylan, don't," she whispered. "You're my doctor, remember?"

The look on his face changed to one of stark, bottomless pain, stunning her to motionless silence. "And you're a reporter. One keeps confidences, the other breaks them."

"Not always," she murmured.

"Always."

Never known for her psychic abilities, she nevertheless felt a wave of sadness run through her, black and empty and terribly real.

"Dylan?" she murmured. "What is it? Are you hurt?"

"If I am, it's my own fault."

His eyes closed, as though sleep were taking him away again, and then his blue eyes were open again and searching her face, an expression of abject torment turning the depths ebony.

"Why did you have to be so beautiful?" His mouth flattened. "Isn't a life in exile enough punishment for one man?"

She took a careful breath. He didn't seem quite awake, and yet his eyes seemed clear beneath the shimmering pain. "I don't understand—"

"Better that way," he murmured, curling his hand around the back of her neck. "C'mere, angel."

"Dylan, stop—" she got out before his mouth smothered the rest of her startled protest.

No Easy Way Out

The fingers holding her were iron. The mouth taking control of hers was soft, moving with slow, provocative deliberation.

His body was hard and lean and angular, honed by more than his duties as a physician. His arms were possessive and roped with the same combination of need and restraint framing his kisses. His heart was slamming against his chest like blows from a sledge.

After the initial shock, she stopped struggling. He wasn't awake, he wasn't aware. Exhaustion would soon claim him again.

When his hand found her breast through the flannel, she jerked backward. At the same time, another sensation, as sharp and piercing as a knife thrust in her side, had her crying out.

The spell was broken instantly. The softness left his eyes and the cruel lines deepened around his mouth. At the same time he gripped her arms, his fingers hard, holding her away from him.

"That's some bedside manner you have there," she quipped through the pain.

His face turned the color of old brick, and a vein throbbed in his temple. "What about you? How far were you going to let me go before you stopped me?"

"Me? What about you? I'm not the only one in this room, you know." Her temper flared. "And just for the record, short of a knee to the groin, how is a woman my size supposed to stop a man your size, anyway?"

"Try saying no," he shot back.

"You didn't give me a chance."

Dylan made himself ignore the growing pallor of her skin and the widening of her pupils. She was right, and he was an unprofessional jerk.

"Go to bed, Arden."

"Not until you get out of my house."

"Damn, woman, why does everything have to be a full-scale debate with you?"

He was out of the chair so fast the footrest hit the floor like a felled timber. Arden managed one step backward before she found herself being swept away toward her room.

His chest was hard, his shoulders rigid. Exertion—or was it anger?—had his neck corded and his jaw bunched. She detected scents of wood smoke and coffee and soap and sensed some powerful emotion coming from him in waves.

He was moving toward the hall almost before she could cry out. Held so securely, she expected pain, but instead, felt only the fluid surging of his stride and the thick security of his massive, warm chest.

There was no sound from Steffie's room down the hall. No sound from his stockinged feet. Nothing but the angry rasp of his breathing.

Her light was still burning, giving her a glimpse of rumpled sheets a split second before he deposited her in the middle of her bed as gently as a newborn.

"Tell you what, Ms. Anchorwoman Crawford," he said, straightening. "We'll make us a deal, you and me. I'll stay out of your life, and you stay out of mine."

"Fine with me. Better than fine."

Turning to leave, he forced himself not to look at her. The tug to apologize was too strong. The need to explain even stronger.

To his shame, he discovered that he couldn't do either.

Chapter 5

The seasoned hickory split straight and true, but Dylan scarcely noticed. He worked steadily, his movements as precise as a machine, his concentration fixed on the pile of firewood that had grown steadily larger with each hour that passed.

Usually he relished physical work, especially chopping his own firewood every few days. It kept his senses sharpened and his wind good.

It also wore him out enough to keep the loneliness from sitting too heavy in the empty rooms on those rare evenings when he made it home before eleven.

At dawn on a blustery morning after a night he'd just as soon forget, however, he didn't care about anything but purging himself of the feel of Arden's body and the taste of her kisses.

Resting the ax against the stump, he managed to wrestle another chunk of hickory onto the block without keeling over. He took a moment to swipe his sleeve over his dripping brow, then took up his ax again.

He brought the blade down hard and true, turning one log into two. Pain shot through his lower back, making him wince. His shoulder muscles were exhausted to the very point of cramping, and his wrists ached.

Tired as he was, need still flamed inside him whenever he thought about the softness cupped against his palm. She fit, too well. He wished she hadn't.

Maybe then he wouldn't be torturing himself now, wondering how the rest of her body would feel against his. Or how snug and moist she would be if he were inside her.

A ragged groan escaped his chapped lips, crystallizing in the frigid air. He hadn't felt a woman's warmth closing around him in over nine years. Sometimes, he'd all but convinced himself he'd lost the ability to function sexually.

Over the years, he'd missed sex, of course. Sometimes, in the early years of his self-imposed celibacy, he'd had nights when he thought he'd go crazy, he'd missed it so much.

Time had eroded most of that kind of physical desperation. Self-discipline took care of the rest. Until last night.

Damn it, celibacy was a choice. A man could change his mind, couldn't he? And then what? prodded his conscience. Risk involving her in the cesspool his life could become again in the wink of an eye or the click of shutter? Stain her and her daughter with the same shame he'd brought to his father and sisters?

Not even he would sink that low.

By the time he had the wheelbarrow full, the freezing rain had turned to hard sleet, and he was shaking so bad he had trouble guiding the wheelbarrow up the path from the woodshed to the porch steps.

His thighs were rubbery, and his arms had about as much strength as those of a prepubescent kid. Thus, stacking logs in his arms was a nearly insurmountable task. Climbing the steps was an exhausting exercise in patience.

It took him four trips instead of his usual two and just about all his wind to fill the wood box just inside the door.

No Easy Way Out

Even then, he'd managed to drop a half-dozen logs along the way.

By the time he'd finished, his chest was heaving and sweat was freezing to his face. It took a large chunk of his remaining strength to wipe down his ax and refill the bird feeder under the window before heading inside.

By the time he had a fire going in the fireplace, he was reeling with exhaustion. Food was out of the question. Even if he could summon the strength to fix something, his stomach would almost certainly rebel.

Somehow he made it up the stairs to his bedroom and out of most of his wet clothes before he collapsed onto the bed. Tired as he was, however, it was a long time before the shame burning in his gut would let him escape into sleep.

Someone had turned off her alarm. Dr. Kincade, she suspected, sometime after she'd gone to sleep and before they'd had their blowup. He was gone, of course. Only the blanket folded neatly on her chair remained.

Standing alone in her kitchen with a wintry sun streaming through the window, she lifted a hand to her mouth and touched her lips with her fingertips.

She found them swollen and tender, sensitized by his demanding mouth and a kind of unspoken yearning she had tried most of the night to understand.

He was an attractive man, even sexy when he forgot to scowl. And, she suspected from the way he kissed, a good lover. Sex partners would be easy for him to find.

As she went about brewing a larger than usual pot of strong coffee, she told herself to forget last night ever happened. What she'd intended as a gesture of caring he'd taken for a sexual come-on. It happened.

And he wasn't an evil man. She'd seen too much kindness in him to ever believe that. More likely, he was simply another spoiled bachelor who thought he was taking something that was being offered.

Except that that particular rationalization didn't work worth a darn. Not when she could still see the agony in his eyes and feel the rough loneliness in his kiss.

She had a feeling he needed more fuzzy blankets in his life and kisses he didn't have to steal in the dead of night when his defenses were down. Most of all he needed someone to bring those long-ago laugh lines to life again.

She, however, was not that someone.

Waiting impatiently for the water to drizzle through the grounds, she found herself staring at the bleak landscape beyond the cold windowpanes.

The deal he'd proposed made very good sense. She had Steffie and the paper and a list of important goals that were entirely hers—for the first time in her life. A relationship with anyone, let alone a man as mercurial as Kincade, was far, far down on that list.

The moment the last drop hit the pot, she had a mug poured and was lifting it to her lips. As she did, a flash of blue from the street below caught her gaze.

It was a truck, all right. But it wasn't his.

"Mommy, where's Dr. Kincade?"

Turning, she found Steffie framed in the kitchen doorway, a look of disappointment creasing her forehead.

"He had to leave, sweetie. Doctors are very busy people, you know."

Steffie's mouth edged toward pouting. "Did you tell him the blanket was from me?"

Arden all but groaned aloud. "I'm sorry, sweets. I forgot, but I'm sure he would have been pleased to know you were thinking of him."

"Yeah, but you promised, and you keep saying a promise is a sacred trust between people and as important as always telling the truth."

"You're right. And I made a bad mistake by not telling him, and I'm sorry."

"I could call him at his office. He said I could."

"I think that would be a fine idea, sweetie, but perhaps you should wait until after breakfast."

"But I want to do it now!"

"Okay, but I doubt he'll be in this early."

"Then I'll call him at home. He wrote the number on the back of the card he gave me yesterday at the hospital, just in case."

Happy again, Steffie skipped down the hall to her room. Seconds later, Arden heard her talking on the bedroom extension. Because the urge to eavesdrop was nearly irresistible, she busied herself making waffles for breakfast, a treat she usually reserved for her days off.

By the time Steffie returned to the kitchen, smoke was billowing from the waffle iron she was trying to scrape free of charred batter.

Unconcerned at the latest in a lengthening series of her mother's culinary disasters, Steffie slipped into her place and took a long swallow of milk before saying brightly, "He was taking a shower, but he answered, anyway."

Hot or cold? Arden wondered, jabbing the tines of the fork at a particularly stubborn bit of ruined waffle. "I'm sure he was happy to hear from you."

"Yep. He said it made his morning."

"Uh-huh." Giving up, she shoved the waffle iron to the back of the counter and reached for the box of cold cereal. Corn flakes might be dull, but they were trustworthy.

"He asked me if you were up and how you were feeling."

Arden poured cereal into two bowls, then set about slicing bananas over the unappetizing flakes. "What did you tell him?"

"That you were drinking coffee and trying to burn down the kitchen."

Arden shut her eyes tightly for a moment. "What did he say?"

"Mostly he sounded like he was trying not to laugh." Steffie took another gulp of milk, then wiped her mouth with the back of her hand instead of the napkin Arden was always careful to provide. "Then he told me I'd better see if I could help you out, 'cause you were still recovering and likely to be a little shaky."

"That's all?"

"Yep, 'cept for the part I don't understand, of course."

Arden turned slowly to face her daughter. "What part is that, sweetie?"

Steffie glanced toward the ceiling as though trying to recall the exact words. "He said to remind you about some conversation you two had about mistakes and, uh, perfect people?"

Arden nodded, uneasiness tickling her throat. "Yes, I remember." She carried both cereal bowls to the table, plunking them down with a tad more force than necessary.

"Well, then he said to tell you that his, uh, behavior, I think he said, last night was all the proof you ought to need that there aren't any." Looking down, Steffie wrinkled her nose at the cereal. "Do you know what he meant?" she asked, looking up again.

"I think he was saying he was sorry."

"Then why didn't he just say it?"

"Because some people have trouble putting their feelings into words." Men more than women. Strong men even more so.

"Do you?"

"No, but that's my job, isn't it? Putting things into words."

She settled into her chair and poured milk she tolerated because it was good for her over cereal she hated but ate for the same reason.

"What's he sorry for?" Steffie's expression was openly dubious, as though she couldn't imagine a man as perfect as Dr. Kincade ever having to say he was sorry. At least not to her severely flawed mother, anyway.

"For doing some things he shouldn't have done."

Steffie thought a moment. "Like yelling at you last night, you mean?"

Arden felt her heart rate falter. So Steffie hadn't gone right back to sleep, after all.

"Yes, for yelling at me." Among other things. Things that were more difficult to understand—and forget.

"How come he did that?"

Arden touched the tip of her tongue to her still-throbbing lower lip. "I don't know, sweetie. Maybe he doesn't, either."

Seemingly satisfied, Steffie attacked her cereal, her expression one of resignation at being served the same old thing one more time.

"Mommy?" she asked, looking up suddenly, as though struck by a thought.

"Yes, sweetie?"

"You like Dr. Kincade, don't you? I mean, even though he yelled at you and all?"

She almost groaned aloud at the matchmaking glint in her daughter's eyes. "I don't know him well enough to know one way or the other."

She stirred her coffee and told herself that she didn't *dislike* him. She just wasn't sure it was safe to let herself *like* him.

"He's a very, very good doctor," she added when she realized Stef was still watching her.

Impatience crossed her daughter's face. "Yeah, but I mean, you like him for a friend, too, don't you?"

Oh no, she thought, recognizing the signs. No matter how much time Arden spent with her, or how many suitable male role models she had tried to introduce into Steffie's life, her sweet, sensitive little girl was still searching for the perfect father figure.

Which Dylan Kincade most definitely was not.

Not if Arden had anything to say about it.

Hiding her distress, she put down her spoon and lifted the mug to her mouth. Three swallows later, she was able to manage a breezy smile.

"Well, I don't really know him that well, sweetie, and we're both very busy."

"But you could be friends, right?" Steffie prompted eagerly. "And maybe we could have him come to dinner sometimes, like Mark used to come to dinner when we lived in L.A. Or like Daddy comes to dinner sometimes, on special occasions."

Arden ached for her little girl. She'd had that same deep longing for her own father's love when she'd been a child. Only, in her case, her father had lived in the same house with her instead of several continents away.

"We'll see, sweetie, but I have a feeling Dr. Kincade might be too busy to come to dinner, and I don't want you to be disappointed if that never happens."

"We could ask him and find out, right?"

"Uh-huh."

Steffie's face fell. "You always say that when you mean no and don't want me to be upset."

"Now, Stef—"

Disappointment flared beneath Steffie's feathery eyebrows. "I *knew* you wouldn't like him, 'cause he's not a wimp like Mark and those other guys you dated in L.A.!"

"I thought you liked Mark—"

"Well, I didn't! He smelled like a girl, and he was always looking in the mirror to check out his hair like one, too." She slipped from her chair and left the kitchen.

Alone again, Arden buried her head in her folded arms and closed her eyes. This was all her fault. If only she'd listened to sound advice for once in her life and stayed in the hospital one more night, she wouldn't have been at the recital, and Dylan would never have been in her house.

Maybe then she really would have been able to think of him as a friend. Instead of a man with torment in his eyes and a knack for kissing a woman until her knees were weak

No Easy Way Out

and the good old-fashioned common sense that had been her salvation more than once had flown south for the winter.

For Steffie's sake, she would be pleasant whenever she and Dylan happened to cross paths. For Steffie's sake, she would even invite him to dinner. When he declined, which she knew full well he would do, she could at least face her daughter with a clear conscience.

Feeling better, now that she had a plan, she lifted her head and squared her shoulders. The princess was in control again.

Dylan put aside the blood pressure cuff and pulled the stethoscope from his ears. Nettie's condition had deteriorated in the three months since her last examination. He'd done all that he could do, but it wasn't enough.

"There's a man in Boston I want you to see. A heart specialist. Man named Cabot, the best I've ever seen in cases like yours."

Nettie adjusted the covers with a hand not yet touched by arthritis. Her mind was as sharp as ever, and she wore glasses only for reading. In all aspects but one, she had the body of a much younger woman.

"No more specialists," she declared firmly. "It's simply a waste of time and money, and we both know it."

"Wrong. New things are being developed every day. This man has come up with a regimen that's had rather promising success with patients worse off than you."

She sniffed her opinion of new things. "I see you've been poring over those medical journals of yours again, and I thank you for caring, but not even willpower as strong as yours can hold back the inevitable."

Dylan perched on the edge of her bed and took both her hands in his. Her skin was cooler than normal, a result of sluggish circulation, and dark moons dotted her nails.

"Stow that fatalistic mumbo-jumbo. You've been a fighter all your life. You can't quit now."

"Yes, my dear Dylan, I can," she said with a gentle rebuke in her tone that nearly broke his heart. "Besides, I have other things to save my energy for. My students, of course, and, well, Norman is coming home and bringing his wife and baby Arthur. He's promised to stay for a good long visit this time."

What, two days instead of one? Dylan wanted to say, but kept silent in deference to the soft light in Nettie's eyes.

Norman MacGregor was her only son and the joy of her life. He was a doctor, too, specializing in cosmetic surgery in Palm Springs.

"How is Norman these days?" he asked as he released her hands and stood.

"Fine, just fine. He and Jane just built a new home. I'm hoping they remember to bring pictures."

"I'm sure they will." He was anything but.

Dylan remembered the first time he'd set eyes on Nettie's son. Known then as Normy, he'd been a college kid with a cocky attitude and a love 'em and leave 'em way with the starry-eyed local girls.

The last time Dylan had seen him, a few years after Norman had finished his residency, Nettie's son had been driving a big black car and smoking big black cigars. When they'd chanced to meet on the street, Norman had made it very clear that even casual conversation with a small-town GP was beneath him.

Still, Nettie doted on him, even though once he was no longer dependent on her financially, she rarely saw him. Dylan considered him a lightweight and a poor excuse for a son. But he *was* blood kin and, as such, was bound to have his mother's welfare at heart. Or so he devoutly hoped.

"Maybe I'll buy him a cup of coffee while he's here," he said as he picked up her chart and signed the patient release form. "Pick his brain about the newest techniques in lifting sagging chins."

Nettie snorted. "It's my heart that's getting old, Dylan, not my brain. You like Norman about as well as I like that crotchety, prune-faced sister-in-law of mine. And the only reason you'd even spend a second of your time with him is so that you can try to get him to talk to me about this Boston specialist of yours."

Heat crept into his face, bringing with it a self-conscious frown as he shoved his pen into his pocket. "Hold on, Nettie. I've never said a negative word about your son."

The fact that he didn't bother denying her other assumption won him a teasing look. "You don't have to. You think he's self-centered and ungrateful and a disgrace to his father's memory."

Dylan opened his mouth, then shut it tight, causing Nettie to chuckle. "Well, you're right. He's all of those things, but I love him, anyway. Does that surprise you?"

"Yes, it surprises me," he admitted with a trace of bitterness in his voice, triggered by the memory of a son's failings and a father's disappointment.

Nettie's gaze turned anxious, and her voice grew gentle. "Don't be upset with me, Dylan. I know I've given you more trouble than any one doctor should have to take, but I've always lived my life by my own lights. I can't change now."

"Damn it, Nettie. I'm not trying to change you. I'm just trying to keep you alive."

"There's a difference between living and breathing."

"Nettie—"

"No, hear me out. Life is more than taking up space. Life is loving and being loved, watching the seasons change and your children grow. And it's friendship and kinship with all creatures and a need to be remembered for more than a pretty face or a fat bank account. My life has been all those things, and more. A trip to Boston, maybe another operation and a long recovery would take precious time away from the things that matter to me."

The thought of her death had him feeling sick inside. He covered it with anger. "That's bull, and you know it."

"You mind your tongue, young man." Her voice gentled. "And stop worrying about me. I know what I'm doing."

He brushed a kiss across her papery cheek, then let his hand rest on her shoulder. It was as close as he could come to telling the woman who'd been like a mother to him for nine years that he loved her.

The *Press* was in trouble. No matter how many times Arden reworked the figures or juggled expenses, the paper she'd put her heart and soul and all of her savings into ten months ago was headed full-tilt down a long slide to bankruptcy.

Somehow she needed to double circulation, attract thousands more per month in advertising or rob a bank. At the moment she was open to all three.

Arden threw down her pencil and tore off her reading glasses. Why, why, why did she ever think she could take a newspaper that had lost money for five years in a row and make it profitable? she wondered, rubbing the aching bridge of her nose.

"Because you're still trying to make Daddy proud of you," she muttered aloud. Since she was alone in her office, with the windows separating her from the pressroom beyond, she allowed her shoulders to slump.

Jacob Roberts Forbes had been born with galley ink in his veins and fingers nimble enough to set type almost as fast as a machine. Or so said the legend she'd heard all of her life.

At the age of nineteen J.R. had inherited the Susanville *Herald* from his father. By the time he'd turned thirty, everyone who was anyone in journalism knew of the small California daily and its crusading, innovative publisher.

The accolades were piled deep by the time Arden had been old enough to understand what they'd meant. His first Pulitzer had come when she'd been eight. The awards ceremony ended up being the day before she'd had her tonsils out.

J.R. had offered to let his managing editor accept in his stead, but Arden had stoutly refused to let him miss out on what he and everyone had been calling the biggest thing to happen to Susanville since the gold rush.

And if, secretly, she'd been hoping he would somehow understand that she was terrified of the surgery and change his mind at the last minute in order to be with her, no one saw her disappointment when he didn't.

His second Pulitzer had come when she'd been a senior in high school. Her own modest recognition as the editor of the school paper had been lost in the deluge of congratulations for her father.

Not that it wasn't deserved. It was.

Everyone who was anyone in journalism recognized J. R. Forbes as a deeply principled man incapable of compromise. His only god was truth. Discovering it when no one else had the strength to dig as deeply, revealing it with clarity, integrity and scrupulous, painstaking accuracy, sticking by it when others threw stones—those were his passions.

Nothing got into the *Herald* that hadn't been checked, rechecked and then checked again. If it saw print, you could trust every word.

J.R. had sent her to college to learn how to write crisp, clear copy. After graduation, he had planned to teach her everything he knew about the business of informing the public about the world around them. Instead, she'd met Mike Crawford and fallen instantly, ecstatically in love.

J.R. had been furious.

"The man's on TV," he'd shouted over the phone after she'd just bubbled for ten solid minutes about the man she was going to marry. "Wears makeup and reads someone else's words. Makes things up if the facts aren't nailed down by airtime."

Arden had loved both men and had needed both men to love her. She tried a compromise. She would marry Mike and go with him to Mexico on his latest assignment. At the same time she would send back features for the *Herald*. Instead, she had gotten pregnant, and that was the end of her writing.

The *Herald* was gone now, burned to the ground by angry loggers after J.R. had exposed corruption in their union. He'd died soon after. Not once, even on his deathbed, had he told his only daughter that he was proud of her.

Catching herself drumming her fingers on the desk, she frowned. By nature she was not a nervous person. Nor was she the same impulsive young woman she'd once been.

Experience, and especially motherhood, had matured her. Her life was made up of well-thought-out goals and thoroughly reasoned aspirations, none of which came close to being extreme or exotic or even all that unusual.

A Pulitzer would be nice, but she'd gladly settle for a thriving, viable newspaper noted for its progressive stance on important issues and appreciated for its service to the community.

A stock portfolio and a stack of triple-A bonds would be lovely, but she would settle for enough in the bank to send Steffie to the college of her choice with enough left over for a vacation in the sun once a year for herself.

It wasn't a bad life. Pretty good, in fact. Except, sometimes, she was so lonely she ached.

And sometimes, when she saw Steffie wistfully watching a mother and father and children strolling together in the mall, she wondered if she would ever fall in love again.

Her mind, usually so willing to slide over the very idea of another man in her life, turned instead to an image of a shaggy-haired, sleep-tamed bear of a man with lost battles in his eyes and a need to be loved he did his damnedest to deny. Which, she reminded herself, he'd made very clear was none of her business.

Fifteen minutes and a fifth rejuggling of figures later, she let out a long, noisy sigh and gave up. Economizing wouldn't do the job, and every corner that could be cut without jeopardizing quality and employee security had been cut.

She needed an infusion of capital, she decided, swiveling her chair around so that she could see the prized painting of her father hanging on the wall.

His expression was endlessly stern, and his eyes bored into her, reminding her of the things he expected her to stand for—honesty, integrity and, above all, the people's right to know.

First, however, she had to keep the doors open and the presses running.

"How come everything always comes down to money?" she muttered, her shoulders slumping.

"That's a question I've been asking since I opened my practice."

The gruff, masculine voice had her spinning around far too quickly, causing her stomach to somersault and her senses to jangle.

Sure enough, Kincade was standing in the doorway, a beautiful pearl-gray cowboy hat in one hand and a beribboned pot of pink African violets in the other.

Coming directly from the outdoors, he was wearing a shearling jacket that added unneeded breadth to his already massive shoulders. His jeans were indigo new and not quite as snug as they would be after a half-dozen washings. She couldn't be certain, but it looked as though his boots had been shined.

Almost formal dress for Myrtle. Certainly for him.

She hid her surprise behind a long, accusing glare. It had been a week since their encounter in her family room, and she hadn't seen him since.

Her incision was nicely healed, and she hadn't had more than a few tugs of minor pain for days. Instead of returning to his office to have her stitches out, she'd removed them herself with her cuticle scissors.

She was honest enough with herself to admit that she'd been deliberately avoiding him. Not because he'd kissed her so much as the reaction she'd had to that kiss.

"That door was closed for a reason," she said haughtily.

"I knocked."

Dylan studied her face, noting signs of fatigue around her mouth and temper in her brown eyes. There wasn't a hint of welcome in her expression. Not that he deserved any, he accepted, but still, sometimes a man hoped for the impossible.

"I didn't hear any knock," she said pointedly, confirming his preliminary diagnosis. A welcome visitor he was not.

"Sometimes a doctor has to take extreme measures if he thinks his patient might be in trouble."

"I'm not your patient anymore, and I'm not in trouble. Besides, I thought we had a deal. I leave you alone, you leave me alone, and the world goes on spinning."

"There are deals, and then there are deals."

He tossed his hat onto the desk, then used his free hand to close the door. If she wanted privacy, he was happy to accommodate her.

"How are you feeling? Any problems I need to hear about?"

"No problems, at least none that should concern you."

He nodded. "Glad to hear it." He glanced around curiously. "Nice office."

She snatched off her glasses and tossed them to the desk. "Do *not* sit down. You are *not* staying."

He felt like an idiot, standing there with a sissy-looking plant in his hand, so he got rid of it by plunking it down in front of her.

"Here. This is a peace offering."

When that didn't win him a hint of a smile, he knew he was in trouble. "It's supposed to like windowsills and not too much water. If you do it founders, or something."

She flicked the pink blossoms a wary glance, clearly refusing to be charmed. "I hate African violets. They always die."

He took heart in the hint of nastiness in her tone. Anything was better than cold rejection. "Try vitamins."

No Easy Way Out

Her gaze came to him slowly, then held. Seeing his own lousy opinion of himself and his behavior reflected in her eyes had him struggling to keep his gaze steady.

"Why are you here?" she asked finally.

He moved his shoulders under the jacket he rarely wore because it reminded him too much of a Bostonian's idea of Western garb.

"Mostly I'm trying to find a way to weasel out of the whopping apology I owe you."

A smile was in her eyes before she could stop it. Relief ran the length of his spine, and he had a feeling he'd taken a big step toward regaining her respect.

"Nice try, I'll give you that much." She sat back and crossed her arms over her chest. Just the sound of skin moving under silk had him thinking thoughts he'd worked an entire week to curb.

"But you want the words, huh?"

"Only if you mean them."

It was hot in her office, and now and then he caught a whiff of her perfume. It reminded him of soft white flannel and pink roses. "I mean them."

He waited, but she refused to let him off the hook. He should have known she would hang tough. He stifled a sigh and gathered his courage. Admitting he was wrong was a habit he'd tried to avoid most of his life. In this case, he couldn't.

"I behaved like a jerk, and I'm sorry."

"That's your idea of a whopping apology?"

She was watching him with more warmth now, and her mouth had taken on a slight curve. He took it as a start on the friendship he wanted to propose.

"I suppose I could take out an ad in this rag of yours, but—"

"Rag!" Her eyes were dancing now, and her voice had taken on a lilt. "I'll have you know the Myrtle *Free Press* has a long and honorable tradition in this county. And an impeccable reputation." She bunched her eyebrows wryly. "Well, for the last ten months, anyway."

"Making changes, are you?"

"You mean you haven't noticed?"

Telling her that he hated newspapers and never read hers or anyone else's was a good way to lose the little bit of ground he'd gained so far. Telling her why he hated them was an impossibility.

"I don't have much time to read anything but medical journals," he hedged.

"That's a good way to stay uninformed, Dr. Kincade."

"I'm informed on things I care about. Besides, in my job I probably get the news before you do, anyway." He considered that, then added with scrupulous truth, "The juiciest parts, anyway."

He hadn't realized how tight he'd been holding his muscles until she laughed and some of the tension gave way.

"You're probably right about that."

Tilting her chin, she offered him a teasing, speculative look that had him thinking about pink panties and cold showers.

"Want to become a part-time reporter? We pay next to nothing, but the benefits are even worse."

She was wrong. Reporters made plenty of money and didn't care whose blood was spattered all over it. Problem was, he was having trouble shoving her into the same damnation he reserved for the rest of her ilk.

It wasn't a particularly pleasing discovery. In fact, it was making his life a damn sight more complicated than he could afford.

"I have a job," he said, taking up his hat. "Which I've neglected longer than I'd planned."

"Thank you for the violet." Her tongue made a quick, nervous swipe over her lower lip, sending his blood pressure into dangerous territory. "I'll do my best to keep it alive."

"That's all any of us can do."

No Easy Way Out

"True enough."

Dylan glanced down at the hat in his hands, gathering his nerve. When he looked up again, his belly was knotted and his palms were sweating.

"Arden, I want you to know, the things I said to you, they came out of a mess I made in my life a long time before you and I met. It had nothing to do with you."

She got to her feet and circled the desk until she and Dylan were only a few feet apart. "I think I knew that, even when you were saying them," she said softly. "But I have a temper.... I said some things I regret, too."

She held out her hand, surprising him. He wiped his palm on his jeans, then touched it to hers. Her fingers curled slightly over his, completing the connection.

"Friends again?" he asked, his tone grave and just a bit husky.

"I don't know about the again part," she admitted, her own voice far from broadcast crisp, "but friends, yes."

Sometime during the black, sleepless hours of soul-searching he'd spent the last few nights, he'd promised himself he wouldn't kiss her again unless she asked him to. But that was before her perfume had a chance to tease his memory again. And definitely before he'd touched her again.

Not even a saint could endure that kind of torture, and he was about as far from being a saint as a man could get this side of hell.

Tightening his grip just slightly, he drew her toward him. She didn't resist. Nor did she show any signs of resisting. Instead, she parted the soft, tempting lips that had haunted his waking moments for days and sighed.

"Arden?"

"Yes... Dylan?"

If you have any mercy in your soul, you'll ask me to kiss you. "Tell me to get the hell out of your office." His mouth slanted, seemed almost to smile. Fascinated, she watched the subtle shift of muscle over bone, giving his face a starkly handsome cast.

"Get the hell out of my office." Her voice had the sting of a soft summer breeze, and the message in her tawny eyes was anything but fierce.

He brushed his mouth over hers, scarcely long enough to feel more than a slight rush. It was all he could safely allow.

He took back his hand and stepped away. "Take care of yourself—and that precocious kid of yours. She'll make a terrific doctor someday."

"Newspaperwoman."

"God, I hope not. I was just beginning to like her." He left before she could throw the plant in his face.

Chapter 6

"Okay, that's settled, then. Page one we go with the story on the mill closure in Drain for the lead and Linda's story on the fire at the VFW, including the color art."

Arden glanced over her glasses at the five members of her editorial staff gathered around the table. "Anything else?"

Wire editor Gordy Voss glanced at the news budgets spread out in front of him. "What about the story from AP about the latest on the wood products trade agreement with the Pacific Rim countries?"

Arden tapped her pen against her teeth as she studied the items already budgeted for pages one, two and three. "If we shorten the piece on Congress and the budget, we would have room at the bottom of page one."

Gordy sat back, grinning. "One line ought to do it." He drew an imaginary headline in the air. "Congress Still Gridlocked."

"Works for me," chimed in Betty Moran, Arden's prized managing editor.

"Me, too." Impatient as usual, chief photographer Nora Bennington gathered up her notes and closed the blue folder containing the photos they'd rejected. Those that would be used were already stashed in the red folder that would go to layout for cropping.

Arden drew off her glasses and rubbed the back of her neck. "Anything else?"

The others looked at one another questioningly. No one spoke. "Looks like that's it, then."

Like children dismissed for recess, everyone but Celia Montrose scattered. "I need some advice," she said when Arden raised inquiring eyebrows.

"I'll do my best, but I'm not promising anything."

Celia smiled. "About this piece on the ambulance fundraising drive. I just can't seem to find the right hook." She sighed. "I know it's extremely important to the well-being and safety of our readers, and I know repeated publicity is vital. But I can only put so much excitement into potluck suppers and raffles with an elkhound as the grand prize."

Arden nodded, her mouth twitching. "I have to admit I was hoping not to win when I bought my tickets last week."

Celia managed a straight face. She'd grown up in the Midwest, so Oregon ways weren't as strange to her as they were to a California native like Arden.

"According to Harve Delacroix, 'that thar hound' is a genuine champion, with the nose of a true thoroughbred, or purebred—something like that, anyway."

Arden digested that for a moment, her mind busy turning over possibilities. "Okay, how's this? We do a piece on the progression of medicine from the turn of one century to the eve of the next. Depending on the photos in the morgue, we could show how new discoveries and modern inventions were introduced here over the years—you know, the horse and buggy giving way to the automobile, that kind of thing—and how a doctor's life changed with those innovations."

No Easy Way Out

Celia perked up visibly. "I like it! It has terrific potential as far as drawing parallels. From the horse and buggy to MRIs in semis that go from town to town on a regular schedule."

"Dylan—Dr. Kincade—mentioned his predecessor, a man named Sennett, I think. See what we have on him. There might be something there you could use."

"Great idea! I'll get right on it."

Arden settled her glasses on her nose again, capped her pen and stood up. "You might ask Dr. Kincade for a comment on the old versus the new. Or perhaps an anecdote about Sennett himself."

"It's worth a try." Celia rose as well, and the two walked to the door. Stepping into the corridor, Arden nearly collided with the receptionist.

"Oh, Mrs. Crawford, there you are." Stark relief shimmered in the young woman's eyes. "You didn't answer in your office, so..." She paused for a gulp of air.

"Anyway, can you take a call from Mrs. Peavy at the school? She's says it's about your daughter, and it's urgent."

Snow was mounded as high as her thighs on both sides of the sidewalk. Icicles dripped from the porch roof of the big, ugly house that had been home and office to old Doc Sennett for his entire adult life.

Now it provided office space for two doctors and living accommodations on the second floor where Dr. Christopher had been living for the past two years.

The waiting room was full. Arden recognized the faces of friends and acquaintances. Several called out greetings which she returned as politely as she could. When she reached the window separating the inner office from the waiting room, receptionist Marjorie Toth looked up from the notation she had just made in the appointment book.

"Where's Steffie?" Arden demanded when she found enough breath. "I came as fast as I could."

"Whoa. Slow down, Ms. Crawford," Marge said with a reassuring smile. "Dr. Kincade has enough patients to handle, what with Dr. Christopher still down with the flu. He doesn't need another."

"Is she all right?" She craned her neck, trying to see past the wall of files to the inner rooms.

Chuckling, Marge stood up and beckoned. "Come on back before you do yourself some permanent damage. And yes, she's fine. Dr. Kincade is just finishing up with her."

Arden beat Marjorie to the door and opened it herself. Inside, she was hit with the pungent smell of antiseptic and old wood lovingly maintained with lemon oil and elbow grease.

"Finishing up?" she demanded somewhat shakily to the older woman's back as they headed down a long, narrow corridor. "Marge, what's that mean, he's finishing up?"

"Your little girl is doing just fine, believe me. Why, already she has Dr. Kincade so wrapped around her finger he's almost mellow." Marge chuckled as she glanced over her shoulder. "Well, mellow for him, that is," she murmured in a low tone.

Marjorie stopped at the last door on the right and rapped lightly before opening it. "Mrs. Crawford is here," she said, stepping aside to give Arden a quick glimpse of Dylan's wide back and her daughter's pale face.

Murmuring her thanks to Marge, she took a deep breath to keep herself calm and stepped into the small space.

Steffie might look "just fine" to Marge Toth, but to Arden, she seemed very young and very fragile lying on the examination table with a cold compress on her head. Her left foot was bare and clearly swollen.

Dylan glanced her way and nodded. He had the preoccupied air of a badly overworked man trying to stretch himself too thin.

"What's wrong? What happened? Mrs. Peavy said it was a playground accident, but she didn't give me any details."

"Possible concussion, a slight sprain."

No Easy Way Out

His fingers were capable and thorough as they moved over the little girl's small bones. Arden remembered those same clever fingers sliding expertly over her skin, testing, probing so gently the pain was scarcely a twinge.

"Is it serious?"

"No. She'll likely be out of school for a day or two, and I want her to use crutches until I see her again in a week."

"My poor sweetie," she murmured, her voice catching in spite of her effort to remain calm. "Does it hurt a lot?"

Steffie's mouth turned down. Not in pain, Arden discovered, but in fury. "It hurts monstrous, and it's all Jimmy Anderson's fault."

"What happened? He didn't hit you, did he?" Arden took her daughter's hand. Her own was shaking.

"No, but it was his fault. He was showing off at lunch for Alison Grieves, trying to be some kind of stupid football star, and he ran right into me."

"Is that Jimmy with the mother who looks like Madonna, or Jimmy with the father who raises horses?" she asked lightly.

"Jimmy the jerk," Steffie muttered. "The one who delivers papers for you." Her eyes took on a cunning glint. "If you really loved me, you would fire him," she wheedled in her most persuasively charming voice, the one she'd inherited from her father.

Arden hid a smile. "You don't really mean that."

Her eyes flashed. "Sure I do. He's a creep, and I hate him."

"Perhaps, but that's between the two of you. I'm not involved."

"You're the publisher of the paper, and besides, you own it, so that makes you the boss. You can do anything, and no one will say anything about it, 'cause they won't want to lose their jobs."

Arden felt her mouth go dry. "Steffie, you know that wouldn't be fair for me to punish Jimmy for something that was an accident."

Stephanie pouted. "Daddy would stick up for me if he was here."

Your father has never stayed around long enough to do much more than spoil you rotten, then leave me deal with the tears and tantrums, Arden wanted to say, but didn't.

"I can't speak for your father. Only for myself. And I don't intend to fire anyone."

To her complete shock, Steffie's brown eyes welled with tears. "All you care about is that dumb paper."

"That's not true," she protested, stricken. "I care about a lot of other things—you, most of all."

"Then take me back to L.A. and my friends and my school and all the neat things I had when we lived there."

"This is our home now, Stef. Remember how we talked about making a change, and why?"

Steffie started to cry. "I don't want to live here anymore. There's no beach and the dumb cable TV only has twenty channels and people look at me like I'm weird, just because I wasn't born here."

Arden had heard those same complaints before, and she had just about run out of reasonable responses. But her daughter was in pain, and Dylan was watching them with far too much interest for her peace of mind.

"Now Stef—" she began, only to be interrupted by another, even more heated, barrage.

"I mean it! I *hate* Oregon. It's boring and stupid and... and *green*. And I hate you for making me come here."

Arden went still with shock, and then anger took over. Steffie had pushed too far this time. Differing opinions she could handle. Disrespect, never.

Not from her ex-husband or her employees or the daughter she adored. Before she could find her tongue, Dylan had literally shouldered her out of the way.

"Here, kid," he said, pulling a lollipop from his pocket and removing the waxed-paper wrapping. "Stick this in your mouth before you really get yourself in trouble. And try not to pick any more fights while I have a talk with your mom in my office."

Steffie's mouth took on a sulky droop, but to Arden's amazement, she did as she was told. There was little time to marvel, however, because Dylan had her by the arm and was walking her out of the examining room and toward his office before she knew what was happening.

Inside, a quick glance showed walls bearing old-fashioned wallpaper meeting a high ceiling, a desk piled high with papers and an old glass-fronted bookcase crammed to overflowing with well-thumbed medical books and dog-eared journals.

"Sit," he ordered, indicating one of two chairs in front of the desk.

Instead of taking his usual place behind the big desk, however, he rested his backside against the desk, crossed his brawny arms and regarded her calmly.

"Okay, here's what I can tell you at the moment," he said before she got a chance to speak. "Physically, your daughter is okay. Emotionally I'm not so sure. She was pretty upset when I brought her here."

"Well, of course she's upset! She's just been run over by a kid twice her size."

"*After* she'd called him a dumb, ugly moose."

"Who told you that?"

"Mrs. Peavy, when she brought Stephanie to the office."

From what he'd been told Steffie was headed down a long road to a self-generated exile and could do with a little help from a friend.

He knew what that was like. And he knew what it was like to find out your friends didn't want to know you anymore.

"Maxine wasn't telling tales, mind you, but from the things she said, it seems Stephanie has a rather, shall we say, dominant personality."

"If you mean that she'd been raised to take care of herself, yes, she does." He could feel her anger. It radiated from her like heat.

"I *mean* she's got a reputation as a sharp-tongued bully who isn't shy about letting everyone know her less-than-positive feelings about Oregon in general and her classmates in particular."

Her color heightened in a swath over each cheekbone, and her chin tipped forward. There was a lot of her mother in Stephanie, he thought again. Most of it, he suspected, as interesting as it was exasperating.

"And before you start calling me a chauvinist pig or whatever term is in vogue these days, I should tell you I was raised by a mother who was a feminist before there was such a term."

"Don't be ridiculous. Steffie doesn't have a mean bone in her body."

Without seeming to, he assessed the color of her skin beneath the quick flush and decided that she looked much better than last night. Medically speaking.

On a personal level, he'd have preferred to see her wrapped in her rosebud flannel, glaring at him from the middle of her bed.

When his mind began recalling the creamy skin barely covered by scraps of pink silk, he reminded himself that she was a patient, and now the mother of a patient, and therefore off-limits.

Just to make sure he remembered that, he walked around the desk and sat down. And just to make sure he was no longer able to smell her perfume, he tipped back his chair until it hit the wall behind.

"I'm not saying she's mean," he said, accepting her affronted gaze evenly. "But apparently she *is* having some difficulty fitting in."

"In *your* opinion."

"Yes, in my *professional* opinion."

Arden invariably felt the first stirring of strong emotion in her chest, right under her heart. She was feeling it now and didn't care who knew it.

"Oh, I didn't realize you were a child psychologist as well as a GP," she said with an astringent force that won her the beginnings of a grin.

"These days we call ourselves family practitioners."

"Well, excuse me."

"Apology accepted."

She worked hard at ignoring the understanding in his eyes. It was the subtle dance of humor that had her mouth twitching. "I guess I'm being an overprotective mother, huh?"

His eyebrows lifted slowly, suggesting that he was giving her question more than cursory attention. She realized that she liked him for that. She liked him for a lot of things, all of which were beside the point at the moment.

"Perhaps a bit," he said slowly. "But I can understand your reasoning. Stephanie can be a handful, yeah, but she's also one bright, loving kid. She'd be easy to spoil."

She sucked in hard. "Are you saying this is all my fault now, because if you are, let me tell you, it's no picnic raising a child alone in today's times. But then, I seem to remember you weren't all that keen on trying, anyway, so—"

It was laughter that had her stopping in mid-rebuke. Roughly like a throaty growl, to be sure, and just a bit self-conscious, but laughter nonetheless. This from a man she suspected seldom laughed out loud.

"Enough! I give up, Mama Bear." He rose and circled the desk much too quickly for his size. Before she could protest, he had her by both upper arms and was lifting her from the chair.

Taken by surprise, she caught the heel she'd hooked on the chair's rung and would have fallen if his hands hadn't been gripping her so firmly.

"Okay?" he asked with a frown between his eyebrows.

"Yes, fine."

His fingers loosened, but his hands remained hard on her flesh. A warm awareness stole over her, making her far too aware of the sexual sizzle between them. Frowning, she angled a look at the big hand still wrapping her left arm.

"Really. I feel great. No side effects at all. I even managed to pull out the stitches without any trouble."

His face changed. "I told you to make an appointment."

"And I would have, if there'd been a need. But I know how busy you are, and I do know how to use a scissors."

She grinned just to show him that there were no hard feelings. "I assure you, there hasn't been one side effect."

"You're sure? No twinges, no nausea?" His eyes bored into hers, searching, compelling—and so strongly familiar she found her own gaze welded to his.

"No, none," she managed to murmur when the frown between his eyebrows etched deeper. "I, uh, assume Stef can go home now?"

"She can—and she can't."

"Now, that's certainly precise."

His mouth softened only momentarily. "From a medical standpoint, your daughter is in no danger if she leaves. However, she definitely shouldn't put any weight on that ankle, which, as I mentioned before, means crutches. Which you will need to rent from Leo's Pharmacy—unless you have a spare pair lying around somewhere?"

She shook her head. "Sorry, fresh out."

"And since you shouldn't be lifting anything heavier than a book for the next few weeks, it's best that she stay here with me until I can bring her home later."

Without giving her a chance to argue, he strode to the door and pulled it open. "About six, I think."

He was gone before she found her voice.

He'd said six. It was almost seven when she opened the door to a rush of cold and a look of contrition in steel-blue eyes.

"You're mad," he said before she'd even opened her mouth.

"How can you tell?"

One side of his mouth softened. "Your eyebrows are smashed together over your nose, and your eyes were shooting gold darts at my head before you'd even gotten the door all the way open."

Arden snorted. "I think you need to fine-tune those diagnostic skills of yours, Doctor."

"Yeah, well, I do my best."

She refused to notice the sheen of rapidly melting snow on his hair, or the way he filled out the shoulders of the heavy coat like a linebacker in civvies. Instead, she focused her attention on her daughter.

"How are you feeling, sweetie?"

"Hungry."

Cradled against his chest and wrapped in a blanket—in addition to scarf, mittens and parka—Steffie looked cozy, warm and adorable. One small arm was around Kincade's neck. The other was holding on to a small white grocery bag, the kind that usually held frozen items.

"It's triple-chocolate sin," Steffie offered when her mother's eyebrows lifted. "It's Dylan's favorite."

"You bought ice cream in the dead of winter?"

"It's cheaper than roses," he said when she looked puzzled. "And besides, it's my favorite."

She refused to take the hint. Instead, she leaned forward to kiss her daughter's rosy cheek before stepping aside. "Take her to the family room, please. I fixed a little nest for her in the recliner."

Nodding, he brushed past her, taking great care, it seemed to her, not to touch her.

She followed, fighting the feeling that her well-ordered domain had been invaded by a large, shaggy and almost certainly dangerous bear who'd been in hibernation too long to be more than marginally civilized.

She hovered over her daughter until he had her settled in the pillow-lined nest. Then, one by one, she helped Steffie out of her things until her little girl was down to her school clothes again.

By the time she finished fussing, Steffie was settled like royalty on a well-padded throne and clearly enjoying the attention.

"How's that, sweetie?" Arden fussed with the pillow behind her daughter's back, adjusting it just so. "Are you comfortable? Can I get you anything?"

"Ice cream?" Steffie eyed the sack on the coffee table with obvious lust.

"For dessert."

"That's exactly what I told her," Kincade drawled. "Only you said it with more authority, of course. Moms always do."

He took Steffie's left shoe from his pocket and set it on the floor near the chair, then stood tall and stretched, looking around curiously as he did. "Something smells great. What are we having?"

"Spaghetti," Steffie volunteered before Arden had a chance to respond. "Only it's just sauce from a jar."

"As long as it's hot."

With her head tilted, Arden gave him an imperious look. "Funny, I don't remember inviting you to dinner tonight."

"Consider it payment for patching up the kid here."

Obviously sarcasm didn't faze him, she thought.

"Yeah, Mommy. You said you were going to ask him sometime."

Trapped, Arden forced a smile. "She's right. It's just sauce from a jar."

"Hey, I'm easy. Feed me enough to fill my belly, and I'm not in the mood to complain."

His eyes rested on her face almost impersonally. Nothing in his stance or demeanor suggested anything more than a purely professional scrutiny. Doctor toward patient, perfectly proper. Responsible.

She had no reason whatsoever to think that he was interested in her as a woman. But that's exactly what she was thinking—and feeling. It wasn't a bad feeling, more like disconcerting.

"Well, that's settled," she said, pressing her hands together. "Three for dinner."

"Hooray!" Steffie shouted, looking happier than she'd looked in months. Arden refused to feel guilty.

He shed his coat, draping it over the nearest chair with one hand and running the other through his hair to shake out the snow. Even though he was quite obviously tired, there was still a vitality about him that seemed to fill up the small room with energy. And sexual heat.

"I, uh, rented crutches." She glanced toward the corner near the upright piano where she'd stashed the child-size crutches after her hasty trip to the pharmacy.

"Yeah, I see."

He was also seeing the quick, wary glances she darted his way every time she thought he wouldn't notice. And the way the pale pink of her fuzzy sweater was reflected in her cheeks.

"Leo down at the pharmacy said metal ones were lighter and easier to manipulate."

"The bows are a nice touch. Was that Leo's idea, too?"

"Not exactly. I just thought they might make those ugly things a little more feminine."

Steffie giggled. Arden was pleased to see sparkle in her eyes again. "Mommy's trying to teach me how to coordinate colors, for when I'm old enough to buy my own clothes."

He thought about Arden's choices. Flannel with pink flowers, boxy slacks, oversize sweaters. Not exactly raw material to run a man's libido to hot, and yet his had been at blast temperature for days now.

Tonight she was wearing jeans, with buttons on the front—the kind that women had appropriated from men a few years back. Cut for a man's flatter behind, they had a tendency to hug a woman's curves with provocative snugness.

"Uh, so how's the paper?" he asked, and then winced inwardly. A man with his education ought to be able to come up with something a little more interesting than that.

"Improving, or so I'm told now and then." She cleared her throat. "How is Dr. Christopher?"

"Lazy and good-for-nothing most of the time, but he's got charisma, something Marge kept telling me the practice needed."

"Funny, I was thinking the same thing the other morning, right about the time you were warning me not to get out of bed—or else."

"Yeah, I'm a real tyrant, all right."

"Hey, you're supposed to be talking about me," Steffie piped up. "I'm the patient now, remember?"

Arden smoothed her daughter's hair. "Yes, sweets, we remember. And we're doing our best to take care of you."

Dylan saw the way her fingers stilled against her daughter's forehead, lingering for an instant, as though the contact was somehow special.

His mind zoomed back a few hours to a time when he'd been the one in the chair, and those same slim fingers had smoothed his hair.

He shifted his gaze and busied himself rolling the cuff of one sleeve above the wrist, then the other. If he concentrated hard enough, he might just succeed in keeping his thoughts out of her bedroom and off the middle-of-the-night fantasies he'd entertained about seeing it again, this time as an invited guest.

"Dinner smells ready," he said when he caught her watching him again. "What can I do to help?"

Chapter 7

"...and Dr. Christopher asked you to bring him some more decongestant and some chicken soup. He said you'd know the kind he likes best."

Portable phone pressed between his shoulder and his ear, Dylan leaned his chair back on two legs and tried to ignore the tiredness tugging at his bones.

"Anything else?"

"That's it, Doc," Grace said with a smile in her voice. "Not too bad this time. Only three house calls."

He tucked his notepad into his back pocket, along with the stub of a pencil he preferred to a pen. "Thanks, Gracie. Keep up the good work."

"You too, Dylan. And try to get some sleep, okay? You sound like your tail is dragging." The elderly operator hung up chuckling.

He was mentally prioritizing the calls when Arden returned to the kitchen. He preferred to think of her as a patient—*had* to think of her as a patient—for his own good and hers.

But that didn't mean he couldn't enjoy the way she looked in the shadowy light. All rosy and soft in sweater and jeans, with outrageous fuzzy slippers on her feet and her hair flopping every which way over sleek, feminine eyebrows.

He tried to picture her the way he'd first seen her, curled up in pain in a sterile, unisex hospital gown, but he kept seeing soft, provocative curves under flowered flannel instead. He decided to concentrate on things he could control.

"How's the patient?"

"All tucked in, and half-asleep already."

Instead of Stephanie, he pictured Arden tucked beneath warm sheets, her hair spread out on the pillow and a secret little smile on her lips. He pictured himself crawling beneath those same sheets and taking her into his arms.

The rush of raw hunger deep in his body told him that it was time he got out of her house. And her personal life.

"There's more coffee," she said when she noticed his empty cup. "How about one for the road?"

He hesitated, then figured a few more minutes wouldn't hurt either of them. "Half a cup, and then I've got to get back to work. Grace has three calls lined up for me before I can call it a night."

"I would offer you more ice cream," she said as she fetched the pot, "but you ate it all."

"With a lot of help from your daughter."

Her lips curved. "No wonder she likes you. Prescribing ice cream for a possible concussion, she's bound to develop a crush on you."

"Kids are easily impressed."

She glanced at him with those careful brown eyes that said she was anything but. He shifted, suddenly restless, and she returned her attention to the coffee she was pouring.

"It looks cold out there, and the weatherman is predicting more snow by midnight," she murmured. "How far is your place from here?"

"Fifteen, twenty minutes on dry pavement."

She shot him a look, her expression droll. "You mean it really gets dry sometimes up here?"

"A day or two every summer—in a good year."

"Define 'good.'"

"I can't. We haven't had one since I've been here."

"Oh, Lord, I think I'm in trouble," she muttered, pursing her lips to hold back the laughter he saw shining in her eyes.

He shook his head, his expression as serious as he could make it. "Not until you go to take a shower some morning and discover you've taken root. *Then* you know you've got trouble."

She tried, but the laughter tumbled out. "I asked for that, didn't I?"

"Maybe a little, yeah."

She skimmed the first steaming sip from her coffee, then cradled the mug against her chin. "You know what, Kincade? You're a lot of fun when you let yourself relax."

"Don't let the Harvard Alumni Association hear that," he said with mock horror. "We weren't trained to be anything but pretentious and rich."

Her lips curved. "You'd better get on the stick, then, because you're not either of those things. In fact, from what I've seen and heard, all those pompous Harvard M.D.s could learn a lot from watching you."

Moved beyond words, Dylan had to swallow hard before he could force down a sip of his own. "Careful, Arden. You'll have my head so swollen I won't be able to get through your front door."

"Don't worry, that's probably the last compliment you'll get from me. Downstairs, I'm known as a real hard case."

Such a simple thing, sharing a laugh with a pretty woman in a warm kitchen, his body relaxed, the aroma of rich food and strong coffee mingling with her perfume. And yet, something rare and precious to a man who had consciously, deliberately cut himself off from the solace of a woman's company.

He didn't want to leave. He couldn't stay.

He drained his cup with one swallow, then got to his feet. She rose as well, a perfect hostess. An enticing woman.

"Thank you for dinner," he said as he carried his cup to the sink in the way a man did when he was used to living alone.

"Thank you for not lying and telling me it was wonderful."

He never lied unless he had no choice, but when he had to, he did a damned good job of it. "It wasn't that bad."

"I suppose not—if you happen to like burned meatballs and curdled sauce."

"Must have. I ate three helpings, didn't I?"

He'd also been so busy trying to keep his unruly hormones in line that he would have shoved down a plate of charcoal and not tasted a bite.

He found his coat where he'd left it and slipped into it quickly. Her scent still lingered in the lining, a warm, sensuous, teasing fragrance that evoked passion and elegance and a man's curiosity to discover all the places where it clung strongest to her skin.

Scowling, he found her waiting for him by the front door. "I have a thermos," she murmured. "And there's plenty of coffee left. Why don't I send some with you?"

He wanted to mistrust the kindness in her eyes. He needed to mistrust it. "I'm supposed to take care of you, remember?"

"You have, and very well, in spite of my, shall we say, lack of cooperation."

"Shall we say, pigheadedness?"

He ran his palms up her arms. Gripping her shoulders lightly, he pulled her closer. He meant the kiss to be friendly, nothing more. Until he had taken her lips again.

"You taste better than any coffee," he said, rubbing his thumb over her lower lip.

When her eyes warmed, then turned softly questioning, he told himself to walk away now, before he crossed a line he himself had drawn a long time ago.

Instead, he brushed his mouth over her lips again, testing, tasting, until he knew he would remember the shape and taste forever. Reining in his impatience, he drew back. It wasn't safe to test too often the walls he'd built.

"I've always made it a rule never to become involved with a patient."

He took a strand of hair between his fingertips, testing the silk texture. Until now, he'd never noticed how many different shades of brown there were.

"But since you're really Neil's patient, that doesn't apply. I just wanted you to know that."

Her breath caught, then released unsteadily. "I won't go to bed with you, if that's what you're asking."

"When the time's right, I won't ask."

Because his control would only stretch so far, he left without kissing her again.

Neil Christopher took one look at Dylan and winced his sympathy. "There's whiskey in the wardrobe, left side."

"Don't tempt me."

Dylan dropped the bag with the soup and decongestant onto the bed near the mound made by his partner's big feet and stripped off his gloves.

It was a few minutes past midnight, and the snow was coming down hard again, making the mountain roads treacherous, even with four-wheel drive. If his luck held, Neil would be the last patient of the night.

"How're you feeling?"

"How do I look?"

"Rotten."

Stuck in bed, his pugnacious jaw covered with several days' worth of whiskers and his coarse brown hair a tangled mess, Neil looked more than ever like the down-and-out druggie he'd once been.

"Busy day?"

Neil leaned against the jumbled pile of pillows and took out the container of soup. Dylan settled into the overstuffed easy chair in the corner and watched his partner slurping down broth like a greedy ten-year-old.

"Busy enough, yeah."

Neil drained the cup and tossed it into the trash basket, which was all but overflowing with tissues. "Then you'll be stoked to hear I'm ready to come back to work. Part-time, anyway."

"Maybe you are and maybe you aren't. I haven't examined you yet."

"No problem, I'll save you the trouble. Temperature's normal, cough is almost gone, and I'm horny as an old goat."

Dylan tried for a smile, but it was too much of an effort. "The temp and the cough I accept. Last I heard, being horny hasn't been recognized by the American Medical Association as a diagnostic tool."

"Maybe not, but it's been a tried-and-true method for this doctor for a lot of years."

"Whatever works." Dylan got to his feet with more energy than he knew he had.

"Dylan, before you go, there's something we need to talk about." Neil was suddenly dead serious, something that was rare for him.

"I'm listening."

Now that he had Dylan's attention, Neil seemed oddly reluctant to continue. "Kels called again this afternoon. About the documentary on rural medicine? Wanted to know if you'd changed your mind about letting SM Productions film here?"

"I haven't changed my mind, nor do I intend to." Dylan knew his voice sounded cold. It was meant to.

"It could mean big bucks for the ambulance fund. Maybe even attract a few more tourists to the area." Neil grinned. "We could even offer ride-alongs like the cops and the firemen. You know, show the city folk how we country docs spend a day."

"Don't you mean how one country doc makes time with an old girlfriend who just happens to be a hotshot producer of documentaries?"

Neil flushed. "Honest, she's really hot to do a piece on country docs, especially after I ran your bio past her."

Dylan went cold. "*My* bio?"

"Yeah. Well, she already knows mine, and to tell you the truth, she's not all that impressed. Dumb, wet-behind-the-ears intern slides off the rails and gets himself canned. Old news in L.A."

He shrugged, but Dylan knew Neil was still dealing with some emotional baggage left over from the cocaine use that had nearly cost him his license.

When no one would give him a job in California, he'd come north in answer to a small ad Dylan had placed in one of the journals. Because Neil hadn't lied to him about his past, Dylan had hired him on the spot, without references and without judging.

So far it had been a good partnership. At least, Dylan was pleased. He realized now that he couldn't speak for Neil.

"Now, you, on the other hand," Neil went on, "are the stuff legends are made of."

Eyes gleaming, he traced a headline in the air. " 'Son of Illiterate Coal Miner, Turned Sophisticated Harvard Cum Laude, Finds Peace and Fulfillment in the Wilds of Oregon.' Kels says it's a natural."

Dylan knew Neil was grateful to him and trying hard to pull his weight. Maybe he thought this was one way of saying thank you to the man he considered his mentor.

He was wrong.

"Find another way to impress the lady. I said no, and I meant it."

Dylan grabbed his jacket and headed for the door.

* * *

Arden put aside her book and leaned back against the piled pillows. It was no use. She'd read the same page twice and still had no idea who had strangled whom or why. Nor, it seemed, did she care.

She'd chosen a thriller because the pace was invariably fast, allowing her to completely immerse herself in the twists and turns of the plot.

Tonight, however, she might as well have been reading a cookbook, for all the enthusiasm she'd been able to summon up. Something was decidedly amiss if a hefty dose of murder and mayhem couldn't keep her attention.

Arden frowned, casting her mind over the last few weeks. Things had been hectic, for sure. Her surgery and Nettie's dizzy spell. Just when things had started to slow down, Steffie had had her accident.

She was used to juggling lots of different balls. In her years as a working reporter, and then later as the highest-rated anchor in the local L.A. market, she and stress had become constant companions. It was uncomfortable, but it was manageable.

The intrinsic loneliness of single life was sometimes a problem, especially since she'd moved to Oregon, but that could be controlled.

On the other hand, Dylan Kincade showed every sign that he couldn't.

For all his gentleness and brooding quiet, he was a very dangerous man. He wasn't overtly or viciously dangerous, but he was definitely threatening.

Inner strength, self-control, a confident man's fierce pride—he had them all. She'd seen those and more in the OR that morning. And she'd sensed other things, as well. Things that were far more difficult to ignore.

Like the lines etched like scars into his wide brow, suggesting that he knew more about suffering than any medical textbook could teach.

Years ago, before her face had become too well-known to make such things unwieldy, she'd done volunteer work in a veterans' hospital. The wards had been filled with men in pain, some from physical wounds, others from injuries inflicted on the inside. Proud men. Men who had medals attesting to their courage.

Dylan reminded her of the men who kept the agony inside, determined to keep their suffering hidden. Private.

Those brooding eyes, his permanently lined brow, even his wildly disheveled tobacco-brown hair, suggested a man more complex than the life he led would seem to indicate.

It might be fun to scrape off some of that prickly male reserve. It might also be the worst mistake she'd ever made, she decided as she turned off her reading lamp and settled down for sleep.

An hour later she was still trying to remember what there was about Dylan Kincade's deep blue eyes that she couldn't seem to forget.

Chapter 8

Two days later, Arden took Stef in for a follow-up appointment. The waiting room was only slightly less jammed, so she wasn't surprised when Marge told her that Dylan was running twenty minutes or so behind.

"He hates to keep patients waiting," Marge added with an apologetic smile, "but Dr. Christopher is still getting his post-flu legs under him, and Doc is taking up the slack."

"No problem," Arden told her, holding up her briefcase. Her years in L.A. had taught her never to go anywhere without work to be done.

Waiting in the examination room while Steffie perched on the nearby table reading a magazine for children, she flipped through the file of clippings she'd brought with her. Everything Celia had collected on the ambulance story.

She had just uncovered a photo of Dylan taken only a few years earlier according to the dateline, when the door opened behind her, and the man himself walked in.

He seemed severely professional in his white coat—until she caught a suggestion of sexual heat in his eyes, quickly masked.

"Sorry to keep you waiting, ladies, but it's been hectic this morning."

"Hi, Dylan!" Steffie closed the magazine and grinned up at him, her pleasure at seeing him again unfeigned.

"Morning, Slugger."

His voice was burred with a rare good humor, and his hands were gentle as he unwrapped her ankle. "Been in any good fights lately?"

She giggled. "Nope."

"Glad to hear it. I'm busy enough as it is." He carefully rotated her foot, watching her face for signs of discomfort.

"Swelling's down. How does it feel?"

Steffie pouted. "It hurts."

"As bad as it did yesterday?"

Steffie shook her head.

He saluted her with a quick grin. "You're a champ, Ms. Stephanie. I wish all my patients were like you."

Steffie beamed. "Really and truly?"

"Really and truly."

He wrapped the ankle, handed Steffie the magazine she hadn't finished and turned his attention to Arden. Caught studying him, she found herself studied instead. Warmth crept through her at the memory of his mouth on hers.

"Did you have any trouble waking her every few hours night before last?"

"No, none. She seemed fine."

"Seems that way to me, too." His eyes narrowed and fixed intently on her face. "You, on the other hand, look like a woman who needs some time off."

So much for the extra blush and concealer she'd used to cover the ravages of a much-too-busy schedule interspersed with bouts of worry over her diminishing back account.

"I'd settle for a nap," she said with a heartfelt sigh.

Something flickered in his eyes, then was gone as he unclipped a pen from the pocket of his coat. Frowning in concentration, he scribbled a lengthy comment on Steffie's chart before glancing Arden's way again. This time she was prepared. It made no difference. She was still drawn to him with invisible strands.

"She's a quick healer, like her mother."

"I take it that's good. Medically speaking."

"Very." He gave her a personal, private look that sent warm fingers directly to her midsection. "Medically speaking."

Telling herself that exhaustion was causing her to read more into those eyes than she should, she forced a smile. "I'm glad to hear it."

"If she's careful, she can go back to school this morning."

Steffie groaned. "Do I have to?"

The same eyes that had all but undressed Arden now seemed benignly sympathetic when directed toward her daughter. "That's up to your mom, of course, but medically, there's no reason for you to stay home."

He replaced her slipper. "Just be sure you use those crutches for a few more days."

Steffie made a face. "'Member before when I said my foot wasn't hurting very much? Well, it is now. A *lot!*"

His expression didn't change, but Arden sensed his amusement. "Sounds like you're not all that crazy about school."

"The kids hate me there, and I hate them back, that's all." Her expression challenged her mother to object. Arden drew a sharp breath, but a swift glance from Dylan had her biting her tongue.

"*Hate's* a pretty strong word, Slugger."

He hooked a stool from the corner and sat down. Steffie refused to meet his eyes. Instead, she appeared fascinated by the tiny smudge of a bruise on the knuckles of her right hand.

"It's true. Some of 'em even say so to my face. 'Specially Jimmy."

Sympathy twisted in Dylan's belly. He knew the look of real misery when he saw it. Arden's little girl was hurting big-time.

"Would it help if I told you the same thing happened to me once when I was about your age?"

This time her gaze came up and stayed on his. The sheen of fiercely held-back tears in those big brown eyes had him biting down hard on his emotions and wishing like hell he'd kept his mouth shut.

"It did? Really?"

"Really." He moved his shoulders, but the viselike tightness wouldn't budge. "We moved from one side of town to the other when I was in fourth grade, just like you are now. I was the new kid in school, short for my age, with big feet I kept tripping over."

He glanced ruefully at the size twelves he'd had since he'd been thirteen. "I begged my father to let me go back to my old school, even offered to walk all the way if he wouldn't drive me, but he refused. Said it was up to me to figure out a way to make friends."

Dylan rubbed the back of his neck. "One morning I got to school early and I saw this kid take money from the teacher's desk." He still remembered the excitement he'd felt at catching rat-faced Leonard Argyle red-handed.

"This guy also happened to be the one who used to call me the worst names at recess, so I figured, Hey! Now I had a way to pay him back, especially when the teacher sat us all down and told us the field trip to the zoo was going to be canceled unless the person who took the lunch money from her desk confessed."

Behind him, he heard Arden murmur something. Turning, he caught the look of sympathy in her eyes. She knew what was coming, even if Steffie didn't.

"What happened next?" Steffie asked impatiently, as though this was a story from a book. If only it had been.

"Leonard just sat there, so, like the smart little kid I thought I was then, I told on him."

Steffie considered that for some moments, a strange look on her face. "Did that make the kids like you better?"

"Just the opposite. From that day until I graduated high school, there were still people who called me 'Snitch' to my face." And worse behind his back.

"Bummer."

"Yeah, only that wasn't the worst of it. My father never stopped telling me how ashamed he was of me." He could still hear the disgust in his old man's voice. A gentleman never broke the unspoken code of honor, not if he wanted to keep the respect of his peers. And his own self-respect.

Dylan pried her hands apart and balanced the right one on his palm. Resting on his own, it seemed so very delicate.

"Do you think maybe you could try a little harder to make friends with Jimmy and some of the others?"

"I wouldn't have to, if Mommy would tell him to stop or she'd fire him."

"That might work with Jimmy," he conceded, "but what about the other kids?"

"She could find a way, if she really tried." Her lower lip edged forward. "In L.A. she was famous. People were always nice to me 'cause she was my mother."

His fingers slowly closed over hers. "Did you ever think that might not be the best thing for you?"

She looked shocked. "Why not?"

He shrugged. "There might come a time when she couldn't bail you out. Might even be a time when she didn't want to for some reason, and then you might just find yourself in a bad way. Might even want to run away and hide because you didn't know how to get yourself out of trouble."

Steffie digested that with a wrinkled brow and troubled eyes. "Mommy says it's wrong to run away from problems."

"Mommy's right." He drew a long breath. A kid's world was so simple—yet so damned hard. "I'm not telling you what to do, mind you, but if I were you, I think I'd try a little harder to make friends instead of acting like you don't care."

"Maybe." Steffie frowned, but capitulation was already in her eyes.

"Good for you. I'm proud of you." He squeezed her hand before returning it to her lap. "Now, suppose you read your book for a minute while your mom and I have a talk in my office."

"About me?"

"No, about her. She's my patient, too. Remember?"

Steffie glanced from one to the other, then shrugged. "Okay by me. Take all the time you want."

Beyond the examination room door, the corridor was empty, although Arden could hear Marge's voice coming from the reception area in the front.

"How did you know what was bothering her?" Arden asked in a low tone when she was sure they were alone.

"Luck, mostly."

"It was more than that. You two were somehow on the same wavelength while I was still a mile behind."

"Maybe you care too much to be objective."

"Maybe, but still—"

"In here."

Dylan opened a door and stepped back, letting her precede him. She had an instant to realize they were in his office, before he had her backed up to the now-closed door, his big hands planted on either side of her head.

"I've been thinking about this damn near half the night."

His mouth came down fast, his hands tilting her head just slightly so that his mouth and hers meshed perfectly. He smelled of antiseptic and tasted like strong coffee and a virile man's hidden need. Beneath the starched linen, his heart was hammering and his thighs were rigid.

When he lifted his mouth from hers, his eyes were dark with hunger, his face flushed and intense. "What time are you free tonight?"

She drew a quick breath. "I'm never free in the evening. The *Press* is a morning paper, which means we're not done with the final layout until midnight or sometimes later."

"And then what do you do, Ms. Publisher-editor?"

"Have a cup of hot chocolate and fall into bed."

He toyed with the hair feathering her neck and wondered when the clean scent of shampoo had gotten so erotic. "I just happen to be crazy about hot chocolate." His thumbs nudged her head to an angle more accessible to his hovering mouth. "You might even call hot chocolate a particular passion of mine."

"Why do I find that difficult to imagine?" Her voice came out rusty.

"Don't know. Maybe you need a little persuasion." His gaze found her lips, and anticipation fluttered in her chest.

"Believe me, that's the last thing I need."

"I'm open to compromise." His mouth brushed the hair tumbled over her forehead. Shivering, she felt his mouth curve. "Feels like you are too, honey."

Laying his lips against her neck, he breathed in the scent hidden there. In the distance a phone rang. Pipes rattled overhead as the steam built. Commonplace things, easily dismissed. Things that posed no threat.

He wanted her in his bed, under him, her skin pearling with the moisture of sexual arousal. He wanted to plunge his body into hers and feel the warmth of her thighs pressing warm and soft and eager against him.

Unable to stop himself, he ground the aching bulge behind his fly against her belly, trying to ease some of the searing heat.

She gasped softly, then went utterly still. "Dylan," she whispered close to his ear. "We...need to stop. We can't do this."

Fighting to clear his head, he dragged his mouth free of her and slowly opened his eyes. "You're right." His voice was thickened with need and none too steady. "It's the wrong place and the wrong time."

Arden drew a shaky breath. Her blood was racing, and her body was supremely alive, more alive than it had been for years.

She'd been a coed when she'd fallen in love with Mike. A virgin. She'd been a brand-new college graduate when they'd married. What she knew of physical love, she'd learned from him.

As careful and meticulous in bed as he'd been in his work, he'd given her a calm, sweet pleasure that was never threatening, never out of control.

"This isn't like me. I don't do things like this. I've never done things like this."

"Like what, honey?"

A small muscle relaxed next to his mouth, suggesting a smile was lurking. The temptation to press her tongue to that tiny spot was strong.

"This," she murmured, gesturing toward the office of a busy man with a hand that felt disconnected from the rest of her body. "Necking in a public place with my daughter's doctor. And a man I scarcely know."

"Come to think of it, neither have I." His mouth took on a cynical slant that sent chills cascading down her spine. "And you know more about me than anyone else in the county." He moved slightly, letting her feel his hard, insistent arousal.

"That's purely physical."

He shook his head. "I seem to remember someone telling me that the mind and body are intimately connected. What touches one touches the other."

He straightened her collar with steady hands, then laid his fingers along the exposed skin. He felt her tremble. His own equilibrium was far from steady.

"Nothing will happen you don't want to happen. You have my word."

"Dylan, please understand. I... It's obvious that I'm attracted to you—"

"Works for me."

"—but there are other things, other people to be considered here."

He heard the faint pleading in her voice and figured she was scared and determined not to show it. He understood that feeling all too well.

"If you mean Steffie, she seems to like me well enough." His tone was meant to be light, reassuring. Instead, it came out husky. "Maybe better than her mom does."

"It's just that she's at that vulnerable stage where she needs her father." She gripped his arms, feeling steel beneath the clothing. Her gaze clung, her need to make him understand strong.

"I know you would never intentionally hurt her, but it could happen. If we got...involved, I mean, and then found it wasn't working out."

His eyebrows rose. "Somehow I never figured you for one of those women who wants an ironclad guarantee before she sleeps with a man."

"I'm not, but I am a mother, and my daughter has been hurt before by a man she trusted."

"Your daughter? Or her mother?"

"Both."

He dropped his gaze for an instant. "I intend to treat you both with great care. I promise." His gaze meshed with hers. "Do you believe me?"

She searched his eyes, looking for a reason not to. She didn't find it. Instead she sensed steady strength and an integrity so solid it awed her.

"Yes, I believe you," she murmured in a clear voice. "And I'll be free at midnight."

* * *

Arden sipped hot chocolate and watched Dylan devouring his second bowl of Steffie's favorite multicolored, marshmallow-studded cereal.

"I can't believe you, as a physician, would actually put that stuff in your body," she said when she couldn't keep silent a moment longer.

"Hey, take a look at the box. This stuff is loaded with nutrients."

"Not to mention sugar and preservatives."

"Sorry to tell you this, Arden, but no one yet has proven sugar harmful to your health."

She snorted. "How old did you say you were, Dr. Kincade?"

He shoveled in another spoonful and chewed diligently before pausing to think. "Thirty-eight. No—thirty-nine. I had a birthday in January." He scraped the last of the cereal from the bowl and visibly savored the last bite.

"There's more," she offered grudgingly.

"Nope. I'm full."

He put down his spoon and splayed his hand over his taut belly. He was dressed more neatly than she'd ever seen him—in a crisp Western shirt and slacks—and his hair had definitely been trimmed between this morning and the stroke of midnight when he'd appeared on her doorstep.

The more conservative style took a few years off his face, but she found she missed the soft tendrils curling over his collar.

"I still say I should have given a cheese omelet another shot."

His mouth quirked. "No sense ruining another pan."

She choked off a laugh. "To say nothing of setting off that stupid smoke alarm again."

"It's a good thing Steffie is a sound sleeper."

"Fortunately, she always has been."

She got up to pour him more coffee, then added a little to the remaining chocolate in her cup. "How many house calls did you make tonight?" she asked, sitting again.

"Just one. Nettie. And it was more in the nature of a social call."

"I had tea with her this afternoon when I picked up Steffie after her piano lesson. I always enjoy spending time with her. Her stories about the old days in Myrtle always lift my spirits, not to mention making me feel more like a part of the community."

"Don't get too used to it. Nettie thinks she's invincible, but she isn't. No one is at seventy-plus, after two myocardial infarctions."

"Heart attacks, right?"

"Essentially, yes."

His frustration was obvious, his affection for his most trying patient even more so. She sensed that she was seeing only the tip of a very deep vein of tenderness, one he would deny with his last breath.

She felt a tug at her own store of tenderness, one she knew better than to show. Instead, she fashioned a teasing smile.

"She thinks the world of you, you know. Even though she likes to give you a hard time. She says you're the best doctor Myrtle ever had or could hope to have."

His mouth quirked, but it was the dark circles under the deep blue eyes that registered even more strongly. He looked even more exhausted than he had the night she'd found him asleep in her family room.

"I do what I do because it's what I was trained to do."

"Why here?"

He concentrated on the coffee. "This community paid three years of tuition plus my expenses through three years of internship and family practice residency. I owed them five years in return." He shrugged. "I found out I liked it here, so I stayed."

"And your family and friends? Don't you miss seeing them?"

He used his finger to capture a stray drop of coffee making its slow way down the side of the mug. Anything to keep from meeting her eyes. "My family's dead." To him, anyway. "My friends are here."

"Nettie mentioned once that your best friend was killed in an auto accident right before you arrived in Myrtle."

Dylan stilled. Common sense told him that people would discuss him with the same vigorous interest they gave to the matter of Nettie's age and a dozen other topics on the Myrtle grapevine.

He told himself to relax and play along, the way she expected. Instead, he found himself tensing even more.

"His name was Aaron Cabot IV." His mouth twisted. "Of the Beacon Hill Cabots."

"What happened?"

"In a way it was my fault." He moved his shoulders. "I wanted to go home to West Virginia for one of those nostalgia things guys do when they're young. You know, see old teachers, visit my folks' graves, impress the bluenoses who thought I'd end up in jail. Things like that. I asked Aaron to go along, mostly so we could take his sports car."

Glancing up, he saw concern on her face and questions in her eyes. Taking about his past was something he rarely did, and only when he couldn't find a graceful way not to.

"We checked into this motel, had a few beers, then went exploring. That night I stayed in to watch a ball game. Aaron went for more beer."

"What happened?" she asked softly.

"I don't know exactly. The sheriff who came knocking on the door said that he'd hit a bridge abutment. Died instantly."

Her soft gasp of sympathy tore him up inside. "The coroner identified him by the wallet in the glove box. Said there wasn't enough left of him to autopsy."

"I'm terribly sorry."

"So am I." His hand clenched around the mug.

"What kind of a man was he? Your friend, I mean."

He lifted his head and found her eyes. For once he could tell the truth. For once he didn't have to hide his feelings. "Actually, Aaron Cabot was a lazy, arrogant, rich man's son who never had to work hard for anything in his life."

"But you said he was your best friend."

"He was. He was also a spoiled bastard. He knew it, too, even took pride in it." His mouth twisted. "Said it was his birthright. That all the Cabots were bastards, his old man being the king of all of them."

According to Arden's father, a good reporter had to develop a poker face and a tolerance for bad whiskey if he wanted to get at the truth. She'd managed the former fairly well. Now she was glad. "Something tells me you loved him very much."

"Actually I detested him." He took a sip of coffee and waited for the tightness in his throat to ease. "Enough about me. What about you? How come you left the fast lane?"

"I got tired of having someone else pull my strings."

He heard a hint of resentment in her tone and read more in the quick tightening of her mouth. "Somehow I can't see you as anyone's puppet," he said, and meant it.

Her eyes came to him, cool and wary the way they'd been that morning in the OR right before she'd gone under.

"I'm not." She got up to pour more him some more coffee, then discovered the pot was empty.

"I'll make a fresh pot," she said when she caught him watching her.

He was about to decline, then decided that her need to make coffee had more to do with the sudden tension he sensed in her than a need to be a perfect hostess.

He leaned back and extended his legs. It felt good to stretch. It felt even better to be in her kitchen watching her measure coffee and draw water.

She was wearing jeans again, this time with a gold sweatshirt. At some point she'd twisted her hair into a tiny ponytail that looked as though it might have been tidy and sedate once, before little tendrils had begun to escape at the nape of her neck.

Letting his breath out in a long slow stream took some of the coiled tension out of him. Not nearly enough, however.

"How'd the kid do in school today?"

"I'm not sure. Better, I think."

She put the pot on the burner and turned it on. Turning, she rested her bottom against the counter. "At least she didn't seem as upset tonight as she did this morning."

"She'll work it out."

A deep sigh escaped her. "I wish I could be as sure of that as you seem to be."

"With her grit and her mother's charm, how can she miss?"

"The grit part I believe, the other is problematical."

"Ah, the lady is modest."

Her eyebrows drew together, and her mouth turned pensive. She had full lips, perfect for making love to a television camera. Or a man.

"The lady knows she's been anything but charming these past weeks, especially to a certain doctor, who, if you will recall, was ready to throttle that same lady in the not too distant past."

"Yes, you have a point." He fought to keep his expression solemn. "Scratch the charming part."

When the coffee was ready, she carried the pot to the table. "I did manage to have a talk with Steffie's teacher and Mrs. Peavy," she said as she poured them both refills. "They pretty much confirmed everything you suspected. Steffie's been a real pill since the day she arrived, and now she's paying for it."

"Sometimes suffering's the only way to learn." His mouth tightened. "The most important lessons, anyway."

She took her place again, then looked across the table with sober eyes. "In case I forget to tell you, I'm very grateful for the interest you've taken in her. And don't say it's just your job," she added when he was about to say just that.

"Not saying it doesn't mean it isn't true."

She conceded graciously, her lips curving only slightly before she raised the mug for a sip. It was enough to show a glimpse of twin dimples, enough to send his imagination into overdrive.

Last night he'd stolen a few kisses. This morning he'd taken again. Tonight he wanted her to come to him. To offer those soft lips willingly just once.

"I notice you haven't mentioned Steffie's father all that much. For that matter, neither has she."

Her mood changed, leaving him cursing the purely masculine itch that made him wonder what kind of a man had managed to win her.

"Mike's not a big factor in her life." She didn't sound angry about that. On the other hand, she didn't sound pleased.

"According to her records, he works overseas."

"Yes, for one of the bigger British networks. He's quite the rage in Europe, I understand."

"Does that bother you?" He saw it briefly, but clearly. More than disinterest, less than bitterness.

"Not anymore." She sipped again, then rested her cup against her chin. "But it took me a long time to quit blaming him for a lot of things that weren't really his fault."

"Like what?"

"Like the fact that I got sidetracked into broadcast news when my first love was print."

"No offense, but isn't TV the cutting edge of the news business these days?"

"Not for the daughter of J. R. Forbes."

He whistled softly through his teeth. "J. R. Forbes of the *Time* magazine cover and the two Pulitzer prizes?"

Surprise flashed in her eyes. That a coal miner's son knew of her father?

"The same." She laughed softly, but without humor. "Daddy had my future all planned. UCLA, internship at the paper and then a small column on the style page—only it was still called the 'woman's' page in those days—until I was ready to tackle 'hard' news."

Pieces fell into place, forming a picture that he understood all too well. "And your ex-husband? Was he part of Daddy's plan?"

"Anything but. Sometimes I think that's why I married Mike. Daddy thought all TV commentators were little better than actors reading lines."

Dylan drew a long breath. "It's a bitch being the heir apparent. I know. I had that dubious honor myself." The words were out before he could stop them.

"You did?"

Dylan cursed the comfortable aura of privacy she'd created. It was too easy to let down his guard when she was sitting so near, encouraging him with sleepy brown eyes and soft smiles.

"All my life," he admitted, because to clam up now would only raise more questions. More dangerous ones, perhaps. "There was never any doubt about it."

Some of the stiffness left her face. "Your father must have been terribly disappointed when you went into medicine instead of the mines."

"Something like that, yeah."

As though sensing his discomfort, she dropped her gaze. "I tell myself that Daddy would be proud to know I'm the publisher of the *Press*. On those rare days when everything is going the way it's supposed to, that is."

Dylan thought about the look in his father's eyes the last time he'd seen him. It would take more than he could accomplish in a thousand lifetimes to make his father proud of him again.

Too restless to sit any longer, he got to his feet and stretched. Looking startled, she slipped from her chair, as well.

"I know what you mean," she said as he brought his arms down again. "It's been a long day."

The lines of strain bracketing his mouth suddenly seemed deeper. "Sounds like that's my cue to say good-night."

It surprised her to realize she was feeling slightly let down, as though she'd expected him to push her for another kiss.

"I'll get your coat." He'd left it in the entry hall, hanging on the doorknob.

"Don't bother. I know where it is." He came toward her, his eyes so intense it took her breath.

He took her hands and put them on his shoulder, then linked his hands behind her neck. "Thank you for the midnight snack," he said, looking at her mouth, his voice gritty.

"You're welcome." She wanted him to kiss her, but he seemed content just to hold her.

"Does that mean I can come back sometime?"

"As long as you bring your own food. I'm not used to feeding a bottomless pit."

"Hey, watch it, lady."

His fingers played with her hair, brushing her skin ever so gently. Small shivers ran over her skin, sensitizing her.

The temptation to rest against him was strong. Even stronger was the urge to press her mouth to his. To feel the quick tensing of his muscles and hear the helpless hiss of his indrawn breath.

Having power over a man was a new experience. Her father, Mike, the news producer that she'd thought she'd loved a few years ago—all three had been strong, forceful and successful.

It had been so easy to nestle in the shadow each cast over her. Until she'd realized just how much of herself she'd given up each time she said yes when she'd really wanted to say no.

"It's better that you go," she whispered.

"If that's what you want." His tone was gruff, his mouth stiff.

If only he would press those stiff, proud lips to mine, she thought, wavering between her own need and common sense. If only he would make the choice, assume the responsibility. Like Mike, a voice inside her head insinuated. Like Daddy. She let out an unsteady breath.

His eyes darkened, then turned bleak. "I'll get my coat."

She stopped him by taking his hand. "I need you to know that I have priorities. Responsibilities. Stef, the paper."

His eyebrows drew into a hard line. "Don't bother letting me down easy. I'm a big guy. I've been dumped before."

"I'm not dumping you."

One side of his mouth jerked. "Call it what you want. I asked, you declined. End of conversation."

She pressed her lips together. Never in her life had she met a more difficult man. Nor more willful. Or more desperately hungry for love.

"Now that that's settled, will you please shove that stiff-necked pride out of the way and kiss me?"

Chapter 9

It was the wobble in her voice that unraveled him. He'd expected sophistication, and there was that side of her, but he hadn't dreamed she might be as wary of intimacy as he was.

Or as vulnerable.

When her body swayed into his and her arms came around his neck, he thought he groaned. He knew he shuddered. His hands roamed her back, memorizing, caressing. The more he touched, the more he wanted to touch.

Her hands framed his face, caressed his neck. Her fingers played with his hair. Intimate gestures, things he'd told himself he could live without—and had, for a lot of years.

"We'll take it slow, fast, any way you want it."

She moaned, a tiny helpless sound low in throat. "Slow," she murmured. "I'm out of practice."

His lips curved, and a beautiful, slow smile started in his eyes. "Honey, you've come to the right guy. I'm not even sure I remember what goes where."

His mouth was thorough, his tongue hot, spreading warmth over hers, leaving her lips tingling and her need unsatisfied as he concentrated next on the sensitive whorls of her ear.

His teeth nipped, exciting sensations that were new to her and so arousing she couldn't quite bite back the moan rising in her throat.

His size made his gentleness irresistible. His mouth made her doubts fade. His fingers were clever and skilled and very gentle as they massaged the tight muscles of her shoulders, working out every last shred of tension.

When he lifted his mouth from hers, his eyes were dark with hunger, his face flushed and intense. "Is there a lock on your bedroom door?"

Her eyes opened, taking focus slowly. "If that's slow, Kincade, I'm afraid to see your version of fast."

"Don't ever be afraid of me, honey. It would break my heart."

It shook her to realize that he meant what he said. "I'm not afraid," she whispered. "Not of you."

Laying his lips against her neck, he breathed in the scent hidden there. Like the delicate hedgerow roses that fought the wilder, thornier brambles for space beneath the trees.

Then, slipping a strong, possessive arm around her waist, he kept on kissing her all the way down the short hall and into her bedroom.

Alone behind the locked door, with only a single light burning, he was suddenly nine years' nervous. Nine times nine, he realized, because Arden was more to him than a one-night stand. More than a woman he'd worked to bed simply for the pleasure she could give him.

At the moment he wasn't quite sure of all that she was to him, or could be, and that was the problem. He didn't want to disappoint her with a body that was no longer young or offend her with a technique that had never been all that terrific when he was in practice.

His hands weren't quite steady as he skimmed his palms over her shoulders and down her arms. She shivered, her eyes clinging to his. When he drew her sweatshirt over her head, she helped by lifting her arms.

She was wearing something with lace, more than a bra, less than a slip. Swelled by her breasts, it shimmered in the light, so thin her nipples shone through like dark, rare pearls.

He skimmed it free, his hands unsteady, his breathing beyond controlling. His heart thundered and his senses were riveted.

"You're so lovely you make my heart stop," he whispered hoarsely. "I'm not sure.... I don't want to hurt you."

"You won't," she murmured. Eyes trusting-soft, her lower lip nipped between her teeth, she reached out to unbutton his shirt. Her fingers fumbled, as though she, too, was out of practice.

Need urged him to tear the shirt off himself, followed by the rest of his clothes and hers. But he sensed that would be rushing her, so he stood stiffly passive, trying to keep from shuddering with each slow movement of her fingers. The tight thermal shirt was beyond her, however, and with a small, almost shy smile, she indicated that he should take over.

He stripped it off quickly, feeling as awkward as a kid facing his first time. He'd grown to fit the size twelves by the time he'd turned seventeen, and his voice had long since hit the lower registers, but the fear was still there, making him acutely aware of all the things wrong with his body. Too much butt, a gut that had expanded an inch or two in the last twenty years, chest muscles that had never pumped iron.

He held his breath, letting her gaze roam as thoroughly as his had earlier. Her brow was furrowed, her eyes dark and impossible to read.

"I knew you were strong," she murmured. "So strong, so beautiful."

When she reached out to touch him, he wanted to grab her hands with his and keep them from discovering all the flaws.

Instead he concentrated on not flinching when her fingers tentatively pushed through the hair on his chest. But when they brushed one nipple and then the other, his body shuddered.

His hands were steadier now, as they reached for her slacks. Hers were impatient with his belt buckle. Between long, probing kisses, they undressed each other, scattering clothes wherever they chanced to fall.

When he took her in his arms again, there was nothing to separate skin from skin. She was warm against him; his own skin was burning. His hands skimmed sweet silk. Hers explored hard planes and imperfect valleys. Somehow they fit.

Drawing back, he used one hand to throw back the covers of her bed, the other to draw her down with him. Her sheets were cool, perfumed by her body when she'd curled and stretched between them. His senses reeled, his body strained.

Her arms linked behind his neck, her lips moist and eager on his throat, wrenching a groan from him even as he was lowering his mouth to nuzzle her shoulder.

His fingers stroked her breasts, her slender waist, the provocative lushness of her belly. Need lashed him as he slipped his fingers into the warmth between her legs.

Gasping, she arched backward, her arms straining to pull him closer, her breath coming now in small labored bursts.

Closing his eyes, he cupped her gently, conscious of the moist heat nestled in the soft triangle beneath his palm. He pressed gently, intimately, and she shivered.

Pressed against her thigh, his shaft swelled and hardened, nerve endings screaming for release amid the hot pooled blood.

"Honey?" he whispered urgently against her throat. "Am I going too fast?"

"No, too slow," she murmured, bucking against his hand, the sensations rocking her mirrored on her face. He watched eagerly, humbled at the way her body responded to his touch. Her hands reached for him, raking his shoulders, the building tension showing on her face, in her soft moaning breaths.

He thought she cried his name even as she arched one final time, her eyes glazing, her fingers clenching. Even as she was shuddering, he was entering her in one desperate movement.

Emotions he'd denied too long hit his gut like doubled fists, stunning him. He stilled, trapped in her moist tightness, part of her now. Imperfect, flawed, and still a man capable of giving pleasure.

Forcing himself to be gentle, he thrust slowly deeper, hot spikes of need raking his distended flesh. When her hands began stroking his back, urging him on, he pulled back with the same aching slowness, feeling her moistness clinging to his skin like hot honey.

Self-control had come hard to him once. Now it seemed a blessing as he measured each thrust by the intensity of her response. Each small moan, each helpless sob, took him higher and higher until she was pressing her face into his shoulder to muffle a scream of release.

He let go then, losing himself in her. Nothing had ever been so sweet.

Arden frowned at the sudden absence of warmth. Opening her eyes, she found the room awash in the light of the full moon.

Dylan was propped on his elbow, watching her. One hand was resting ever so gently against her cheek, as though he'd been trying to touch her without stirring her awake.

"Mmm?" She felt her smile come from very deep inside. A drowsy search of her memories failed to find a time in her adult life when she'd felt as serenely happy.

"Go back to sleep, honey. It's too early to get up." His voice was graveled, his face lined as though he hadn't slept.

"You're not leaving?" She reached toward him, but he captured her hand before it could reach his face. His grip was firm, his fingers stiff with tension.

"Have to. My truck's still downstairs in your lot and your daughter's asleep in the next room. I wouldn't want to stir up gossip."

"What time is it?"

"Almost three."

Her fingers played with the soft hair on his chest, making small whorls against his sun-bronzed skin. His brow furrowed and his eyes heated. "I have to warn you, honey, you're taking us into dangerous waters here."

"I know." Scooting closer, she touched her mouth to his, her tongue probing very gently until he parted his lips. "I can swim. Can you?"

"Barely," he replied in a strangled tone.

"We'll take it slow." Her tongue teased his, until fire was kindling and blood was pooling.

"In that case, there's something important I need to tell you." He captured her hands and used them to pin her to the mattress.

"Huh?"

"It doesn't get light until five."

As had been her habit since college, Arden woke a few seconds before the alarm buzzed. She knew immediately that she was alone in her bed, and had been long enough for the sheets where Dylan had lain to have lost the heat of his body.

Smiling and yet wistful, she slowly stretched, feeling each small twinge and ache with sublime satisfaction. Smiling, she plucked the pillow he'd used from the cold sheet and pressed it to her face. It smelled like him, clean as a surgeon's hands, masculine as a lumberman's sweat. She couldn't wait to see him again.

* * *

Arden signed the last of the month-end payroll checks and put down her pen. There was enough money in the bank for four more months. Five, if she cut her own salary to bare bones. After that, she would have to find a buyer or fold the paper for good.

What she needed was a story, she thought, digging her toes into the carpet under her desk. Something timely and important and fresh. An errant politician, perhaps, though that was getting to be old news. So was the environment, although the issues still needed a thorough, objective airing from time to time.

No, she needed a scoop, something similar to J.R.'s exposé of the corrupt logger's union.

True, J.R. had lost the *Herald* because of that one, but she had no intention of losing the *Press*. She'd worked too hard at proving to herself that J.R. had been wrong about her. She was just as good a newspaperman as he'd been.

She intended to become better.

She swiveled her chair to face his portrait, her eyes traveling up the line of vest buttons to the unforgiving mouth.

When she'd been a child, he'd been like a god to her, full of wisdom on any and all subjects, always willing to take time to teach her something new about the business he loved.

What he hadn't been was willing to listen to her when she'd come running to him with her first imperfect spelling paper or her first broken heart.

He had cared about her because she was his daughter. And he had tended to her needs for that same reason. Things her mother had handled until her death when Arden had been eight.

After that, he'd simply done the things he'd considered appropriate—taken her to San Francisco twice a year to buy clothes that fit and would last, made sure she'd had her physical checkups and inoculations on schedule and taken an active interest in her schoolwork.

No Easy Way Out

But there'd been no gentle teasing in him, no laughter that didn't have an edge of sarcasm to it, no passion for anything that couldn't be reduced to six columns across.

It wasn't his fault he'd had no love left over for her.

Arden drew a heavy breath and dropped her gaze. Love was such a simple thing, really. A smile that warmed, a commiserating or admiring look when a woman was feeling blue and unattractive. Little things given out of a desire to please, instead of obligation.

Dylan had given her those things without even knowing it. A smile curved her mouth as she thought about seeing him again. Tonight, she thought. At midnight. For hot chocolate.

He undressed her slowly, deliberately, his big hands steady and sure this time. Nearly every day for a month, every chance they'd stolen or manufactured, they'd made love.

In the bedroom while Steffie was at school and Neil was on call for emergencies. On the floor in front of the stove in the living room where they'd picnicked on ham sandwiches and chocolate ice cream. Curled like contortionists in her old chair.

He couldn't get enough of her. And even though he knew it was selfish, he couldn't make himself worry about the consequences when the affair had to end.

"I can't believe you really took the morning off," she whispered against his throat. Her breasts were soft against his chest, the nipples already hard from the services of his tongue.

"About time, don't you think?" he asked, cupping her buttocks in his palms. She fit snugly against him, warm cream, supple flesh. He was already hard and ready, his body as responsive as a boy's.

"Steffie's been nagging me to ask you to dinner again." She nuzzled his shoulder, her hair feathering over his skin, sending hot prickles through his flesh.

"I accept, on one condition. No more spaghetti."

She laughed, tiny puffs of air that tickled his throat. "I was thinking of lasagna. There's this recipe on the box of noodles—first you boil water, then you plunk in the noodles."

"That's it?"

He stroked the naked line of her back, his fingers lazy, his wrists relaxed. He'd been in the OR every morning for the last four days. It felt good to use his hands for something other than surgery.

"Well, naturally you have to open the jar...."

He took her mouth in punishment, his tongue plunging, his hands wrapping her waist. She arched on tiptoes, rubbing her thighs against his, her breasts against his chest.

His arousal throbbed against her belly, and his mind began to fragment. His control over her was absolute, his surrender a certainty every time she looked at him.

He took her down to the floor, sprawling on top of her in a tangle of arms and legs. Her mouth was everywhere, her hands impatient.

Her moans, her frantic touch, had him so worked up he couldn't think, couldn't reason. He wanted her, needed her. She was color in his life after years of gray. Laughter in the dark.

His kiss was hard, explosive. There was no gentleness in him now, only hunger. Beneath her clinging hands, his neck was corded with tension, his shoulders bunched steel under the warm, smooth flesh. His chest was heavy against her breasts, his arousal stabbing heat against her thighs.

Arden met fury with fury, passion with passion. His hands were in her hair, his fingers tense and desperate, his tongue plundering.

His breathing was rasped with a need so vulnerable she felt tears welling behind her closed lids. She responded instinctively, holding nothing back. She writhed beneath him, as wanton as any courtesan, every slow, deliberate move drawing sharp gasps from his already straining throat.

No Easy Way Out 151

His mouth left hers, only to press hot, out-of-control kisses against her throat. She was the one moaning now, feeling each brush of his mouth in every part of her.

Her hands were tangling in his hair now, her nails raking his scalp, her head thrown back to give him better access to her exposed throat.

He explored thoroughly, reverently, his tongue exquisitely rough on her skin. His body was hot as a furnace, his restraint raw and barely holding.

His hunger was empowering, giving her a boldness she'd never before known. He was strong as oak, heavy with muscle and sinew and a man's thick bones, but somehow she found the strength to shift him to his back.

His groan was half protest, half surrender, arousing an exultation in her that urged her to do more to him, for him. His heart was racing because of her. His body shuddered with each touch, each slow slide of her crooked leg over his thigh.

If he wasn't ready to accept words of love, she would show him with her hands and her mouth and her body how much she adored him.

Finding pulse points in his strong, taut neck was a joy. Wringing harsh, helpless moans from that strong, tanned throat was ecstasy.

Her hand kneaded and rubbed, exploring each chiseled muscle of his chest. Her fingers stroked and plowed the soft, fine hair softening the hard planes. When her nail raked the tiny flat nipple, he yelped like a man on fire, his body arcing backward like a bow under maximum pull.

He cried out her name, his voice shredded, his face contorted with the last of his control. Her own heart racing and her body pearling moist with exertion, she trailed her lips lower, tracing the erotic arrow of hair toward the dense thicket between his legs.

When her lips found hot distended flesh, the groan wrenched from his lips was low and primitive, the guttural cry of a man reaching the limit of human endurance.

And then his arms were around her and he was rolling her to her back. His mouth covered hers—hot, bruising, and yet at the same time the sweetest of kisses.

She whispered her need, urging him to hurry.

And then he was thrusting into her, his need a living breathing presence, his hunger, too long denied, beyond controlling.

On fire, she matched him movement for movement, need for need. She was alive, powerful.

The giving was mutual, the taking pure ecstasy. When finally pleasure exploded, reverberated, released, she knew at last what it meant to be totally loved.

Chapter 10

A storm hit the valley the last week in March, sending trees toppling and the county's two rivers spilling over their banks.

Power lines were down everywhere. Both the hospital and the *Press* were forced to rely on gas-powered generators for twenty-four hours before power was restored.

Fortunately, because it was spring break for the students of the Myrtle district, the schools had been closed, and most of the children had been safe at home when the worst of the flooding hit.

Nevertheless, homes in low-lying areas were inundated, and several streets became rivers, stalling cars and stranding residents in their homes.

Dylan never left the hospital for two solid days, treating everything from cuts and bruises to a near drowning. He slept in snatches, an hour here, two there, taking turns with Neil, who was equally busy.

Arden and her crew worked around the clock, getting out a special edition with emergency information and advice. By the time the sun was shining again and the waters were receding, they were all exhausted.

Dylan had taken to leaving his Bronco at the office and walking to her apartment, arriving after Steffie was in bed and Arden had finished downstairs.

On their first free night after the flood, Arden was late getting upstairs. Steffie had been given permission to remain up late, and Arden found her and Dylan sprawled on the kitchen floor, covered with paste and papier-mâché, making a replica of Crater Lake for her school science project.

It was clear, from the way Steffie was bossing him around, that he was the grunt labor and she was the exalted artist.

"All put to bed down there?" he asked, his tired eyes lighting up at the sight of her.

"All sixteen pages," she murmured, her throat tightening with love and her eyes filling. He looked worn-out, and yet he was patiently layering strip after strip of paper according to Stef's direction, as devoted as any father.

More, in fact, than most.

It shook her, suddenly, how much she loved this man. And how very much she wanted them to be a real family. But though they'd talked about everything else, neither had brought up the subject of any kind of permanent commitment.

"We saved you some ice cream, chocolate chocolate chip," he said, head bent over the strip of wet, gooey paper he was patiently fashioning into the valleys and hills of a lake bottom.

Steffie looked up, grumbling. "Dylan and Jimmy ate almost half before I made them stop."

"Did Jimmy get home safely?" Arden asked, pouring coffee and, at the same time, surreptitiously wiping her eyes with a tea towel.

"Uh-huh, and he asked me to his birthday party next Saturday. I need to get him a present."

No Easy Way Out

Once Steffie had set her mind to it, she'd worked diligently to mend fences and make friends. Dylan claimed she was as single-minded as her mother. Arden figured she was simply practical. Once Stef had found out that love was far more satisfying than hate, she'd gone for it.

"Remind me tomorrow," Arden said, taking a greedy sip before carrying her cup to the table. "There's a new discount store in Riddle, and I hear it has a great children's book department."

"I'm scheduled to be in Riddle tomorrow to give flu shots at the senior center," Dylan said, wiping his dripping hands on a scrap of paper toweling. "If she wants, she can hitch a ride. I'll even buy her lunch if she agrees to carry my bag for me."

"All *right!*" Steffie exclaimed, grinning.

Arden slipped off her shoes and rubbed her aching insteps one by one. "What time do you have to leave?"

"Early. Six at the latest."

"I don't mind," Steffie put in before her mother could object. "I like getting up early."

Arden stared. "Stephanie Crawford, that's a bald-faced lie and you know it. Why, just this morning I had to drag you out of bed at noon, just so I could change the sheets."

Steffie looked sheepish. "Well, anyway, I could try to like getting up."

Dylan got to his feet and carried the bucket of flour and water to the sink. "Tell you what, Stef. I'll come by early and honk. If you're up, you can go with me."

Steffie gathered up the papers they hadn't needed and put them by the wastebasket. "Maybe you should just stay here tonight. I mean, everyone knows you and Mommy are sleeping together, so what's the big deal, anyway?"

"Out of the mouths of babes."

Dylan ran his hand down Arden's arm and stared at the muted flicker of flames behind the stove's opaque glass door. Steffie had been in bed for almost an hour. Downstairs the presses were silent, the reporters' cubicles empty.

"She's got the Forbes nose for a scoop, all right." She snuggled closer to his chest, too tired to move an inch from the couch, even for more ice cream.

"Does it bother you to have your name linked with mine?"

His voice was a tenor rumble in his chest, deep enough to be soothing, gentle enough to be endearing, but the slight edge of wariness was still there.

"Actually, I'm told that's quite a coup, considering your reputation."

His hand stilled. "What reputation is that?"

She summoned enough energy to pull free of his arms in order to see his face. "Extremely moody, almost gothic in your need to be alone, although no one knows why. Sexy." She grinned. "In other words, every woman's idea of the perfect man."

Instead of smiling back at her teasing as he'd been slowly learning to do, he frowned. "I have to tell you, honey, I'm anything but perfect."

She kissed his jaw where it had gone hard. "You're too modest," she murmured, and then would have kissed him again but his hands were suddenly framing her face, holding her still.

"Arden, what if I told you there were things in my past, things I did, that make my gut crawl just thinking about them? What would you say?"

It was a small thing that warned her, the tiniest flattening of a muscle, the flick of his blunt eyelashes, but Arden knew raw shame when she saw it.

Something to do with the death of his friend, she suspected. Something that had driven him to exile and his heart into hiding.

"I'd say that you were human, just like everyone else I know, and as you were trying so sweetly to impress on Steffie, we own up to those mistakes and try to do better. To *be* better."

His eyelashes flickered, a telltale sign of emotion beyond his control to prevent. "That's the question, though, isn't it? How does a person know if he's changed enough? If he can *ever* change enough to balance the scales?"

She touched his shoulders, felt stone beneath her fingertips. Hard, punishing stone, as though he'd tried to make himself into a man with no softness to him, a man who couldn't feel. Because, in reality, he felt too deeply. Whatever was tearing at him had taken away his ability to know, or perhaps accept, the kind of man he truly was.

"I guess you look at yourself and the things you do through the eyes of people you respect, people you care about, people like Nettie and Neil and Steffie. And me." She curved her lips, loved him with her eyes. "If they've accepted you, it might be a start on learning to accept yourself. And if they love you, which they do, perhaps someday you can learn to love yourself."

His throat worked, his chest heaved, with the effort of a very deep, very slow breath. "You make it sound awfully simple, honey."

Her lips curved. "I'm not sure anything worthwhile is ever simple. Certainly it's never been that way for me, but..." She shrugged. "I spent half my life trying to be someone's perfect daughter, someone else's perfect wife, the perfect mom. I was so hungry for acceptance, for love, that I did things I shouldn't have done, for all the wrong reasons. I told myself I was doing it out of love, but in fact, it was just easier that way."

She felt tension run through him, like a fast-running current. "Easier?"

A month ago she would have read nothing more than mild interest in his lazy question. Now she knew better. The more important something was to him, the less he appeared to care.

"Sure," she said, keeping her own voice light. "Why make choices when someone else could make them for me? If something went wrong, it certainly wasn't my fault."

She grinned, but her insides were twisting. "My marriage failed because Mike was a rotten husband. I mean, hadn't I done everything he'd told me to do? And if Daddy was disappointed in me, so what? Hadn't I been a good girl all my life?"

Because he was still holding her away from the chest she longed to nuzzle, she contented herself with rubbing her forehead against his stubborn chin.

"Isn't it weird what the need to be accepted can make a person do sometimes?"

She felt him take in air, then let it out slowly. Instead of answering, he drew her into the circle of his arms again and tucked her head against his shoulder.

His arms closed around her, holding her securely, his breathing deep and regular. Arden closed her eyes. When he was ready, he would tell her, she thought.

About the things in his past that had left him so wary of loving and being loved. And about the pain he still carried. Someday, he would trust her.

When that day came, she would know, with certainty and without reservation, that he loved her.

"Dylan?" she murmured, nearly asleep.

"What do you need, honey?"

She smiled sadly at the telltale choice of words. How could a man so giving ask so little for himself? "Nothing. I just wanted to tell you something before I fell asleep, which is about to happen any second now."

His chuckle warmed her to the bone. "What's that, honey?"

"Nothing all that important. Just that I love you."

He scraped the last of the whiskers from his jaw, then ran the straightedge under the water to cleanse the honed steel.

No Easy Way Out

His body was tired from a week of overwork and lack of sleep. And his mind was fuzzy.

Snatching a towel from the rack, he held it to his face and closed his eyes. He'd left Arden asleep on the couch, curled into a ball under the same blanket she'd once used to cover him.

He'd driven home without remembering much of the trip. He'd showered and shaved on automatic pilot, his movements mechanical and precise while he'd run through the list of patients and appointments on his schedule for the day.

Replacing the towel neatly and tidying up the bathroom were part of his routine, done without thought. Naked, he padded through the bathroom door into his bedroom, oblivious to the curtainless windows.

No one, not even an occasional lost hunter, came to this part of the woods. It was too remote, too lonely. The ex-logger who'd traded him the land for gall-bladder surgery claimed the place was haunted, although Dylan had never found any evidence of ghosts. Not the traditional kind, at any rate.

He dressed quickly, with no extraneous movements, no dawdling over matching shirt to trousers, color to color—trappings of a gentleman he'd abandoned during his first month on rotation as a raw intern. Every second spent on needless chores was a second lost to sleep.

He jerked the thermal undershirt over his head, his skin cool now where she had warmed him. His mouth softened at the thought of Arden curled up next to him, asleep in the bed behind him that was still neatly made.

He'd never brought a woman here. His house was designed for a bachelor, without any provision for a woman's clutter. Or for a child's rambunctious play.

He hauled on his jeans, clean socks, found a flannel shirt, then discovered a long rip along the armhole. Tossing it aside, he grabbed the one hanging next to it and slipped into it quickly.

A fast check of the clock had him frowning. He'd told Steffie six sharp. No way was he going to disappoint her, even if he had to go without breakfast.

He strapped on his watch, collected his keys and wallet and headed for the stairs and the pot of coffee he'd brewed as soon as he'd hit the door.

Once a kid with slipshod ways and a flexible conscience, he had trained himself to be a careful man of careful habits, and his thermos was clean and waiting.

It reminded him of Arden and the time she'd offered to send him out into the night with hot coffee for company. Trying to take care of him in spite of his bad manners.

He poured coffee and drank it down, then poured more. Instead of coffee, he tasted shame, as strong as it had been nine years ago.

The hatred for the man he'd been had dulled during the years of devotion to his patients. Now it churned with even stronger vehemence in his gut.

He'd pushed himself into her life because he'd been so sure he'd turned himself into a better man. A decent man. A friend worthy of her respect.

The word *love* hovered in his mind. It wasn't a word he used or particularly respected. It was a word he'd learned never to trust.

Coming from Arden's lips, however, it was a word he hadn't been able to ignore as he had in the past. Nor shred to confetti with brutal, cynical logic.

He wasn't ready to hear it. He wasn't ready to believe it, but God, he wanted to be.

It was two weeks after the official beginning of spring. The river was back to normal, and the children were back in school. Steffie's science project had won first place. Arden was catching a cold, and she was in a rotten mood.

The computers were down, the men's bathroom had sprung a serious leak, and her best advertising rep had just announced that she was pregnant and going on early maternity leave.

A sense of doom hovered over her office, as thick as a cloud. On the windowsill, the violet Dylan had brought her looked almost as dispirited as she was feeling, in spite of the tender loving care she'd lavished it on it every day.

Outside the frosted window, snow came down in wind-driven swirls, and the mercury hovered near zero. The spring promised by last week's thaw now seemed more distant than ever.

Still, every time she thought about the contentment she'd found in Dylan's arms, she found herself smiling. Love was like that, she thought. Even the worst of days didn't seem quite so black.

Too restless to sit, Arden got up from her desk to pour another cup of coffee. Still standing, she sipped slowly, watching the activity on Main Street. Beyond the frosty pane, a feeble ray of sunlight struggled to melt a mountain of soggy, gritty snow piled along the curb.

Her second winter in Oregon, she mused, watching a dirty pickup back out of a space across the street. Seconds later, Dylan's blue Bronco wheeled into the same space, spattering slush to both sides.

He climbed out with the fluid grace of a dismounting rider, slamming the door like a man on a mission, and his stride seemed determined as he headed toward Leo's Pharmacy.

He was wearing fur-lined boots in honor of the fresh snow, laced up tight against strong calves and brown canvas jeans.

It was easy to picture this man sending the business end of a timber ax deep into age-hardened wood as though it were butter.

It was equally *difficult* to imagine those big, rough hands manipulating a scalpel with the deftness of a fine artist. But that's exactly what he'd done, cutting into her flesh, then closing the wound with stitches as delicate, and knots as tiny, as any high-priced Beverly Hills cosmetic surgeon.

Her body tingled still, not from the neat incision, but from the pleasure he'd brought her with those same talented fingers.

Bringing her hand to her mouth, she smiled at the extra fullness his kisses had given her lips, and the generous blush his midnight shadow had rubbed into her cheeks.

She was still smiling when he came out again. In one hand he carried a small white bag with the distinctive blue Rx on the front. The other hand was wrapped around the biggest chocolate bar Leo stocked. The kind with almonds, it was already half-gone.

With the same economy of motion, he climbed into the Bronco, fired the engine to life and pulled out as quickly as he'd come.

She hadn't seen him for three days. Chicken pox had come to the valley, and he and Neil were spread thin, trying to take care of all the cases.

Since Steffie had escaped the virus so far and was thus still susceptible, they'd agreed that he should stay away, just in case. But she missed him terribly and couldn't wait to see him again, even though she knew that they had to be discreet. Myrtle was a small town, with small-town ways and prejudices, and they both depended on goodwill for their livelihoods.

More important, they both liked and respected their neighbors. Neither wanted to offend the very people they called friends.

Then there was Steffie.

She was at that difficult age, Arden thought, and then grimaced. When wasn't she?

With a heavy sigh, Arden returned to her desk. Perhaps it was the late arrival of spring that was making her so moody. That and the lack of increased advertising revenue in spite of several innovative changes she'd made in the *Press*'s look and editorial style.

No Easy Way Out

Still, there were signs she just might be turning the corner on her financial problems. If she didn't have to buy a new computer system, that is. And if the old pipes in the building could be patched up one more time. And if she could find a crackerjack ad rep to replace the one she was losing in less than a month.

Arden flipped open the folder of former job applicants left by her predecessor. Somewhere in the stack there had to be the person she needed.

There were several—all happily employed elsewhere, she'd discovered after six disappointing phone calls. And she was almost to the bottom of the stack.

By the time the phone at her elbow buzzed, she was ready to split nails.

"Hello, Arden Crawford here."

There was a slight pause before a woman's voice came through the wire. "This is Kelly Saint-Marie from SM Productions. Did I catch you at a bad time?"

"Nothing that won't wait. What can I do for you, Ms. Saint-Marie?"

"First off, you can call me Kels, since we met once at the Emmy Awards two years ago in Studio City. I was with Peter Weston. You and your date sat at our table."

Arden went blank. She knew Peter, of course. They'd worked for the same station for years.

"I'm sorry, I... Wait a minute! Of course, I remember you. You won an Emmy for a documentary you made on health care in the inner city."

"Yes. 'Healing Angels in the Devil's Backyard.' And thank you for the nice note you sent me afterward. It was the only one I got." She chuckled. "So much for sisterhood in this wacky business."

Tucking the phone between her shoulder and ear, Arden kicked off her shoes and curled into her chair. A voice from the past was a welcome diversion, one she intended to enjoy.

"It was a terrific piece, and I especially liked the emphasis on the good things that are happening in the city instead of the bad. I wish I'd thought of it."

"Good! That makes it easier to beg a favor."

"Oh yes? What kind of favor?" She found herself immediately on guard. Old habits were harder to break than she'd figured.

"I'm working on an idea for a new piece, this time on rural medicine. On the same lines as the piece on the inner city, actually. With real patients, of course, and real problems."

"Sounds interesting," Arden offered cautiously, "but I'm still not sure why you're calling me."

"It's simple. You've lived in a city and now in a small town, and you're also a trained observer. I'd like you to be the camera's point of view."

Arden frowned. "It's been a long time since I was a field reporter."

"That's just it. You won't be a reporter. You'll be a patient. One of several."

"You mean to film here in Myrtle?"

"I would like to, yes."

Suddenly alert, she sat up and dropped her feet to the floor. The diversion she'd been anticipating had taken an intriguing turn. "It's an interesting concept, but I'm not sick."

"Ah, but according to my source, you've undergone emergency surgery in the hospital there. And your daughter—" there was a pause, followed by the sound of paper shuffling "—Stephanie was recently treated for a playground accident."

Arden was grateful the anonymity of the telephone kept her surprise from showing. "What source would that be?"

"You know I can't tell you that, but I will say my source is plugged in to just about everything that goes on in the county, medically speaking."

Arden felt an uneasy feeling creeping up her spine. "Why do I feel as though I'm being used?"

To her amazement, Kelly Saint-Marie burst out laughing. "Because you are—at least, I hope so." When she went on, her tone was serious again. "Think of it, Arden. It's a perfect opportunity. Almost custom-made, in fact. When I heard that you of all people, a trained reporter with a high recognition quotient and a terrifically photogenic face, had settled in the very community we had targeted as one of four possible locations, demographics-wise, I got goose bumps all over."

Arden had the sudden feeling that all she had to do was close her eyes and she would be in L.A. again, fighting the same old battle for ratings and playing the same old power games.

"A definite sign, not to be ignored, right?"

"My point exactly. I just *knew* you'd see the symmetry in it!"

She stifled a sigh. "Symmetry, yes. Advisability, I'm not so sure. After all, I am in the newspaper business now, so in practical terms that makes us competitors."

"Not if you were a coproducer." There was another pause, slightly longer, before the other woman added briskly, "Which, of course, means you would get a percentage of the net when the piece sells."

"If it sells, you mean, don't you?"

"Not in this case. I've already got one of the networks interested in it. In fact, the same one that put on 'Angels.' They're even talking about sharing rights with subsidiaries in Britain and France. Your share should come in at mid to upper five figures."

Arden grew very still. She didn't really believe in miracles. Nor did she give credence to the idea of a guardian angel. But fifty thousand dollars, even after taxes and expenses, would go a long way toward saving the *Press*.

"It's tempting," she said, far too aware of the adrenaline starting to flow in her veins. "But I can't help wondering why you would be so generous. No offense, but the idea of anyone sharing anything in L.A., especially money and/or credit, isn't the way I remember things being done."

Ms. Saint-Marie chuckled softly. "Generous, I'm not. But I am pragmatic, *and* I'm in a bind."

Because she was alone, Arden allowed herself a cynical smile. Here it comes—the pitch. "I'm listening."

"In a nutshell, the one person whose cooperation I need for the project to move ahead has turned us down flat."

"Who's that?"

"A stubborn, publicity-shy GP named Kincade. And your job, Ms. Crawford, should you choose to accept it, is to get him to change his mind."

"I . . . see." Arden barely managed to keep a sudden disgust out of her voice. "In other words, you're offering me a bribe."

"You could call it that, yes." Ms. Saint-Marie's voice was decidedly cooler, but still very calm. "I'm more interested in the bottom line than semantics, however. And this bottom line means more than just money for SM Productions and Kelly Saint-Marie or Arden Crawford, for that matter. It means much-needed publicity for people who are fighting against a tidal wave of apathy and corruption in this country to make a difference. People like the doctors and nurses and social workers in my first piece. People like that bullheaded Dr. Kincade you have up there."

Arden turned her chair and stared up at the face of her father. What would he have done if the *Herald* had been at stake? she wondered. And then she knew that J.R. would have made a pact with the devil himself to save the newspaper he'd loved.

Arden's conscience didn't quite stretch that far. But she was willing to negotiate. "Myrtle needs a new, high-tech ambulance. Suppose we were to make this documentary. Would SM Productions be willing to match whatever donation I might make out of my share?"

"Depends on how much we're talking about."

"The county is trying to raise sixty thousand. As it stands now, the total amount of pledges is around fifteen."

"Okay, say twenty thou from you, twenty from me on the day we wrap, with the town picking up the slack. Agreed?"

Arden dug her fingers into the sudden knot at the nape of her neck. Personally, she had everything to gain and nothing to lose. Her fellow citizens, including her employees and friends, would benefit. Almost certainly lives would be saved sooner.

On the other hand, Dylan must have had a reason for opposing the project. Didn't she have an obligation, as a matter of courtesy if nothing else, to find out what that was before she committed herself?

"When do you need my answer?" she asked, avoiding her father's fixed stare.

"Two weeks ago," Saint-Marie shot back with a laugh. "But I'll settle for twenty-four hours."

"Fair enough."

"In the meantime, I'll fax you everything I have on the project so far. Except for the name of my source, of course."

"Of course," Arden replied dryly before they both hung up.

Arden adjusted the focus on the microfilm viewer and the grainy photograph sharpened. At her request, the *Press*'s librarian had given her everything to do with doctors and medicine in Myrtle County since the paper's first issue came out in August of 1910.

So far she'd found herself fascinated by the tidbits she'd gleaned about Myrtle's earliest days. Dr. Sennett had been a genuine horse-and-buggy doctor, welltrained for his day, and as progressive as the times and limited funds permitted.

When he'd died in his sleep at age ninety-two, the void he'd left had been enormous and far-reaching. According to her notes, the county had been without a doctor for nearly five years after his death.

What doctor in his or her right mind would set up shop in a poor timber town in the back of the beyond with no hospital and nothing but overwork and poor pay to look forward to?

One article after another attested to the hardship—and, far too often, the tragedy—of having to travel forty miles or more over dangerous canyon roads in order to reach medical care.

It was then, it appeared, that Arthur MacGregor had taken charge, forming a committee to raise money through fund-raising and public-health grants to bring a qualified GP to the area.

He had also represented the town at a meeting in Boston with the man the committee had considered number one on the list, one Ezekiel Dylan Kincade, a native of Skunk Hollow, West Virginia, and a top-flight student at Harvard Medical.

An interview with MacGregor upon his return had described the young man in glowing terms. "Dr. Kincade is the son of a workingman, a coal miner. He grew up poor but hardworking, like most folks around here. Knows all about the problems and foibles of small towns."

The next few years made only occasional mention of Dr. Kincade and his progress through his internship and residency at Massachusetts General. Other articles were related to local accidents and the continuing need for a resident physician.

Arthur MacGregor's death was one of those. The irony was tragic. The one man who'd fought the hardest to bring medical care to Myrtle had been the last to die because of its lack, bleeding to death from a mill accident before his men could get him to the nearest hospital.

Finally, in a July issue dated nine years earlier, she saw banner headlines proclaiming the long-awaited arrival of Myrtle's new doctor.

The accompanying photo was of poor quality, but the likeness was recognizable. Dylan was clearly younger and much thinner.

The force of his personality had been less obvious in those days. Much less, in fact. And the confident brace of his big shoulders was missing, as well.

Apparently the photographer had caught him by surprise. In fact, she wondered if he hadn't actually tried to avert his face from the lens. So he'd been wary of public notice even then, she mused. But why?

Slipping her glasses halfway down her nose, she rubbed the aching bridge and tried to figure possible reasons for his reticence.

As a child she'd had a habit of biting her lip when she was particularly troubled or upset or feeling lost. It was a habit she'd managed to break a long time ago. But now, thinking about Dylan and the feelings he aroused in her had her teeth worrying her lower lip before she could stop herself.

Telling herself the key to breaking a bad habit was a suitable diversion, she picked up her pencil and gnawed that instead. It didn't help.

She was still uneasy and growing more and more so the longer she studied the distinctive lines and angles of his face. It seemed so familiar to her now. As though she'd known him all of her life.

And yet, she knew that she hadn't.

Sighing, she selected another reference and adjusted the focus. The photo was a recent one, the last on the list, in fact, taken the night of the kickoff dinner for the ambulance drive.

The photographer had caught him head-on from only a few feet away. He'd been unsmiling as usual, his expression half wary, half resigned. His eyes seemed to hold hers, so vividly memorable, even in a black-and-white photo.

She froze, her gaze glued to the image on the screen. Her breathing quickened, and her hands grew clammy. Her mind flew back ten years.

She and Mike had been living in Mexico then, but they'd subscribed to the *New York Times* and several other dailies, just to keep from feeling too cut off and homesick. The story had been on the national wire service, old news in Boston by the time the papers arrived a week late.

She drew a deep breath, her heart racing now. Her memory of the details was sketchy, but instinct told her she was on the right track.

She flipped off the viewer, hastily gathered her notes and headed for her office. Ten minutes later, she was talking to the chief librarian at the *Boston Globe*.

By the time the last fax rolled out of the machine, Arden was numb. It was all there, splashed over four columns. Dylan's face over another man's name.

Aaron Cabot IV, handsome and imposing in a dark suit and conservative tie. Scion of the wealthy, powerful Cabot clan of Boston and Newport.

The man she knew as Dylan Kincade. The man who had lied to her and everyone else. A sorry excuse for a doctor, an even sorrier excuse for a man.

A man under indictment for involuntary manslaughter, out on bail and visiting another state with his old college roommate in order to get away from the scandal. A man who used a grisly mistake in identity to escape justice.

A murderer.

Dexedrine, for God's sake, she thought, the cramming student's faithful friend.

Only he'd taken uppers by the handful, and right before going into surgery. Not only had his hand slipped, but his mind had gone blank in the middle of major surgery.

The accident victim on the table had died, along with the fetus she'd been carrying. Worst of all, no one would have known that he'd been strung out on uppers, had it not been for his fiancée, a graduate student at Wellesley majoring in journalism.

No Easy Way Out

No wonder he hated reporters so much, she thought, staring at the wall. Fiancée or not, if the woman hadn't done the honorable thing and gone to the district attorney with the information about the pills, he would have never been called to account.

How many others would have died since then? she wondered cynically. Dozens? More?

The door to her office opened suddenly to admit Celia, who was obviously deeply absorbed in the copy in her hand. She was almost at the desk when she looked up and started.

"Oh, I'm sorry, Arden. I thought... My God, are you all right? Has something happened to Stef? You're white as this paper."

Hands shaking, Arden gathered the faxes together without regard for order or neatness and shoved them into her top drawer.

"No, I'm fine. Uh, what time is it?" Even as she was asking, she was glancing at her watch. "Omigosh, I'm late picking up Steffie at Nettie's."

Arden shot out of her chair and grabbed her purse. Seconds later she was heading for her car, but not before she'd remembered to lock her desk drawer.

Chapter 11

Arden was stamping the snow from her boots when Nettie answered her knock at the back door.

"Come in before you freeze solid," the sprightly little woman ordered with a papery chuckle. "As soon as I heard your knock, I poured your tea, and if you don't mind an old lady saying so, you look as though you could use it." Her black eyes grew conspiratorial. "Or perhaps you'd prefer brandy?"

Arden forced a smile, her conversation with Boston still vivid in her mind. "I would, but the tea will have to do. I still have a paper to get out, remember?"

"You work too hard, child. You need to take time out for yourself. Do something for fun."

"I have fun," Arden replied, pulling off her gloves. "Visiting with you is one of my greatest pleasures."

"Mine, as well." Nettie chuckled, looking pleased.

"Is spring always so late in arriving up here?" she asked as she busied herself unwrapping her scarf.

"As a general rule, I'd say no. But the past few years have been unpredictable. This winter has been especially severe."

"I'm not surprised, considering the way my luck has been running lately."

Arden hung her scarf on the peg by the back door. Her ratty muskrat followed as she slipped out of her boots. "Where's Steffie? Doing her homework?"

"No, she finished about twenty minutes ago, so I gave her permission to watch TV in the parlor."

"How'd she do with the new recital piece?"

"About as well as expected," Nettie said with a twinkle in her eye.

"Uh-oh."

In stocking feet, she followed Nettie through the old-fashioned mudroom into the spacious kitchen. The old house reached out to welcome her, its high ceilings and large rooms offering a sense of shelter. She could almost hear the laughter of a long string of happy families echoing from the sturdy walls.

The sound of weeping was there, too, left by grieving widows and orphaned children, or perhaps a broken-hearted young woman whose beloved suitor had been killed in battle or lost at sea during the countless wars that had been fought during the house's lifetime.

At the moment she was ready to join in the wailing. She was heartsick and confused, but that wasn't something she intended to foist off on Nettie.

Assuming a gay air, she took her usual chair at the old pine table. As promised, her tea was waiting, served in Nettie's best bone-china cup.

"I love your house, Nettie. It's so much like you."

Nettie glanced up from the plate of cookies she was meticulously arranging and smiled. "I'm hoping to persuade Norman to keep it in the family for his son."

"What about Norman? Isn't he fond of the house?"

"Oh yes, of course. Very fond. But his practice is in Palm Springs and Jane's parents live there." Her hand fluttered over a perfectly formed macaroon. "Did I tell you Norman and Jane are bringing baby Arthur for a nice long visit next week?"

Arden nodded. Four or five times at least, she thought, but would never repeat that thought aloud.

Nettie fine-tuned the arrangement on the plate, fussing over each cookie like a doting mother, before she was finally satisfied. "It'll be nice having the rooms filled again. The happiest years of my life were spent under this roof."

Arden breathed in the scent of freshly baked cookies and smiled. "I can imagine."

"Arthur was the fifth MacGregor male to bring a bride home to the marriage bed upstairs. I was just eighteen, and my father was sure I'd be back home within a week."

Nettie carried the cookies to the table and sat down. "Arthur and I fooled him, though. We had forty-nine wonderful years together in this house, and I never did go home for more than a few hours at a stretch during all those years."

"You loved him very much, didn't you?" Arden had noticed that love in every photograph of the two of them together. It had brought a lump to her throat every time she'd seen it.

"Oh my, yes," Nettie said, suddenly as lovely and in love as she must have been at eighteen. "He was the kind of man who'd let it be known right from the start that he intended to have things his way or else. And then proceeded to indulge me shamelessly every chance he got."

Her eyes turned luminous. "He had such a kind heart, but then, many strong men do, don't they?"

Arden nodded, thinking of another man. A man she'd considered strong and honorable... and honest. It hurt so much to know that she'd been so gullible. So wrong.

"I've seen pictures of him, of course. He was very good-looking."

No Easy Way Out

Nettie looked puzzled. "Now, that's very strange. I don't remember boring you with my picture album these past months."

"You could never bore me, Nettie." Arden lifted the fragile cup to her lips and took a testing sip. The tea was still too hot to drink, and she returned the cup carefully to the saucer. "And I would love to see your albums someday, but actually, the pictures I saw were in our morgue."

Nettie shook her head. "Considering all the times my face has been plastered on the pages of the *Press* over the years, I suppose you have pictures of me in that morgue of yours, too."

"I certainly do."

"No doubt drying up as fast as I am, too."

The two women shared a laugh. Reaching for a cookie, Arden breathed a silent prayer that Nettie would be around for many more years to come.

"Actually, they're all on microfilm now. Mr. Winston had started the changeover before he was killed. We finished a few months ago."

"Very progressive. Myrtle needs more people like you."

"Thank you. I'm flattered."

Nettie waited until Arden had polished off her cookie and was reaching for another before asking blithely, "If it's none of an old lady's business, just say so."

"Pardon?"

"I've been waiting for you to tell me why you happened to be looking at pictures of Arthur."

"I was doing some research on the community," she hedged. "Just to keep my hand in, you might say."

"I do the same thing myself," Nettie said with a nod. "Every night after dinner, I sit down for an hour of practice." A fond smile crinkled her face. "Sometimes, when Dylan drops by, I can occasionally talk him into playing a duet or two before he has to leave."

Arden was immediately on guard. She hadn't intended to discuss Dylan with anyone, not until she'd had a chance to confront him.

"He played once with Stef. Mozart, from memory."

"Yes, it's one of our favorites." Nettie was suddenly terribly interested in stirring her tea. "You know, he's tried so hard not to care about you, but he does, deeply. I see it in him every time he mentions your name."

To her chagrin, Arden discovered she'd sloshed tea onto Nettie's snowy tablecloth. "Oh, I am sorry—"

"Don't think a thing of it, my dear." Her eyes took on a sudden gleam. "You must know by now that nothing is ever secret in Myrtle for long."

Arden went still. "I sincerely hope you're wrong about that." She busied herself with her napkin until every drop of tea had disappeared from the damask tablecloth.

"I didn't mean to embarrass you. But when one gets to be my age and time is short, one tends to be blunt."

Arden felt a faint burning behind her eyes. Nettie seemed so frail all of a sudden. As though her life force was diminishing with each breath she took.

"You're not all that old and you know it," she said a shade too heartily, fooling neither of them. "And I like people who tell me the truth. It's the people who... lie that hurt the most."

"Yes, although I have found that sometimes a kind lie is necessary, even preferable to the truth."

Arden shook her head. "I don't agree. In fact, that goes against everything I've ever been taught, everything I believe in." Arden nibbled a macaroon to be polite, but she might as well have been consuming cardboard.

Nettie watched her carefully for a moment, then cleared her throat with a charming delicacy. "So tell me, my dear. What's happening down at the *Press?* Anything exciting? Did that youngest Voss boy ever get rid of his terrible acne problem?"

Arden managed a chuckle. Nettie never failed to enjoy Arden's stories about the paper and its employees, most of whom she knew. "He did. In fact, he's considered quite a stud among the younger set."

Nettie broke off a bit of macaroon and savored it slowly before taking another sip. "Celia called me a few days ago about the article she's doing on Horace Sennett. I knew him, you know. Celia and I had quite a chat about him."

Arden thought about the ambulance and the difference it might make someday to Nettie and others like her. "This morning I had an interesting phone call from a producer I know in Los Angeles. She wants to make a documentary about rural medicine, and she wants to set it in Myrtle."

Nettie paled visibly. "She mustn't," she cried softly. "You mustn't let her."

Arden cried the old woman's name in alarm. "Are you all right? Should I get your pills, or call Dylan?"

"No, no, I'm fine now. Just a bit shaken." She shook her head slowly, as though mourning the passing of a very dear friend. "I think I've been dreading this since Dylan arrived."

Arden narrowed her gaze. "I'm not sure I get the connection." But she did, all too well.

Nettie took a quavering breath. "Arden, do you love Dylan?"

"I...thought I did." Her gaze dropped. "He's a complex man, Nettie. A wonderful doctor, but...well..." She couldn't go on. Telling Nettie what she'd discovered would only hurt the old woman beyond bearing.

Glancing up, an excuse to leave already forming on her lips, she discovered Nettie watching her with deep sorrow in her eyes.

"It's all right, my dear. I know what you're so very kindly trying not to tell me."

"I'm not sure I understand."

"Dylan Kincade is an impostor."

"You know?" Arden whispered, incredulous. "About Aaron Cabot and what he did?"

Nettie nodded. "Apparently so do you."

Arden nearly wept in relief. "I kept having this feeling I'd known Dylan from someplace, but I couldn't quite remember where. And then when that TV producer told me how resistant Dylan was to what I considered a very reasonable request, I got curious."

"And being the competent newswoman you are, you discovered the truth."

Arden nodded. "How did you find out?"

"I was on the committee to select a grant recipient from the applicants Harvard sent us. When Arthur traveled east to conduct the interviews, I went with him."

She plucked at her napkin with thin fingers, her expression turning sad. "I liked the man I met then, although I didn't get to know him well. Still, Arthur and I agreed that he was conscientious and would make a good doctor."

Arden stared at her. "But when the man you met and the man who arrived here five years later weren't the same, why didn't you say anything?"

"Because of Arthur. He told me once never to take action on anything until I was sure of my facts. So I got the facts." Her smile curved in a gentle rebuke. "I'm a librarian, remember? I know how to do research, too."

Feeling suitably chastened, Arden concentrated on her tea. Now tepid, it tasted of lemon and a slightly bitter herb she couldn't identify. "You could have told the authorities, had him arrested, sent back for trial."

Nettie nodded. "Yes, I could have done all those things, and I confess, that was my first thought."

"But you didn't."

Nettie shook her head. "Myrtle desperately needed a doctor. My own dear Arthur's death was proof of that. And from what I was able to find out about Aaron Cabot, he'd shown excellent promise as a surgeon—until he'd mistaken ambition for dedication."

No Easy Way Out

Arden drew a shaky breath. "Does Dylan know?"

A cloud passed over the elderly woman's face. "No. I suspect the real Dylan Kincade never told his friend Aaron about meeting me, although I believe he must have told him about Arthur's death. Otherwise, I doubt that Dr. Cabot would even have attempted to take his dead friend's place."

"But over the years, when you became friends, you never said anything. Why?"

"If I had told him, he wouldn't have stayed. His conscience wouldn't have let him, so I kept silent."

Nettie lifted her teacup to her mouth, every inch a lady. Her wedding band caught the light, gleaming dull gold as she delicately returned the cup to the saucer.

"I know what you must be thinking, my dear, but I wasn't really being irresponsible. I knew I might be risking lives by remaining silent, so I made it a point to watch our new doctor very carefully for a very long time. From that moment to this, I've never had one reason to regret my silence."

Her expression grew almost as tender as it had when she'd been speaking of her husband. "Over the years, he came here more and more. To check on me, he would say, and he did, very carefully indeed. But I think he also needed to be with someone who made it a point to show him she'd accepted him as the honorable, trustworthy man he's tried so hard to become."

Arden blinked away tears. She'd had that feeling sometimes, too. Especially when he'd held her so tenderly after they'd made love.

"He's worked so hard to make up for that one mistake, Arden. Hours and hours devoted to his patients, quite often without any expectation of payment. Sometimes, before he persuaded young Dr. Christopher to relocate to Myrtle, he would arrive here so tired he would fall asleep in that chair where you're seated now, right in the middle of a sentence."

"I know," Arden murmured. "He's done that at my house, too."

Nettie saluted that with a small, sad smile. "He's been alone all that time, and lonely, I think. Desperately, desperately lonely. That's why, when you seemed to care for him so much, I was hoping... Well, I'm an old woman with an old woman's romantic ideas. Of course, times are different now."

"Oh, Nettie, I still don't believe it. He even admitted to the district attorney that he had gone into the operating room under the influence of Dexedrine."

Nettie's gaze came to her face. "Yes, he did. And never once offered an excuse or even an explanation, other than to assume full and total responsibility for his patient's death."

"What kind of an excuse can he possibly give? What he did was wrong, period."

"Yes." Nettie sighed. "And he's suffered for it. He was a broken man when he came here nine years ago. I've never seen a man hate himself as much."

Arden dropped her gaze. "I think he still does."

"Yes, but not nearly as strongly, I think, and even less so since he's met you."

Arden bit her lip, unable to form more than random thoughts. It hurt too much to concentrate.

"He needs you, Arden. Not only to love him, but to believe in him. If you can't, I think it might destroy him."

Arden rasped on a shaky indrawn breath. "Dear God, Nettie, how can I just sit on this? How can I just go about my business, knowing that he was still treating patients, accepting people's trust—yours, mine—as though he had a right to it?"

"Because he does," Nettie said with a rare sharpness in her tone. "And he's earned that trust, Arden. The man we know as Dylan Kincade, the man others call Doc. The name doesn't matter. It's the man inside that counts."

"But what about the lies! The deceit." She waved her hand. "Not only here, but in Boston where the wrong man in buried is the Cabot family plot? What about his family—his father and sisters? Don't they deserve to know he's alive?"

"From what I've read, they cut him dead as soon as he confessed."

"Still—"

"Hi, Mom! I didn't hear you come in." Steffie came bounding in, all signs of her sprained ankle long since gone.

"Hi, sweetie. Mrs. Mac and I were having some tea and conversation."

Steffie's eyebrows met in a frown. "You look like you've been crying," she said, making it sound like an accusation.

"Do I?" Arden swiped at her eyes with her napkin. "I'm probably just coming down with a cold."

"Stephanie dear, how would you like to spend the night here with me?"

Arden had her mouth open to protest, but the sudden flash of anticipation crossing her daughter's face had her shutting it again.

"Can I, Mommy? It's Friday, no school tomorrow, and Mrs. Mac has the neatest dolls. Some even have tiny little button shoes with real buttons."

"Sounds like it's two to one, so I guess I'd better make it unanimous."

"Hooray!" Steffie threw her arms around her mother in a fierce hug which Arden returned just as fiercely, tears very close to the surface again.

"Well, I have a paper to get out," she said, when Steffie released her. Standing, Arden telegraphed her gratitude to Nettie with her eyes and received a gentle, understanding smile in return.

Nettie walked with her to the mudroom. Arden noticed that she was careful to shut the door to the kitchen before she murmured with obvious concern, "You will talk with him, won't you? Give him a chance to tell his side?"

Arden nodded. "Yes, I'll talk with him. I only hope he'll talk with me."

"Okay, that's it. No more changes. She goes as she stands." A quick glance at the clock had Arden frowning. Five past midnight and still no word from Dylan.

"Looks great to me," Betty said, fighting a yawn. "I'll buzz Eddie, let him know we're ready to roll the presses."

Arden nodded her gratitude. Her head was buzzing and her eyes were gritty. "I'll be my office for the next ten minutes if anyone needs me, and then I'm out of here." And on her way to Dylan's house, she hoped, and the words of reassurance she so desperately needed to hear.

Her office was icy cold, but she didn't bother to turn up the heat. Instead, she hurried to the desk and checked the stack of messages left by the night operator next to the phone.

Her heart sank. Not one word from Dylan in response to the messages she'd left at his office, on his home answering machine and with his service.

Catching up the phone, she dialed the number still on the pad. When the answering-service operator answered, she gave her name and asked again for Dylan.

"I'm sorry, Ms. Crawford," the pleasant voice answered. "Dr. Kincade has yet to call in for his messages. Since Dr. Christopher is on call tonight, I can't say when I'll hear from Dr. Kincade."

"I see."

There was a brief pause before the woman came on the line again. "Perhaps you didn't know this, but tonight is the first night Dr. Kincade has had off in nearly three weeks. Personally, I hope he's spending it sleeping."

"Yes, I see your point." Arden thanked her and hung up.

Still standing, she turned slowly until her eyes met her father's. "I love him, Dad. I know that's not a concept you considered very important, but I do." Her eyes went out of focus, her father's face blurring.

Dylan had warned her that there were things in his past that filled him with shame, things he needed to tell her. Things he might even now be gathering the courage to tell her.

Perhaps she should wait.

No, she decided firmly, taking up her purse and car keys. That would be letting someone else make her decisions for her again.

This was her story. Her responsibility.

Her heart was breaking.

Chapter 12

His house was no larger than a nineteenth-century woodsman's cabin. Constructed of logs that appeared hand-hewn, it nestled alone in a grove of giant myrtle trees.

The winding lane had been scraped free of snow, piled so high on the sides she felt as though she was driving through a tunnel.

At the end she parked next to the Bronco and shut off the engine and the lights. Darkness closed in, broken only by the gleam of the single light glowing next to the front door.

It was warm in her car, but the wind outside was fierce, kicking up gusts of snow and denuding the branches of ice. Taking a deep breath, she left the car and picked her way through the drifts, following the crisscrossing tracks made by Dylan's big, heavy boots.

The steps leading to the decklike porch had been cleared since the last snowfall, but the boards were icy and she had to grab the railing to keep from going down.

She banged her elbow and cried out, the sound echoing across the stillness like a lonely wail. Half expecting lights

No Easy Way Out   185

to blaze at the windows and Dylan to appear at the door, she didn't know whether to be relieved or disappointed when neither of those things occurred.

Since there didn't appear to be a doorbell, she rapped hard on the door with her knuckles. Muffled by her gloves, the sound nevertheless seemed loud enough to wake the dead.

When Dylan didn't appear, she knocked harder.

Still nothing.

Worried now, she tried the doorknob. It turned easily, releasing the latch, and the door swung inward of its own volition.

"Dylan? Are you there?" she called through the opening. "It's Arden. I'd like to speak with you."

She heard the distinctive crackling of burning logs somewhere close and smelled wood smoke, but heard no answer.

Gathering her courage, she slipped inside and closed the door behind her. Sure enough, a fire was smoldering in the grate of a freestanding fireplace in the center of a large, wood-paneled room.

Burned nearly to embers, the fire provided meager light. Still, it was enough to give her a glimpse of the austere way he had chosen to live out the remainder of his life.

The room was a decent size, but furniture was sparse. There was a couch, a lamp table piled with books, and a table with a lone chair. There were plenty of windows, but no curtains to keep out the biting cold and no rugs on the simple pine flooring.

The kitchen was small as a ship's galley, its stone counter bare except for a heavy-duty coffeemaker and a solitary mug.

Uncertain now, she slowly turned in a circle, trying to decide if she should stay or go. When she spied the winding staircase leading to a loft above, she knew where he was. And that she couldn't leave.

There was a box by the door, containing his boots, several split logs and an ax. Frowning, she slipped free of her own boots and one by one peeled away the layers of outer clothing until she was down to her jeans and sweatshirt.

Her socks made no sound as she crossed the room and climbed the narrow, steep stairs. At the top she paused, her eyes gradually becoming accustomed to the near darkness. It was warmer under the severe slope of the roof, but no less barren.

Half the size of the room below, it contained a double bed, a fir dresser that served as a desk of sorts with a phone and a blinking answering machine taking up half the space and a stack of medical journals covering the remainder. A companion to the chair downstairs sat next to the bed and was presently piled with clothes.

Dylan was lying on the bed, facedown with one arm wrapped around a spare pillow and a rough wool blanket tangled around his waist.

"Dylan?" she whispered. "It's me, Arden."

Groaning as though in deep pain, he rolled to his back, his hand forming a fist on his midriff, as though, even in sleep, he was unable to relax.

She called his name once more, louder this time. His eyelashes fluttered, but he didn't wake. Biting her lip, she glanced around the Spartan quarters, hurting for the man who hid here alone with his guilt as his only companion.

Guilt that only a few hours ago she had halfway believed that he deserved. And perhaps the man that had lived his life as Aaron Cabot IV did indeed deserve that kind of hell on earth.

But not the man she and everyone else knew as Dylan Kincade. Not the man who had saved countless lives and worked hard to give solace and comfort to those he barely knew.

He was the man she loved.

No Easy Way Out

She tugged off her jeans, then slowly freed the covers from the tangle his restlessness had created. He was naked, his body vulnerable in sleep.

She climbed in quickly and nestled close. When he was awake and aware, they would talk. Until then she would simply love him.

She had dozed. Coming awake with a start, she realized that something was terribly wrong.

No longer motionless, Dylan was now mumbling, wildly trapped, she suspected, in the throes of a nightmare.

"Sorry, oh God, I'm so sorry.... Please don't let her be dead, please, please...." His pleading voice thinned to the strangled cry of a strong man brought to his knees.

His eyes opened, his unfocused gaze searching the room blindly. He started to sit up, but she eased him back to the mattress.

"It's all right," she whispered over and over until his body slowly, gradually relaxed. Linking her arms around his neck, she lay on top of him, warming him with her body until he relaxed and his tortured breathing eased to a regular rhythm.

At first he thought he was dreaming. Then he knew he'd gone to bed half-crazed with exhaustion and unresolved guilt and was now waking up just plain crazy.

He knew he was in his own bed, with familiar shapes and shadows all around him. But for the first time since he'd dragged the mattress and box springs up the stairs, he wasn't alone.

He was lying on his back, something that was rare for him, and Arden was using him for a pillow, her hair splayed over his chest and her knee resting on his thigh.

Afraid to move, he lay quietly, consciously adjusting his breathing to hers, but control of his other bodily processes were beyond him.

Blood that sleep had already pooled low in his groin began heating, surging into capillaries and tissue until his flesh was hard and throbbing.

His heart raced, just thinking about the possible reasons she'd come to him in the middle of the night. To make love was only one of many. At the moment, however, it was the only one that he couldn't seem to get out of his head.

Why else would she be wrapped so snugly around him, wearing only panties and a shirt, her arms locked in a stranglehold around his neck?

He brushed his mouth over her hair and received a mumbled protest in return. Grinning, he murmured her name.

"Mmm?"

Stirring slowly, as though reluctant to leave the cozy place she'd gone to in sleep, she rubbed her cheek against his chest, sending fire through his veins.

"Ah, honey," he ground out, his voice still sleep-harsh, "that's not such a good idea right now. Not until I figure out why you're here."

She stretched, sliding her leg slowly down his. A groan escaped his throat, and she stiffened. Suddenly awake, she shot bolt upright, her gaze riveted to his face.

"Is it morning?"

"Yes, sunshine. Close enough, anyway."

She pushed her tumbled hair out of her eyes and glanced around quickly, as though afraid someone was watching.

"No one can see us, if that's what's worrying you."

"It's not." Her voice was calm, but a closer look revealed the signs of slight edema around eyes that were far from tranquil. Something was definitely wrong with his lady, something that had her running to him for comfort.

Lifting his hand, he ran it from her shoulder to her hand, feeling the tension beneath the fleece. "Talk to me, honey. Let me help if I can."

"Not here. Downstairs."

Slipping free, she left the bed and got quickly into her jeans, her gaze everywhere but on him. "I'll make coffee."

Without giving him another glance, she took off down the stairs, her feet whispering over each step.

Cursing silently, Dylan jammed his legs into the jeans, yanked them over his hips and zipped them tight. At the same time, he ran a hand through his hair, hooked his shirt from the chair and, because habit was strong, and he was first and foremost a doctor before he was a man, even a puzzled one, he stalked to the answering machine and pressed the message button.

Two were routine, nothing that couldn't wait. The third was from Arden herself, asking him in a slightly rushed tone to call her at the paper as soon as he checked his machine.

Badly worried now, he put an arm through one sleeve, then another, buttoned every other button and headed downstairs. As soon as she turned to look at him he knew.

"How did you find out?" he asked quietly.

Surprise raced over her face, followed by a terrible sadness that nearly knocked him to his knees. "I got a call from an acquaintance in L.A. She produces TV documentaries and wanted my help in persuading you to agree to her filming one about you and Neil and your practice."

The words he used were crude, but they got the point across. "She knew Neil when he interned in L.A. They've kept in touch."

She nodded slowly. "I couldn't understand why you were so opposed to the publicity, especially when it could mean so much to the town."

"I couldn't take the chance someone would recognize me."

"No, of course not."

The ache in her voice was all but shredding his control. Needing time, he walked to the wood box and gathered the last of the logs he'd brought in sometime yesterday and rebuilt the fire. By the time it was blazing, he had gathered the guts to face her again.

"It couldn't have been hard for you to put the pieces together after that."

Arden carried the coffee and two mugs to the table and sat down. Her hand was shaking so hard she slopped more coffee onto the table than she got into her mug.

"Here, let me." His big hand covered hers, helping her pour two full mugs before he released her. He took one for himself, then leaned a shoulder against the wall and stood watching her.

"How much do you know?"

"Enough. Too much." She tried for a laugh and failed miserably. "As soon as I started putting bits and pieces together, I called the *Globe* and several other papers in the area."

"Very competent. Your father taught you well."

She couldn't believe how calm he seemed, how unruffled, even slightly bored, as though they were discussing the weather or the price of fuel oil. It was then that she saw the tiny movement at one corner of his mouth, like a muscle held too tightly suddenly letting go.

Drawing on the facts as a crutch, she told him about her research in the morgue, the old photographs and the flood of memories they'd released.

"Unfortunately, you have unforgettable eyes," she added wistfully when she had finished. Beautiful, sad, sensitive eyes and so wonderfully soft when he was making love to her.

"The curse of a long-ago Irish grandmother," he said before lifting the mug to his mouth. He poured half its still-steaming contents down his throat before lowering it again.

"The Cabots, of course, still speak of that branch of the family tree in guarded whispers, in case any of the other stuffed shirts might be listening."

She stared, shaken. "Is that all you have to say?"

He lifted one shoulder. The man who had gradually come to trust her with his smiles, charmed her daughter and fused his body with hers was gone. He'd been replaced by an icy, distant stranger.

"What do you want me to say? That I'm not Aaron Cranston Cabot IV? Or that I wasn't high on dexies when I cut into a twenty-two-year-old mother and killed her and her unborn baby because my knife severed an artery I didn't see?"

His mouth twisted and his eyes grew stony. "It's true, all of it. And if I'd gone to trial, the jury would have convicted me hands down. Sometimes I wish they had."

He drained his cup, set it on the table and walked to the double windows facing the rear of his property and looked out. He stood stiffly, his hands jammed in the back pockets of his jeans, his feet planted wide.

"When are you going to break the story?" he asked without turning. "Or is that the reason you called? To tell me to check today's headlines?"

Arden gasped. "I don't deserve that."

He turned slowly, his face set in harsh lines. "No, you don't. I apologize."

"Is that all you have to say?"

He stood unmoving, his expression stony, his eyes nearly black. "You came here hoping I would tell you this is all a mistake. A bad dream, maybe. Or a miscarriage of justice." His mouth slanted. "I'm guilty, of murder or manslaughter or whatever they eventually would have decided to call it. And I'm guilty of using a dead man's identity to keep from going to prison. End of story, or whatever you put at the end. Thirty?"

"Yes. Thirty." She got up from the table and walked numbly to the wood box. Her hands were surprisingly steady as she slipped into her boots and pulled on her fur coat. Turning, she found him in the same place, watching her with that same lack of expression.

"Tell me one thing before I go, Dylan or Aaron or whatever your name is. How do I explain, to a little girl who loves you, what you did?"

He flinched, the first chink in his control. But he didn't answer. Nor had she expected him to. For once, he had run out of lies.

Dylan stood back from the window, watching without being seen, making sure she made it safely to her car.

She was crying, great racking sobs that shook her small body as she walked. Her face was white and shiny with tears that were already beginning to freeze to her face. Tears a better man would have spared her.

A minute, perhaps two, passed, while she started the car and let it warm. And then she was gone, the plume of hot exhaust slowly evaporating into the colder air.

Arden dropped the lipstick into the drawer and shoved it closed. Concealer, blush, a bright silk blouse to draw attention from her puffy eyes—she was using every trick she knew to hide the telltale signs of tears.

She'd been home for more than an hour. A shower had taken some of the chill from her bones, but she had a feeling the remainder would be with her for a long time to come.

One last look in the mirror had her frowning to herself. Makeup and jewelry and designer shirt aside, she was a different woman than she'd been the last time she'd studied her face in this same mirror.

Then she'd just come from the bed she'd shared with a man she'd known as Dylan, her cheeks rosy from his kisses and her heart soaring with love. Now, however, she felt empty.

Used.

She made a face at herself, straightened her shoulders and left the bathroom. As soon as she'd had a chance to look through the first copy off the press that Eddie had left on the table in the kitchen, she intended to phone Nettie with an invitation to be her guest for breakfast.

She'd take them all to Napoli's, three modern, self-sufficient women—well, two and a half. And if she felt really reckless, she might even order a glass of champagne to go along with her orange juice.

The thought of raising her glass in a salute to the biggest scoop of her lifetime brought a cynical curl to her lips. A Pulitzer had to be worth a broken heart, right? An even swap?

Adjusting a slipping earring, she wiggled her feet into pumps that pinched after so many months of lying forgotten in the bottom of her closet.

She had just entered the kitchen and flipped on the light when the phone rang. A glance at the clock had her wondering who would call so early.

"Hello?"

"*Mommy!* Something's happened to Mrs. Mac. She got this phone call and then she went all white and funny and then she grabbed her chest." Steffie paused to gulp air. "And now she's just lying there, looking really sick."

Heart racing, Arden closed her eyes, trying to think. "Steffie, right now Mrs. Mac needs your help, and it's important that you stay calm and that you listen to me very, very carefully, okay?"

"Okay." Steffie sounded only marginally calmer, but Arden didn't have time to soothe her further.

"Find Mrs. Mac's purse and look inside for the little enameled pillbox, the one she had at the auditorium, remember?"

"Uh-huh."

"Take out one pill—just one—and make sure she puts it under her tongue. If she can't help you, open her mouth and put it there yourself. Do you understand what I'm telling you?"

"Yes, but—"

"Then, after you've done that, go into the bedroom and get a blanket. Cover Mrs. Mac as carefully as you can."

"Mom—"

"Do it, Steffie, right now. I'm going to hang up and call the ambulance. It should be there in five minutes, but you stay right next to Mrs. Mac and hold her hand tight until it comes, okay?"

"Mommy, wait! Call Dylan, he'll know what to do."

"I will, sweetie. Now hurry and do what I told you."

She jabbed the disconnect button, then dialed 911. Five minutes later she was on her way to Nettie's.

Chapter 13

"How long's it been now, Mommy?"

Arden glanced at the clock on the wall. "Almost an hour, sweetie, but these things take time."

She had made it to Nettie's in three minutes flat. Nettie had been conscious, but in great pain. Her breathing, already labored when Arden had arrived, had grown steadily more erratic, as had her pulse.

A second call to 911 had had Arden screaming at the operator and frantically trying to impress upon her how critical the situation really was. Critical or not, the operator had informed her, the ambulance was out of service, waiting for a part being trucked down from Portland. A police cruiser had been dispatched instead.

Five minutes later she'd been preparing to carry Nettie to her own car and drive to the hospital, when Harvey Delacroix had come careening into the driveway, siren wailing.

Between the two of them, they had gotten the pain-racked old woman into the back of the squad car. Harvey had driven as fast as conditions had permitted, with Steffie sitting white-faced and stiff beside him, and Arden crouching in the back, holding Nettie steady on the seat.

They'd no sooner gotten to the hospital than Dylan's Bronco had roared alongside the police cruiser, nearly sideswiping a post and skidding to a stop only inches from the building itself.

The two men had carried Nettie inside, while Arden had done her best to comfort her daughter. Now, after what seemed like an eternity, she and Steffie were huddled in the cramped waiting room off the hospital reception area, along with Harvey and Geneva Harkness, who had just gone off duty. Dr. Christopher had arrived minutes earlier and was now behind closed doors, trying to help Dylan save Nettie's life.

"Maybe it wasn't really a heart attack," Arden murmured when she caught Geneva's eye.

"I pray not, Arden, but don't get your hopes up. Nettie's been living on time Dylan has somehow manufactured for her for years."

"Stubborn woman shoulda gone to Boston like Doc Kincade wanted," Harvey put in from his spot by the coffee machine.

Arden felt a shiver. "He wanted her to go to Boston?"

The chief nodded. "To this, uh, cardiologist in a big fancy hospital there. Someone Doc knew when he was goin' to school there, I expect. Accordin' to Nettie, he's done everything but hog-tie her and haul her there himself."

"She refused?"

"Hell, yes—beg pardon, ladies—heck, yes, she refused. Claimed she was born here and was aimin' to die here, and since Doc couldn't give her a guarantee the surgery he was proposin' wouldn't kill her, she decided to put her life in God's hands instead."

Geneva left her chair to plug fifty cents into the machine. She selected hot chocolate, waited for the cup to fill, then brought it to Steffie with a cajoling smile. "It's pretty weak stuff, but it'll take away some of the chill."

Steffie gave her a wan smile along with a mumbled "Thank you."

"You're welcome, hon."

Geneva resumed her seat, outwardly calm. "This town has gotten used to Dylan pulling miracles out of that scruffy old bag of his. I hope folks can understand if this time that bag turns up empty."

Arden stared into her half-finished coffee. "You think a great deal of him, don't you?"

"Yes, I do. Professionally and personally." The veteran nurse hesitated, then added softly, "He's not an easy person to know. Virtually impossible, in fact, which is why some folks meeting him for the first time think there's more stone under that white coat than flesh and blood. But I've known a lot of doctors in my almost thirty years as a nurse, and I've never met one who cared about his patients more than he does."

"Caring isn't always enough, though, is it?"

Geneva's kind eyes clouded. "No, and I have a feeling no one knows that better than Dylan."

"I still think Doc shoulda hauled Nettie off to see that there Dr. Cabot whether she liked it or not," Harvey muttered darkly.

Arden had to draw a quick breath. "Dr. *Cabot* is the cardiologist in Boston you were just talking about?"

"Yeah, supposed to be one of the best, too. At least, that's what Nettie was a-telling me when we got to jawin' about it and—" He was interrupted by the violent slamming of a door, followed by the sound of angry male voices.

A moment later Dylan and his partner came into view, both walking fast and both clearly grief-stricken.

"Damn it, Dylan, let it go." Dr. Christopher surged ahead far enough to enable him to plant his one hundred seventy pounds plus in Dylan's path, forcing him to stop. "You did everything you could for her. It's not your fault her heart was worn out."

"Get out of my way, Christopher, or I'll go through you."

"Dylan, wait—"

Dylan's hand shot out fast, connecting with Neil's shoulder so violently the younger man was nearly knocked off his feet. Seemingly oblivious to his surroundings or the people watching, Dylan headed toward the rear exit alone.

His jaw white, Dr. Christopher stood stiffly, watching until Dylan disappeared around a corner. He turned then, to face the shocked faces of Nettie's friends.

"We lost her," he said, lifting both hands and then letting them fall. "Dylan did everything he could. More."

Harvey looked stricken, then mumbled something about calling the people who needed to know. Geneva bowed her head.

Steffie's eyes clung helplessly to her mother's. "Mommy, does that mean Mrs. Mac is d-dead?"

"Yes, sweetie, she is." Arden gathered her daughter into her arms and held her tight while Steffie sobbed out her grief.

"I know you'll miss her, and so will I," she said, her own tears flowing freely. "But she had a wonderful life and she told me once that she had no regrets, which is a wonderful way to end your life."

Arden drew back and fished in her purse for a tissue, which she used to mop Steffie's cheeks, then her own.

"Mommy, is this my f-fault? For calling Mrs. Mac to the phone, I mean?"

Arden and the doctor exchanged looks. "What do you mean, sweetie?"

"Mrs. Mac was getting breakfast, and when the phone rang, she told me to answer, so I did. It was a man and he told me to go get his mother. He didn't sound very nice."

"Norman MacGregor," Geneva said with a disdainful twist of her lips.

"Mrs. Mac's son," Arden amplified for Steffie's benefit.

Steffie sniffled. "At first Mrs. Mac was all happylike, talking about her baby grandson and all, and how she couldn't wait to see him. And then she was quiet for a long time, you know, like listening?"

Arden nodded, and Steffie went on. "And she got sort of sad-looking and starting telling this guy that she understood and asking if maybe they could come for Christmas instead, and how she really wanted to see the baby and all."

Steffie stopped, her eyes huge with pleading. "I didn't know that man was going to say nasty things to Mrs. Mac, Mom, I swear. But he must have, because that's when she got all funny and sick, right after she hung up."

Sick inside, Arden gripped her daughter's arms and shook her slightly. "Stephanie, listen to me. None of this is your fault, not any of it. And I want you to promise me you won't even think about blaming yourself, okay?"

"Your mother's right, Stephanie," Geneva chimed in, her eyes still streaming. "If anyone's to blame, it's that selfish brat of a son Mrs. Mac doted on."

The doctor nodded. "Good thing Dylan doesn't know about this," he muttered, glancing again at the spot where he and his partner had nearly come to blows. "If he ever found out, I really think he would kill him."

Arden saw pain and sympathy in the young doctor's eyes, and anger as well. But there was distance there, too, protecting the man from the inevitable defeats that came to all doctors sooner or later.

Dylan had no such protection. Not anymore. Perhaps not ever. The terrible nightmare she'd witnessed was proof of that.

"Mommy, can we go home now?"

Arden started to nod, then glanced at Geneva questioningly. "I think I should be with Dylan," she murmured. "At least for a while."

Geneva nodded. "I'll take Steffie home with me. Eddie's probably watching some mindless sports thing on TV, and Steffie and I can pop some popcorn and play cards. Okay with you, toots?" she asked, shifting her attention to the child.

Steffie nodded wanly. "Maybe Eddie could play, too. I like the way he grumbles when he loses."

Geneva and Arden shared an understanding look. A child's way of coping with grief was different perhaps than an adult's, but just as valid. Perhaps more so.

"Let's go find out, shall we?" Geneva suggested, rising.

"Okay, Mommy?" Steffie asked as she put on her coat.

"Yes, sweetie." Arden took her daughter's face between her palms and kissed her nose. "You mind Geneva now, and I'll see you when I can."

Steffie's expression grew troubled. "Are you going to see Dylan?"

Arden nodded. "Yes, why?"

Steffie blinked, her small mouth trembling. "Ask him when he's coming home."

His Bronco was in its usual place.

She parked quickly, then left the car and started up the heavily trampled trail, only to gasp in horror.

Every window in the front of the cabin had been broken; shards of glass littered the porch and glittered on top of the snowdrifts.

The front door had been knocked from its hinges and now lay at a crazy angle against the porch railing. From someplace inside came the sound of glass shattering and wood splintering.

Arden ran toward the sound, the heels she'd put on earlier making each step treacherous. At the gaping doorway, she paused, her gaze frantically searching the interior.

Dylan was on the other side of the room, his hair dusted with wood slivers and bits of glass, his ax in his hands. His eyes were wild with grief, his face smeared with blood from numerous cuts.

One of the two huge windows was already shattered. Glass crunched under his boots as he raised the ax and swung. Steel hissed through the hair, flashing silver a moment before the window exploded outward.

Needlelike shards showered the deck and tore into the bare flesh of his forearms. Blood ran down his wrists and smeared the ax handle, but he took no notice. Instead, he turned, air hissing through his teeth. His suffering was a living thing, like a beast clawing at him without mercy.

As soon as he saw her, his teeth bared and his chest heaved. His shirt was bloodstained and damp where sweat had gathered along the long line of his spine.

"It's not safe for you here," he ground out with barely leashed fury.

"I'm not leaving." She took a step forward, then stopped as he stiffened. "Not until you stop punishing yourself and talk to me."

He knew all about talk. Talk was cheap, as cheap as life. "Words are your thing, not mine. I make sick people better, remember? Patients, people who trust me, like Nettie. She's lying on a slab right now because I'm so good at what I do." His face contorted, his eyes showing that he'd sealed himself off again.

"Dylan, please, just listen to me for—"

"No, you listen. Get the hell out of my house, or stand back. Your choice."

Turning away, he raised the ax with bloody, powerful arms and swung like a pro, lean muscle and steely sinew working smoothly together, each movement fluid and powerful. Moisture glistened on his forehead and turned the hair touching his skin to dripping ringlets.

Steel flashed, biting deep and true every time. Splinters flew, littering the floor in his wake.

As far as Arden's horrified gaze could determine, he missed nothing, not a stick of furniture, a cabinet, a plate or a glass, until finally, only the fireplace and the stairs remained intact.

He lowered the ax then, letting it fall from his bloody grasp at his feet. Breathing hard, he faced her. "Satisfied now, Ms. Crawford? I put down the ax."

"No, I'm not satisfied, and I'm not leaving here until I'm good and ready."

He narrowed his eyes, shrugged. "Suit yourself."

She snagged his arm, keeping him from turning away. Her nails dug deep, but it was shame that had him jerking away.

She flinched, stood her ground. "I'm not leaving, not until you stop blaming yourself for Nettie's death."

He tasted shame, felt it settle in his belly like sickness. "Don't kid yourself. I'm not the kind of guy to take the blame for anything."

"There's no blame to it," she cried. "None."

He almost laughed. "Believe that if it helps. Me, I know better."

She drew an impatient little breath, annoyed now. "Don't be ridiculous, Dylan. Everyone knows how sick she was, and how hard you tried to keep her alive."

"Oh, yeah, I tried." His mouth had hard angry corners. "Even tried to charm her into seeing my old man." He snorted. "He's a hell of a surgeon, even if he is an unfeeling, unforgiving bastard." His hand slashed the air, cutting off the protest she'd been about to utter.

"Of course, I couldn't try too hard, could I? Father knew Dylan Kincade, might even have decided to consult by phone with him about the referral. And as you mentioned, I haven't quite gotten rid of my Yankee vowels." He swallowed hard, then drew air. "Once you'd heard that mountain twang of Dyl's, you never forgot it. I even called him Hillbilly sometimes."

He stopped, staring fixedly at the floor for a long moment, suddenly seeing the long, bony face splattered with freckles and naive blue eyes that never looked for ugliness in anyone.

"He was a good doctor, a good friend," he said in a low, thready voice. "Better than I could ever be." His head came up again, the eyes calmer.

Arden was afraid to breathe. Afraid to move. "What really happened?" she asked softly.

"Same story, different names. I was sacked out while he took the Vette and went for beer. He had my wallet because I was fronting the bills. We were close in size, had the same coloring."

There'd been differences, too. Dylan had been a runner, had a runner's long lean muscle, while Aaron had rowed varsity crew and needed shirts two sizes bigger. Significant differences in life, minor when a coroner was presented with mangled flesh and shattered bone.

His gut knotted. He hadn't seen the body. He hadn't had to. "Once that bridge smashed him to bits, the mistake in identification was inevitable. When the sheriff came to the door, I didn't bother to correct him. Guess I was too numb."

He raked a tangle of wet, matted hair away from his forehead with an angry hand. Arden waited, sensing that he had more words dammed inside, more he needed to let out.

"I checked out, took a bus...somewhere. Found a place to crash, and then got drunk. I stayed drunk for two days. When I sobered up, my father had already been notified and the papers had printed my obit."

A terrible grin slashed his face briefly. "Funny how death can twist things. The reporters were almost kind to me when they thought I just might have hit that bridge deliberately."

"Speak no evil," she murmured quietly.

"Yeah, I guess. One or two even wondered if I might not have been set up to take the heat for a lot of things that were wrong at Mass General then." Like thirty-hour shifts for interns, and attendings who took money for operations actually performed by residents.

"Was that what happened? Were you a scapegoat?"

If only that were the case. But it wasn't.

When the chief of surgery, a man he'd all but idolized, had shaken him out of the first deep sleep he'd had in days and told him about the pileup on the freeway, he'd known he hadn't been fit to operate.

The chief had known it, too, and had brought a small bottle of pills with him into the residents' sleeping quarters.

"No. I wasn't a scapegoat, but I wasn't all that anxious to go back and face the punishment I had coming, either." He frowned, backed off from the memories that never changed, no matter how many times he'd gone over them.

"Dylan had planned to take the train from West Virginia. I was to drive back to Boston alone," he said, choosing fact over feeling because it was safer. "His bags were still mixed with mine. I had his ticket, his papers, his clothes. Even his driver's license and birth certificate, things he figured he'd need with him. The rest of his stuff had already been shipped."

He saw comprehension in her eyes. He didn't dare look deeper. "What family Dylan had left was scattered all over the hills, so I knew the chances were good none of them would know or care if I took his place. The rest just... fell into place."

She smiled, but her eyes were still dark with questions he could never answer, seeking excuses he would never give. "What about your family?"

"Trust me, they're better off without me hanging around, staining the precious family tree with a prison record."

"Maybe they don't agree."

"Don't bet on it. You'd lose." He looked away, his profile a stark silhouette, pride holding his shoulders rigid. "Hettie, my youngest sister, lost her fiancé because of the scandal. My...mother had a heart attack two days after my arrest. Died forty-eight hours later."

His tongue slid over his lower lip, moistening the suddenly parched skin. He had sealed that memory tight, though not tight enough. "But not before she got a chance to tell me how terribly I'd disgraced the family name."

Arden's hand flew to her mouth, her eyes liquid. Dylan looked down, lifted his hands and studied them. He'd wanted to hold his mother, to beg her to understand. Instead, he'd watched her die, knowing that he'd killed her as surely as he'd killed pretty young Anna Martin and her unborn baby.

Arden touched his arm, felt layered muscle tense, let her hand fall away. He wasn't ready to let her love him.

"There was a funeral," she murmured. "Your family attended, they mourned. I saw their faces in the clippings. One of your sisters was crying. Your father looked... old."

He told himself he wouldn't care. Almost believed it.

"Father was born old. Cut his teeth on the Cabot family coat of arms." He grunted. "All my life he pounded it in, what it meant to be the fourth Aaron Cabot, the fourth doctor." Until he was sick of the name. Sick of knowing he could never be good enough, no matter how hard he studied or how diligently he worked.

"The family resemblance is strong." The same strong face, the same stiff shoulders. The shared pride. So much pride and hurt.

She reached up to brush his hair away from his forehead. Misreading her intent, he flinched, but didn't draw away from the blow he expected.

"Would it help if I really did punch you in that imperious Yankee nose of yours?" She molded her voice with laughter. It won her a surprised look that she considered a vast improvement over the jagged pain in his eyes.

"Yeah, it just might," he said, his mouth quirking as he drew a long, shaky breath.

"But it's such a noble nose, almost Roman." She lifted a hand toward his face. He stopped it in midair by manacling her wrist with his fingers. "Don't," he whispered hoarsely.

She let out an unsteady breath. "Nettie and I had a talk about you yesterday."

She saw the flash of pain, the mistaken assumption. "I didn't tell her about Aaron Cabot," she rushed to reassure him. "I didn't have to. She knew who you were, who you *really* were, and what had made you the way you are now." Briefly she recounted what Nettie had told her.

He winced. "She never said a thing."

"She loved you like a son. She told me that, too."

His chest ached with emotion that he couldn't release, and his eyes burned. "I wish I could believe that."

Lifting a hand, she succeeded this time in brushing his hair into clumsy order, then smoothed away some of the blood. "Believe it. I do."

He brushed his knuckles very gently over her cheek and nudged her chin higher. Hesitation was in each movement, something she'd never seen in him before.

"I need you to hold me," she whispered, sensing his need also. His arms hesitated, then wrapped around her loosely, as though he were afraid to offer more. "You're not the only one grieving for Nettie," she whispered. "I am, too. And I need to know that life goes on. Love goes on, the kind she had for her Arthur. The kind I have for you."

She raised to her tiptoes and brushed her mouth over his. He stiffened as though she'd branded him. Smiling, she linked her arms behind his neck and took small nipping bites of his stubborn chin.

He responded stiffly at first, as though he didn't quite trust her motives, but with each gentle kiss, each press of her fingers against his scalp, she seemed to be stealing a bit of that awesome control of his.

When she lapped a slow trail along the rigid muscle in his neck, he shuddered, his hands grasping her arms with just enough force to get her attention.

"Honey, I'm filthy." His voice was a rasp, his heated eyes intense. "Probably smell like a goat."

She sniffed the air. "No, but one of us has been doing a lot of sweating."

He groaned, then lowered his mouth to hers, his kiss as gentle as a spring breeze across her lips. Just when she was starting to sway, he stopped and took his mouth away.

"The shower still works, I have plenty of towels." His face took on a sheepish look. "Well, two."

A shivery feeling invaded her stomach. "Now, that's a deal no sane woman would turn down."

No Easy Way Out

His mouth quirked at that. "No sane woman would still be here." He lowered his head again and nuzzled her mouth with his, as though he couldn't get enough of her. "I need you, honey," he murmured against her mouth. "It scares me, but it scares me worse to think about letting you go."

Even though he kept his tone light, she felt the taut stretch of shoulder beneath her hands and knew what he was really asking and why. He was giving her one last chance to get out of his life.

"Where's that shower of yours?" she whispered, rubbing against him like a cat desperately needing to be stroked. His hands weren't quite steady as they slipped her coat from her shoulders and let it fall, and his eyes were naked now, his need raw. With one last quick kiss, he took her hand and led her toward the staircase.

The bed was just as he'd left it, with blankets trailing to the floor and his pillow punched into a ball against the headboard.

A barren room occupied by a lonely man, she thought, her eyes smarting again. Controlling the need to comfort, she instead reached for the buttons of his shirt.

"No, I'm too raunchy," he said, gently removing her hands. Two seconds later, he'd stripped off both shirt and boots and was working the jeans over his hips.

Feeling awkward, Arden slipped out of her shoes and began to undress. Before she could get more than the top button of her blouse undone, he'd taken over. His hands were reverent as they slipped the silk over her shoulders. Light as air, it fluttered to the floor where it lay like an exotic butterfly.

His fingers slipped between the straps of her bra and gently eased them free of her shoulders, as well. The hook was in the back. As he worked it, he kissed first one shoulder, then the other.

When her breasts were free, he cupped them in his palms and kissed each one in turn, paying particular attention to the nipples until they were hard and aching and her breasts were heavy with passion.

Her hands gripped his shoulders, her head arching back. Tiny shivers ran over her skin, bringing his gaze up quickly.

"I need you."

"I know. And I need you."

"What about Steffie?"

"She's with Geneva."

He looked startled, then pleased. "Then you can stay here, with me, beside me."

Arden's mouth curved. A plea buried in a demand was still a plea, especially when his eyes were so dark, so hungry. "All right."

His hands slid down her sides, framing her waist for a beat, before they found her belt buckle. His fingers dipped between her slacks and her flesh. Wool caressed her legs as the trousers slithered free.

Dylan kissed her slowly, carefully, then drew back. Under the conservative tailoring, she'd worn tights so slinky and sexy just looking at the naughty curves of her sassy little butt was making him hard.

His hands slid lower, his fingers kneading the softness under the slippery material. Her body was firm, and yet so feminine he was having trouble remembering why he'd suggested they take a shower first, before falling into his already tangled sheets.

Spreading his legs, he flattened both hands against her bottom and pulled her closer. "You know I'm going to look like a clumsy fool if I try to peel you out of those things," he whispered against her throat. "Maybe you should do it," he said, struggling to control his voice while conceding that she had more control over his body at the moment than he did.

Her fingers played with his hair until his shoulders were freckled with bits of glass and wood.

"Patience is a virtue you obviously need to cultivate." She concentrated on cleaning him up then, very gently removing each speck, her fingernails scraping his skin until every nerve ending was screaming and his blood was aboil.

"Enough, woman," he ordered gruffly. "A man can only take so much before he has to show his woman who's boss."

"Is that so?"

"Hell yes, that's so. From now on we're doing things my way."

"Mmm. Is this what you mean?" She moved, adjusting her body to his, her somber expression would have him believe. Pure torture was what it really was. Each shift of her hips had him more aroused, and she knew it.

When she turned it into a slow, grinding dance, he knew he was a goner. "Ah, Arden," he ground out through a tight jaw. "I... You're enjoying this."

"Tremendously," she murmured, taking a small, tidy nip of his shoulder.

That did it. He bundled her into arms, slinky black tights and all, and carried her into the bathroom.

Arden was laughing, even as she held on for dear life. He was scowling, his jaw thrust forward, his breath rasping. But the torment had left his eyes, and his mouth no longer seemed bruisingly vulnerable.

His bathroom was as austere as the rest of the house. It smelled like him—a little soapy, a little antiseptic and very masculine.

Muttering something about pushy women, he set her on her feet in front of the shower stall, then muscled his way past her to turn on the water.

"Take 'em off," he said, glaring at her, "or be prepared for the consequences."

His fingers slipped under the spandex to cup her intimately, choking her protest into a gurgle of surprise. With his other hand he tugged on the waistband until it dipped lower.

She gasped, then her hands were tugging at the band of his briefs. Between kisses, they got rid of his briefs and her tights. Between kisses, he touched her and she touched him.

By the time he stepped into the shower and drew her to him, his skin was already slick with desire. Water pounded his back, washing away the blood and grit.

Her skin was satin and cream, slick as glass under his fingertips as he rubbed lather into every inch. Water turned her hair to shiny brown silk and dripped from the tips of her long lashes.

When his hand slipped between her legs to lather her thighs, she shivered, then arched into him until her breasts were molded to his chest and his hand was pressed between soft, slick thighs.

The scent of soap and the heat of steam enveloped them like a cocoon. Arden was alive, her body soft and warm, her skin tingling wherever his big hands had stroked and petted and laved.

At the same time she reveled in the play of need over hard bone and taut flesh. His hands were everywhere, telling her things he would never put into words.

Understanding, accepting, she pressed her lips to the hollow of his throat while she breathed in the hot scent of his skin. When she felt him begin to shake, she pressed her tongue to the shallow indentation in his shoulder, then used it to swirl the hair into wet tufts.

His muscles went rigid, his hands pulling her hard and tight against him. She skimmed her hand down his back, sending soap and water flying. His buttocks bunched, his thighs hardened.

His breath escaped in a deep, guttural moan, and then he was having trouble breathing. She arched against him, feeling the hard flesh burrowing along her thigh. And then he was lifting her up and away.

His flesh was slick with soap, hot from within. He filled her slowly, inexorably, until she was trembling, her body already taking its pleasure in tiny spasms.

Arms linked around his neck, she pressed her mouth to his. Her thighs rode his hips, as he drove into her over and

No Easy Way Out

over again until their cries filled the small enclosures and wave after wave of pleasure rocked them both.

When it was over, Dylan carried her—still wet and clinging to him—to the bed and deposited her gently on the side he never used.

She whimpered slightly when he pulled free, but he stilled her with a long, lazy kiss. Returning to the bathroom, he sluiced the water and lingering suds from his chest and legs, then grabbed both towels from the rack and returned to the bedroom.

He dried her tenderly, patting each inch, caressing her still-throbbing breasts with extra care. "Turn over for me a minute," he whispered, only to smile when she gave him a drowsy frown.

"What?"

"Over, lazybones," he murmured, helping her with a gentle nudge. Her buttocks were warm and rosy and so tempting he felt his body stirring again, something that should be damn near impossible for a man of his age.

He dropped a kiss on one rounded cheek, then the other, before concentrating on the rest of her slim white back. When he was finished, he tossed the towel to the floor, climbed over her to the other side, tugged the knotted sheets into some kind of rough order and pulled her into his arms.

"Now, sleep," he ordered, and Arden nestled close, thinking of Nettie's theory about strong men and how they showed love.

Chapter 14

Arden woke to the glitter of late afternoon sunshine dancing over her eyelids and the sound of a dresser drawer sliding into place. Still drowsy, her body warm and utterly relaxed, she turned lazily toward the sound.

Dylan was already dressed, his hair brushed and his jaw shaved. He was wadding a sweatshirt into a ball. The small suitcase on the chair was already filled.

"Going someplace?"

He turned at the sound of her husky whisper. In spite of the fresh shave, his face was drawn, his eyes brooding. "Boston."

"When?"

His mouth curved. He should have known she would get right to the point. A reporter's instinct, he thought, and then realized with considerable surprise that the bitterness he'd once felt toward reporters and the press was gone.

"Tomorrow, the next day. As soon as the services for Nettie are over."

No Easy Way Out

She sat up, her chin taking on a familiar tilt. He would miss seeing the sudden flare of temper as she prepared for battle.

"There are things we can do," she said firmly. "Petitions, letters to the prosecutor's office. I've seen it work more than once."

"No letters, no petitions. They wouldn't do any good, anyway, because I intend to plead guilty."

The D.A. had offered him a deal once. He might again. A plea of guilty in return for a reduced sentence. A year or two in a minimum security facility. If he was lucky, they might let him work in the infirmary.

He clamped down on a sudden jolt of panic. No matter what kind of punishment he got, he'd vowed to take it without complaint and do his best to handle it.

Finished with all but last-minute things, he slammed shut the lid of his case and slipped it under the bed.

"Move your buns, honey," he said, brushing her temple with his mouth. "We've got work to do."

She blinked. "We do?"

"Yep. I've got about a ton of glass and splinters to shovel out of my house, and you've got a story to write. Might even win you a Pulitzer."

"No! I won't. I can't. I couldn't possibly be objective."

He laid his hand against her cheek. "You'll be objective, and you'll be fair. What you won't do is pull your punches."

Arden opened her mouth to argue. The steel in his eyes had her closing it again. He had made up his mind. Nothing would change it. Tears sprang to her eyes. She dashed them away.

"All right, but I reserve the right to express my opinion on the editorial page."

She took his hand and pulled him down for a kiss. It was an hour before she let him up again.

The story broke on Monday morning. Arden had wanted to wait until the day after Nettie's funeral on Wednesday.

Dylan had insisted on the town knowing the truth as soon as possible.

"No more hiding," he'd told her when she'd questioned him. Once he was done with something, he was done. She wondered if that meant her, too.

As soon as the paper left the presses, he called Boston and spoke with the district attorney's office. He would surrender in two days, after Nettie's funeral, he told the shocked assistant D.A. After speaking with Harvey Delacroix, they agreed and were sending an officer of the court to escort him east.

Arden had already explained to Steffie why Dylan was leaving and why they might never see him again. They'd both cried, and to Arden's amazement, Steffie had ended up comforting her.

"Dylan loves us," she'd said with an unshakable little-girl certainty Arden envied. "When he gets out of jail, he'll marry us and give you a baby because that's what my friends' stepfathers always did."

Arden had laughed through her tears, but the sadness that had been with her day and night since she'd left Dylan's home late Saturday deepened.

As she'd expected, the story burned up the wire-service lines like a match to a fuse. The switchboard had been jammed ever since, with calls from broadcasting and print media, wanting more information, more details.

Arden felt like crying every time she complied.

Nettie's service was beautiful in its simplicity. Her son and his wife had come to Myrtle after all, sitting stiffly in the front row of the church, two strangers in black. The baby Nettie had so longed to see had been left with his nanny in Palm Springs.

Dylan sat between Arden and Steffie, holding hands with both of them, accepting the stares and behind-the-hands whispers without flinching. But when the minister began the eulogy, he bowed his head and his shoulders heaved. Sometimes a strong man cried without shedding tears.

Arden sat stiffly, her goodbyes to Nettie already said, letting him squeeze her hand until it ached.

The church was nearly silent as the mourners followed the casket down the aisle. Norman MacGregor had asked Neil to be a pallbearer along with Harvey and Eddie and several other men Arden scarcely knew. He hadn't asked Dylan. It was the worst kind of snub, but one that he had expected. She hadn't.

Nor had she expected the conspicuous lack of support from the community for a man they'd known and relied on for nine years. Dylan had expected that as well, even welcomed it. It made leaving the only option open to him.

He'd worked well into the last three nights, going over each of his patients' files with his partner, giving him advice, clueing him in to the best way to handle each one.

The remaining hours he'd spent with Arden and Steffie.

The church was almost empty by the time the three of them reached the door. Dylan saw the man in the dark suit a split second before Arden did. When she did, she stiffened, and her hands clutched his arm in a death grip.

He covered her hand with his, then gently pried her loose. At the same time the man in the suit, eyes hard and watchful, stepped forward. In one hand was a badge. Handcuffs dangled from the other.

"Dr. Aaron Cabot?"

Dylan nodded. It gave him a strange feeling to answer to the name he'd spent years trying to forget.

"I've been empowered by the City of Boston in the Commonwealth of Massachusetts to place you under arrest as a fugitive from justice and return you to the jurisdiction of the superior court of Boston for trial."

The cuffs were on his wrist before he had a chance to take Arden into his arms for the last time. Her gaze clung to his helplessly, tears glistening in her eyes.

He made eye contact with the Boston marshal. "Give us a minute to say goodbye?"

The man's bored gaze flicked to Arden, and then to Steffie, softening momentarily at the sight of her small, stricken face.

"One minute, no more. We got us a long trip back." He returned to his spot by the door, his gaze deceptively lazy.

Dylan dropped to his knees and took Steffie's small hand in his. "It was a pleasure knowing you, Slugger. I'll never forget you."

He kissed her hand, then held it to his cheek for an instant before releasing her.

"'Course you won't," she said, nodding so vigorously her hair flopped in her face, making her look so much like her mother it hurt. "''Cause you're coming back to marry my mom and be my stepfather, right?"

"It would be my honor to do both those things," he said very gravely because he was on the verge of breaking down, "but I can't. Someday you'll understand why." He got to his feet quickly and turned toward Steffie's mother. His iron control nearly broke then.

"Hold me," she whispered, her voice tearing.

He raised his shackled arms and she slid beneath them. He held her as close as he could, his linked hands fisted against the small of her slender back.

Her arms circled his waist and held on tight, as though she would fight the devil himself before she let him go. She would, too, he thought. And win.

"Let me come, Dylan," she whispered fiercely. "There are things I can do—"

"No. We've been all through this. I have to do this alone."

"But I can help."

He shook his head. "Having you there, seeing you without being able to touch you, would only make it harder for me."

He brushed his mouth over her temple and breathed in the scent of her. "Promise me you'll honor my wishes."

"I promise." Her voice broke, and he kissed the spot where her teeth were worrying her lip. "Oh, Dylan," she whispered. "I hate the fact that you'll be alone."

He smiled then. "No matter where they send me or for however long I have to stay there, I'll always wish I was with you, holding you, making love to you," he whispered.

She sobbed against his throat, her tears leaving a stain of wet on his collar like a bittersweet souvenir. "Take... take care of yourself."

"You, too."

He fought the need to bury his face against her throat, and realized that this was a heck of a time to realize he was helplessly in love with her.

He kissed her once, hard and fast and with a bone-deep sorrow beyond bearing. Then, jerking his hands free, he turned and walked out the door, the marshal in his wake.

The trip took nine hours, counting layovers and delays. By the time they'd reached the city jail, Dylan was numb.

As he was pushed and prodded and led through the processing routine, he discovered that very little had changed in nine years. The booking routine was designed to strip a man's dignity and crush his spirit. Dylan understood the rationale, even admired it in a way. He still came close to losing his temper a dozen times before it was over.

Relieved that he would finally be left alone, he was surprised to discover the guard leading him to a small anteroom reserved for client-attorney conferences instead of the cell he'd expected.

"Your attorney is waiting," he was told when he questioned the man.

"My what?"

"Your lawyer—Mr. Tolliver. Rules say you can have twenty minutes."

Dylan kept his surprise to himself. He had a feeling he'd better get used to keeping a lot of things to himself.

One of Boston's most feared—and expensive—criminal attorneys, Graham Tolliver had been a classmate of his father's and a close family friend since that time. His son and Dylan had played on the same prep-school rugby team.

He was already seated at the small metal table, New England dour and incorruptible, reminding Dylan of the hawk he was reputed to be in the courtroom.

He nodded when Dylan was brought in, curving thin white lips into a brief, humorless smile. "Welcome home, Aaron."

"Just tell me one thing," Dylan said when the guard left them alone. "How fast can we get this over with?"

Tolliver folded spare, well-manicured hands over the slim briefcase on the table. "Depends. Are you still planning to plead guilty?"

"I *am* guilty."

"With your record of the past nine years, I believe I can convince a jury to find you not guilty. Providing we handpick jurors who are, shall we say, *appreciative* of all the Cabots have done for this city."

Dylan hid his surprise. Surely his father had withdrawn the protection of the Cabot name by now. Emotion stirred. He refused to call it hope.

"No jury. No tricks. I'm done with being bailed out."

Leaning back, Tolliver studied him, his thin lips pursed. "You've changed," he pronounced at last. "For the better, I believe."

Dylan said nothing. He had no confidence that he'd changed at all.

Another moment passed before Tolliver was ready to rise. When he did, he stood as straight and tall as ever, every inch a man of substance as he consulted the heavy gold watch in his vest pocket.

"I believe we have a few moments left," he said, tucking away the watch again. Scrupulously polite, he lifted his eyebrows. "Is there anything further you need to tell me?"

"I've said my piece."

No Easy Way Out

Amusement flickered in his eyes, then retreated. "I, as well." He cleared his throat, then glanced toward the closed door. "If you have no objection, your father would like a few moments alone."

Dylan's jaw dropped. "Father is *here?*"

"For some hours, I understand. We weren't told the exact time of your arrival."

Stunned and still a little disbelieving, Dylan watched silently as Tolliver rapped on the door with bony knuckles.

It was a different guard who answered, clearly annoyed to have been summoned early. His annoyance changed quickly, however, as Tolliver explained coldly that he was fetching his client's father from the waiting room, adding even more icily that he fully expected his client to be waiting when he returned.

The guard grumbled at the obvious bending of the rules, but he was also a prudent man. And Graham Tolliver, Esq., was a very powerful man with powerful friends at court. And above.

Dylan was standing at the window, looking out at the wall across the compound when he heard the door swing open behind him again.

He had no doubt—would never doubt—that leaving Arden had been the hardest thing he would ever have to do in the time left to him. Turning to face his father, he discovered that this moment was nearly as rough to handle.

His father's face was paler than he remembered. The hair a bit thinner, the unyielding jaw somewhat leaner. Only the ice-blue eyes hadn't changed. They still had the power to tie his belly into knots.

"Sir." It was his standard greeting for his father, one that had been ingrained in him by his mother well before he'd been old enough to enter kindergarten.

The proud head dipped. His father rarely displayed emotion. Nor did he now, though Dylan thought there might have been a moment when his eyes softened.

"Aaron. You're looking fit."

"So are you, sir."

"I understand from Graham that you intend to plead guilty." The accent was pure Harvard Yard, and it made him think of Arden and the sly little smile that came into her eyes whenever she teased him. Pain stirred like knives in his gut. He accepted it because it was all he had left of her.

"Yes, sir."

"You are aware, too, that Graham has ample reason to believe he could win an acquittal should you change your mind and opt for a trial?"

Dylan tamped down his impatience. What the hell did the man want? Him on his knees begging for mercy? He narrowed his eyes, set his jaw.

"I won't change my mind."

The older man regarded him intently, very like Tolliver had done earlier. Then, with a curt nod, he pulled an envelope from the inside pocket of his suit coat.

"Perhaps this will," he said, holding it in front of him.

Dylan took the envelope from his father's hand slowly, his gut giving him fits as he opened it and took out the single sheet of thick parchment stationery.

The letter was addressed to his father. It was the scrawled signature at the bottom, however, that made his heart thud. Dr. Lowell Amherst, the man who'd given him the Dexedrine and all but ordered him to take it.

Glancing up quickly, he caught a look of pain in his father's eyes, quickly gone. "It came shortly after your funeral," he said. "Lowell had just found out he had terminal cancer. He wanted me to know the truth before he died."

Dylan took a slow, careful breath. He wasn't sure what to say. What to think. "Dr. Amherst was a fair man," he said at last. "I don't think he realized..." He shrugged. "I'm sorry he's dead. He was a good doctor."

He folded the letter along the heavy creases and carefully returned it to the envelope. "Thank you for letting me read it," he said, holding it out toward his father who shook his head.

"Keep it. Use it, if you wish. I doubt that any jury would convict you of anything more than poor judgment once it's read in court."

Dylan lowered his gaze. His own instinct told him that his father was right. His body pumped adrenaline, even as Arden's face leapt into his mind.

Freedom! He was holding freedom in his hands.

The shame, the humiliation, the lies.

It was over. He could breathe again. Practice medicine under his own name. Marry the woman he loved and spoil the dickens out of a little girl he had already come to think of as his own.

Closing his eyes, he thought about the happiness on Arden's face when he suddenly walked into that ratty kitchen of hers with an engagement ring in his pocket.

He took a deep, shuddering breath, then remembered that he wasn't alone. "What about you, Father? What kind of a verdict would you bring in?"

The old man's blue eyes held rock steady, with not even a flicker as he said with deep conviction, "On the basis of all I know now, I would vote not guilty."

Looking into his father's face, he saw the same familiar features, the hated Irish eyes. For the first time, however, he also saw the strength of character that his own face had lacked. And integrity, hard as Plymouth rock and just as sacred.

Dylan started to speak, then realized his throat was constricted with emotion. With hands that were as steady now as they were when they manipulated the most delicate of instruments, he slowly ripped the letter into shreds and dropped it onto the table.

Shock broke in his father's eyes. "You're still going to plead guilty?"

"Yes."

"For God's sakes, Aaron, do you want to go to prison?"

He acknowledged his father's glaring challenge with a stiff smile. "No, sir, I do not," he said, his tone emphatic. "It makes me sick just thinking about it."

"Then why?" His father gestured toward the table.

Dylan shoved his hands into the pockets of the baggy jumpsuit that still felt strange to him after years of jeans and plain work shirts.

"There's this little girl I know. Cute kid, daughter of a friend. Tough as nails. A lot like her mother. We had a talk once about owning up to mistakes. Seems she had this idea that it was okay for her mother to use her influence to bail her out of her problems."

It was a mistake talking about the two females he loved, he realized, when his control started to splinter. A mistake even thinking about them.

He shrugged. "Let's just say that little talk was one of the reasons I came back to clean the slate, and let it go at that."

For the first time he saw a flicker of something personal in his father's eyes. "You've never married?"

"No, sir." He moved his shoulders. "I had enough sins on my conscience."

He stared at the clogs now replacing his familiar boots. If he'd asked, Arden would have said yes. And then what? Assume a dead man's name without knowing it? Love a husband who lied to her every day, every hour?

Taking a deep breath, he returned his gaze to his father's and held out his hand. "Thank you for coming, sir. It was good to see you again."

His father looked startled, his mouth firming to the hard, forbidding line Dylan remembered even when he'd trained himself to forget almost everything else. His hand remained at his side.

Dylan's resolve nearly broke then, but the image of a woman's soft brown eyes filling slowly with love gave him the courage to keep his hand steady and his gaze holding firm. "I'm very sorry I let you down, sir," he said in a clear, firm tone. "I hope someday you can forgive me."

No Easy Way Out 223

"On one condition," his father said as he took his son's hand. "That you forgive me, as well."

Dylan had to swallow twice before he could speak. "It's a deal." It was a long handshake, one that had been overdue for a long time, and both men knew it.

When it ended, both men were smiling. Aaron Cabot III had tears in his eyes. His son's were clear.

She put it on the front page. Chapter and verse, the history of Dr. Dylan Kincade, country doctor.

It was all there, the long hours he'd put in, the endless research into new procedures for patients like Nettie and the Grossmans, every kindness he'd tried to hide, every success pulled off against incredible odds.

It took some digging, but she found out that most of the anonymous contributions to the ambulance fund had come from him, fully half his salary.

It took less digging to find out about the clinics he conducted without charging for his services and the house calls he'd made without any hope of receiving payment.

Words poured from her fingers onto the composing screen, words of respect and admiration and gratitude, followed by other words. Harsh, angry words that stripped away the community's right to judge, to censure, to condemn. Words that stirred and provoked and ultimately shamed.

By the time Dylan was led into the courtroom for sentencing, the judge's bench was piled high with letters bearing Myrtle postmarks, pleading for leniency on his behalf.

The same letters went to the licensing board, petitioning that he be allowed to practice medicine after he'd served whatever sentence the judge imposed.

The judge, generally accepted as the toughest jurist in the commonwealth, read some of them into the record, mentioned others, from the Grossmans and Harvey Delacroix and every single member of the Myrtle hospital staff, from the board of directors to the maintenance crew.

There was a letter from Steffie, too, and one from Neil recounting how Dylan had been the only one to offer an ex-drug addict a second chance. But it was the open letter printed in the *Press* that had him digging deepest for control.

As the D.A. had promised, the judge gave him a year on the charge of involuntary manslaughter, then suspended the sentence. Also as promised.

This time, however, there was also a lesser charge. Flight to avoid prosecution.

The D.A. wrangled with Tolliver, then agreed to two years' probation, subject to the judge's approval.

The judge gave Dylan two years, all right. In prison.

Effective immediately.

Chapter 15

Arden was late arriving for the editorial meeting. Steffie's new piano teacher lived in a neighboring town, forcing mother and daughter to make the twenty-mile round-trip two days a week.

Today was one of those days. On her way back, an accident involving one of Oregon's infamous triple trailers had held up traffic for nearly an hour.

Myrtle's new ambulance had whisked the injured trucker to the hospital almost as quickly as any helicopter. Shifting tons of mangled steel and spilled logs off the roadway had taken more time.

"I hope you got pictures while you were stalled in traffic," Gordy said, grinning.

It had been her idea for the editors, as well as reporters and photographers, to carry cameras in their vehicles at all times. So far, they'd come up with three prize-winning photos and several runners-up.

Matching him grin for grin, she reached into the pocket of her blazer and took out a roll of film.

"Here you go, ready to be processed for page one," she said, flipping it to him. He caught it in midair, then bowed modestly to a burst of applause.

Arden took her usual chair at the head of the table and opened the news file she'd prepared earlier.

"Okay, let's see what we have here. Page one." Chewing her lip absently, she ran her finger down the list. "Nothing here looks any more important than the crash of that triple. Suppose we go with that for the picture." She looked up and grinned. "If the esteemed photographer on the scene happened to catch a decent shot, that is."

She expected a round of laughter, maybe a few pointed comments, especially from Gordy. Instead, she was greeted with a silence that was suddenly crackling with tension.

"Hey, don't look so stricken. I was only kidding."

Betty Moran and chief photographer Nora Bennington exchanged uneasy looks. Gordy cleared his throat. "Uh, this came in on the wire while you were gone," he said, passing her a sheet of paper.

Scanning it quickly, she suddenly felt a stab of pain worse than any inflicted on her by her inflamed appendix. Two years, she repeated to herself. How was a man as sensitive and restless as Dylan going to bear it? How was she?

Glancing up, she saw understanding in the faces of people who cared about her. And pity. She took a deep breath and fought the need to scream.

"He thought it might be possible, but his attorney, the D.A., they were so sure they could work a deal." More cynical, Dylan had cautioned her not to count on it. She hadn't listened.

She'd been so sure the letters and petitions would help. So smug about the power of the press.

She had been terribly, terribly wrong.

"I..." she cleared her throat of threatening tears. "This is certainly the lead," she said, her voice calm. "Unless someone has an objection?"

No one did.

No Easy Way Out 227

Arden made a note, then turned to her chief photographer. "What do we have in the way of pictures to go with this?"

Nora hesitated, then pulled a wire-service photo from a folder. "How about this one?" It had been taken only a few hours earlier, as the marshal had led Dylan from the courtroom after his sentencing.

His eyes blazed defiance at the camera, his face set in harsh lines that broke her heart. His big hands, so sure and gentle and loving, were heavily manacled and affixed to a chain around his waist.

"No," she said, her voice fierce. "Not this one. This isn't the man we know." *And love so much.*

She ran through the photos in the files, so few really, then lifted her chin. "We'll go with the one of him and Nettie dancing at her seventieth birthday party."

The photographer had caught him laughing at something Nettie had just said, and those brooding blue eyes had been filled with love for his most troublesome patient.

"I agree," Celia said spiritedly.

"So do I," Gordy chimed in. "No one in this town thinks of Doc as some kind of criminal. Not after Arden set them straight, that is." He sent her a grin which she did her best to return.

"It's ridiculous to think of him as anything but Doc," Betty said emphatically. "Why, if it hadn't been for Doc Kincade, we would have lost Peggy before she took her first step."

Like a dam breaking, her colleagues rushed to share their memories of a man they called Doc and the man she loved.

Arden stood it for a few minutes, then excused herself in a strangled voice and fled to her office.

There, in her big chair with her father's stern eyes looking on, and Dylan's violet cradled in her arms, she cried.

Summer came early to the East Coast, bringing hot, humid days that had Aaron, as Dylan had now come to think of himself, eagerly seeking the sun during the day and sweltering behind the locked door of his room at night.

He'd been sent to a minimum-security prison, where the inmates lived two to a room instead of in cages and the rules were strict but not oppressive.

Still, his door could be locked only from the outside and was—every night from nine until six the next morning. And the facility was rimmed with a twelve-foot fence topped by barbed wire, and the guards carried guns.

Visiting hours were rationed, the rules strict but fair. His father was waiting for him at one of the picnic benches in the yard.

Even though this wasn't the first visiting day father and son had passed together, Aaron was still uptight in his father's presence. He had a feeling that would never change.

Always the gentleman in spite of advancing years, the senior Cabot stood to greet him. They shook hands, still far too wary with each other to do more.

"You're looking good," his father said after a moment's dispassionate scrutiny.

"So are you."

His father nodded gravely, then snorted. "We're both lying bastards," he muttered as he took his seat again. "You look worse than you did last month, and you looked like hell then. As for me, we both know I'm a bad-tempered curmudgeon who should have retired years ago."

"Why didn't you?" Aaron asked, taking a seat opposite his father on the hard metal bench.

"Haven't found a doctor I could trust to take over my practice. Until now."

Surprise moved through Aaron, but confinement had put an edge on his already considerable control. "Is that an offer?"

His father still had the power to impale him with a look. "If you want it to be, yes. Your license is still good in Massachusetts, even if the board did put a few restrictions on you."

His record would be reviewed each year for five years. If, after that time, his professional performance was found to be without fault, the restriction would be lifted.

"I appreciate the offer," he said carefully. And he did. He just wasn't sure what to do about it.

"Think it over. You have time."

"Eighteen more months."

"Precisely."

Both men glanced at the newspapers stacked neatly on the table between them. Because Aaron wasn't permitted to receive newspapers through the mail, his father had taken out a subscription to the Myrtle *Free Press* in his own name.

Aaron's fingers itched to open the one on top, but he knew he wouldn't stop until he'd devoured every word on every page, including the ads.

They'd written, she more often than he. So had Steffie. He'd sent cards for holidays, had his father send flowers for Arden's birthday, champagne for the Pulitzer nomination, condolences when she didn't win.

"How is she?"

His father's face softened slightly. "Neil tells me she's fine. Prospering nicely now."

"And Steffie?"

"Thriving. I understand she's becoming quite a good pianist."

Aaron cleared his throat. "Did Neil mention anything else?"

His father developed a sudden interest in the vista beyond Aaron's left shoulder. "Not that I recall."

Aaron had almost let himself relax when he saw a stain of pink on his father's cheeks. "Haven't there been enough lies between us, Father?" he asked softly, but with just enough force to answer the unspoken question he saw leap to his father's eyes.

Dr. Cabot looked down, then sighed. "As a matter of fact, Neil did mention something about her ex-husband. It seems he's had second thoughts about divorcing her and has come courting."

Aaron nudged the top paper with his fingertip. A man pushing forty had no business feeling like a lovesick kid in the throes of his first crush.

Sometimes, when he was lying in his narrow bed at night, listening to the pipes creak and his heart beat, he missed her so much it took all his strength to keep from breaking down.

"Does Neil know if this ex-husband has been successful?"

His father flicked him a look rife with sympathy. "He's not sure, although he did say to tell you she still smiles whenever your name comes up."

He grunted. "That's something, anyway."

It seemed that neither had much more to say. They sat in silence for several long moments before his father cleared his throat.

"Ms. Crawford has an impressive background, I believe. Her father had a reputation for integrity and honesty that was unimpeachable. Her grandfather, as well."

Aaron stiffened, wary. He had never hit his father, nor would he. But that didn't mean he intended to let the condescending old bastard say or even think ill of Arden.

"Arden is very proud of her family background, but she's made her own way," he said very carefully.

Cabot, Sr., snorted. "Take that chip off your shoulder, son. From all that I've gathered, Arden Crawford is a very remarkable, very *loyal* woman. Besides, I'm not about to say anything uncomplimentary about the woman I hope will someday become my daughter-in-law."

Aaron's jaw dropped, eliciting a bark of laughter from his father. His eyes, however, glittered with a sudden emotion.

"If she's the woman who gave you the courage to like yourself again, I'd welcome her with open arms, whatever her lineage." The older man paused, his throat working. "I care about you, Aaron, and I very much regret the unhappiness I have caused you by expecting you to be a man without flaw when... when I'm so far from that myself."

No Easy Way Out

It was the longest speech his father had given him since their reconciliation. It was also the closest he'd ever come to telling his son that he loved him.

Pressed by a strength of emotion he hadn't felt in six months, it took Aaron a solid minute to pull himself together again.

"I... thank you, sir." It was the closest he could come to telling his father that he loved him, too.

The two men exchanged a long look before the elder Cabot drew a long breath and dropped his gaze to the stack of papers. "Have you asked her to wait for you?"

"No. How could I?" Aaron glanced around the compound that didn't look all that much like a prison when viewed from the outside.

"If she loves you, she'll wait."

Aaron looked up to find a clear, steady light of conviction in his father's eyes. Memorable eyes, she'd said. Cabot eyes. "That's the question, isn't it?"

His father simply nodded. Both knew that it was also a question that couldn't be answered until he was free.

"But it's *my* party!"

Steffie didn't actually stamp her foot, but only because she was perched on a ladder, hanging streamers from the ceiling.

"I know it's your party, but eleven is still too young for makeup and high heels." Arden managed to keep her tone teasing, but her patience was becoming as ruffled on the edges as the hundred or so crepe paper strips she must have twisted in the last hour.

"Birdie Klein wears makeup." Steffie climbed down carefully, her lower lip pushing forward in a pout.

"Birdie Klein is not my daughter. You are, and as long as you're living under my roof, you may not wear makeup until you turn thirteen."

"Dylan would let me," she muttered before stalking to her room and slamming the door.

But Dylan wasn't there. He was out of prison on parole, living with his father on Beacon Hill, helping with his father's practice, and reporting to his parole officer once a week.

He'd reconciled with his sisters, spoken with all the relatives he'd been able to locate of the real Dylan Kincade, and made arrangements for Dylan's body to be reburied next to his parents.

He was working hard, trying to be a good boy and not tick anyone off. He missed her, he'd written, and Steffie. And he was sorry he couldn't come to Stef's party. Maybe next year, when there were no longer any restrictions on his movements.

She pressed a tired hand to her aching back and slowly bent backward, trying to work out some of the kinks. In less than four hours, the apartment was going to be filled with thirty of Steffie's nearest and dearest friends.

"Why did I agree to this?" she asked Neil with a helpless frown. "Why am I doing this to myself?"

"Because you're a devoted, dedicated mother." He tied off another balloon and grinned. "And almost as much of a sucker with kids as Dylan used to be."

Arden had become adept at talking about Dylan almost offhandedly, as though they'd simply been good friends who had regrettably lost touch.

If occasionally friends remembered that she'd once been desperately in love with him, they were too diplomatic, or perhaps too kind, to mention it.

"He told me once that he wasn't all that crazy about kids. Could take 'em or leave 'em, he said."

Neil shot her an incredulous look, then shook his head in wonder. "You didn't believe him, did you?"

"Actually, at the time I did." Just as she'd believed that he'd loved her and would come back to her as soon as he'd completed his sentence. But she'd been wrong. He *hadn't* come back.

Neil put the finishing touches on the floret of balloons decorating the table and stepped back to admire his handiwork. "Without doubt, the work of a true artist," she said, grinning.

"Without doubt." He helped himself to coffee, poured a cup for her and led her to the sofa. "Now sit. There's something we need to talk about."

Arden curled into the corner, drew up her legs, and rested her mug on her knees. "Why do I think I'm not going to like this?"

Neil sat in her old recliner, but didn't lean back, remaining stiffly upright, holding his coffee with both hands. Nor, she realized, did he look particularly comfortable with what he was about to say.

"If this is about Dylan, you might as well say whatever you don't want to say, and get it over with."

Neil's eyes flashed a moment of brief admiration. "I had to call him the other day. About the practice, the remodeling we need to do on the house... other things."

"What other things?"

Seeing her so calm, he had begun to relax. Now he stiffened again. "The patient load... well, it's at the point where I just can't handle it alone anymore." He stopped to take a thirsty drink of his coffee. "To tell you the truth, I don't know how Dylan—Aaron—managed all those years." He snorted. "That's not true. I do know—by working himself to exhaustion every day year after year, that's how."

Arden's smile felt soft on her lips, the way it did when she was alone with her memories of Dylan. "Yes, that's exactly what he did, and without resenting a minute of it."

Neil nodded, then drew a long breath. "Well, anyway, I couldn't put off mentioning that to Aaron when we were on the phone about a patient early last week." He grunted. "Actually, I came right out and asked him when the hell he was going to get his tail back here and boss me around again."

"What did he say?"

"He said that I was the boss now. That I should make the decisions, and that if I needed help, I should look around for another doctor to bring into the practice."

Arden's breath hissed through her parted lips. "And...are you? Going to hire another doctor to take Dylan's place?"

Neil surged to his feet and went to the window. It was fall in the mountains, and the sharp hills were blazing with autumn color.

"No one can take Doc's place, Arden." He turned slowly, faced her squarely, his braced shoulders and self-confident expression reminding her of Dylan. "But I am going to hire another doctor. I have no choice."

"Of course not." She took her time finishing her coffee. Neil watched in silence. When the mug was empty, she set it carefully on the table in front of her and lifted her gaze to his sympathetic gray eyes.

"He's not coming back, is he?"

"I don't know. He seemed ... evasive whenever I tried to pin him down to a date."

Arden smiled. He'd done the same with her. "Well, I'd better get to work on Stef's cake, or I'm going to have thirty angry eleven-year-olds on my hands."

She got to her feet and looked around for her moccasins, then realized she'd never taken them off.

"Arden, there's one more thing."

This time it took two deep breaths before she could find her poker face. "Out with it, Doctor."

His jaw tightened, then relaxed. "Aaron asked me to have Jack Fitz get in touch with him. He's planning on selling his cabin."

Arden made a small, helpless sound, her hand going instinctively to her mouth. "I...see."

Neil moved his shoulders in a helpless gesture of sympathy. "I'm sorry, Arden. I love him, too."

He took her in his arms and hugged her close. She shivered, but managed to keep from crying. Today was Stef-

No Easy Way Out

fie's birthday, and she'd be damned if she'd spoil it for her child.

"Thanks, Neil," she said, pulling free. "For telling me about your conversation with Aaron, and for being my friend."

His mouth quirked. "Anytime, and I mean that."

She nodded, then broke eye contact. Neil was too honorable to come on to her, nor would she want him to. But they were friends and always would be. And they had both loved Dylan Kincade.

"See you at four," he said with a quick wave before letting himself out.

"Yes," she murmured. At four. For Steffie's party.

Black, acrid smoke billowed around her head, nearly choking her. Helpless tears of frustration ran down her face as she stared at the chunks of thick, heat-resistant glass now littering her freshly scrubbed floor.

She'd just gone downstairs for a minute or two, just to check on a few things. And the recipe had said thirty-five minutes. It hadn't been anything close to that.

Had it?

"You ruined my cake!"

Startled, Arden turned quickly to find her daughter gaping at her from the doorway, staring at the mess with shock on her face. Guilt gave Arden a hard, swift kick.

"For God's sake, Stef. I didn't do it on purpose. That stupid door was already cracked, but it shouldn't have just...exploded like that." She fanned the air furiously with a pot holder, trying to clear away enough of the smoke so that she could find the cake.

"It's all burned and the house smells yucky. My friends'll think we live like this all the time."

Actually they did, but Arden decided that she was just as happy Steffie didn't realize it. "Now, Stef, it's not that bad. We've got plenty of room deodorizer, and Neil can pick up a cake at the store."

Summoning her courage, she plunged into the smoke and pulled out a smoking, blackened lump that was supposed to be a devil's food cake.

Turning too quickly, she slipped on a piece of glass and lurched sideways. At the same time, the smoke alarm in the hall began wailing like a furious banshee. Startled, she dropped the cake, then yelped when the corner of the hot pan hit her toes.

"That's it!" she shouted furiously while hopping around on one foot, the other pressed between her hands. "I *hate* cooking! I'm no good at it, and no one likes what I make, anyway."

"I do."

Gasping, Arden dropped her foot and spun around, her mouth still open, her eyes wide.

He was bigger than she remembered, taller, wider through the chest if that was possible. And he was wearing a conservative blue suit and a tie that actually seemed to match.

Aaron Cabot IV, M.D., every long lean inch of him.

Steffie took one look and flung herself in the strong, masculine arms already reaching for her. "I knew you'd come," she exclaimed, hugging his neck fiercely. His arms strained to keep from holding her too tight.

"Happy birthday, Slugger."

The Yankee vowels were more pronounced, the voice huskier than Arden remembered. Much, much huskier.

"Did you bring me something?" Stef asked.

"You bet." Shifting her arm, he reached into his suit pocket and pulled out a small silver package.

Steffie's eyes rounded. "It looks like jewelry."

His blue eyes rested for a long, intense moment on her small face, and Arden's heart began a slow tumbling. "Why don't you open it and see?" His gaze shifted, found Arden's. Held. "If it's okay with your mom, that is."

"Of course, it is," she managed to get out before Stef could ask.

He put Steffie down, then slowly straightened. Steffie hurried to the couch and sat down, the ribbon already torn away from the paper.

Forgotten until now, the smoke alarm continued to wail. Arden frowned, then started toward the hall.

"Let me," he said, his mouth twitching. "I've had practice."

By the time the shrieking had stopped and he'd returned, she had finger-combed her hair into halfway decent order, stopped gnawing her lip and cautioned herself twice not to expect anything more than an in-person goodbye.

"I, uh, guess I won't ask how you're doing." His gaze took in the mess, came back to rest on her face.

"Please don't." She found she was pressing her hands tightly together and dropped them to her sides.

"I should have written, phoned—"

"That's not necessary. You're always welcome here."

"That's something, anyway."

She hated the polite way they were treating each other. She hated not knowing why he'd come and how long he intended to stay. She hated the fear that made her unable to demand an explanation.

"The thing is, I wasn't sure I'd know how to say the things I've come to say." He slipped open the button closing his coat and shoved his hands into his trouser pockets. His waist was still lean beneath the beautiful tailoring, the white shirt an unfamiliar addition, and far too sexy.

"How about straight-out?"

"Sounds easy when you say it. Doesn't feel all that easy when I try it."

"Look what Dylan gave me, Mommy," Steffie called softly, her voice reverent. Arden jerked her attention to her daughter, who was cradling a tiny gold locket in the palm of her hand. Even at a distance, the superior craftsmanship and fine quality were readily apparent.

"It...belonged to my mother," he said when Arden's wondering gaze came back to his. "I hope you don't mind."

Too moved to speak, Arden slowly shook her head.

"Put it around my neck," Steffie ordered like a pint-size martinet, holding out her hand.

"Yes, ma'am." His face was grave, his tone solemn. Steffie giggled as she held her hair off the nape of her neck.

His mouth twitched and his gaze found Arden's. "Hasn't changed much, has she?"

Arden shook her head. No, Steffie hadn't changed, only grown taller, more secure in her school and friendships.

But he had. Not only the clothes, but the way he was looking at her, the way he sounded and walked. It was almost as though he was a different man.

"Turn around," he ordered gruffly.

"Yes, sir," Steffie shot back.

Wrinkling his brow in concentration, he slipped the delicate chain around her neck and fastened the minuscule clasp with a surgeon's deftness. It was then that she noticed the heavy gold signet ring on his finger. No doubt bearing the Cabot coat of arms.

"There, all finished." Dipping his head, he kissed the back of her neck, then stepped back.

"How do I look?" Steffie demanded, her preening gaze moving rapidly from one admiring adult to the other.

"Beautiful," they said in unison, then shared a startled look.

"I just gotta go down and show Eddie and the guys before the kids get here." She was already at the back door when she turned suddenly to give him a worried look. "You're not leaving?" she asked anxiously. "I mean, you're staying for the party?"

His mouth relaxed, and his eyes softened. "I'll be here."

The worry darkening her brown eyes disappeared, replaced by an excited sparkle. "Super!" The door banged behind her as she clattered down the steps.

Arden managed a smile. He shifted his feet, his shined shoes completely out of character for the man she remembered.

No Easy Way Out

"I understand you intend to sell your cabin."

He nodded. "Once I have a few things repaired." His smile was slow, even tentative. Arden's heart beat faster.

"Like just about everything," she murmured.

A muscle pulled in his jaw. "I acted like a jerk."

"You were hurting."

"I still miss her. Just driving past the street her house sits on made me realize how much."

"I miss her, too. I think we all do."

Silence fell. Was that the way it was going to be between them from now on? she wondered.

"I'm glad you and your father have reconciled," she said when she couldn't stand the tension a moment longer.

"Thank you. He sends you his regards."

"That's very kind of him."

His mouth moved. "I'll tell him you said so." He pulled his hands from his pockets and walked to the window. "Town looks good. More prosperous."

"Things are a little better. There's a new mill opening in a few months, and the hospital is adding a wing." She hesitated, then added softly, "Thanks to the generosity of an anonymous benefactor."

When she fell silent, he turned slowly to look at her.

"You?" she asked when their eyes met.

"And Father."

She studied his face, seeing deeper creases, new lines. A deeper strength. "Was it as bad as you thought? Prison, I mean."

Aaron moved his shoulders. "Not as bad as it could have been." Worse than he'd expected, however. Especially the black nights when he wasn't sure he would ever get out sane.

He waited, longing to see the welcoming smile he'd been imagining for two long years. Wondering if he'd misread the leap of joy in her eyes when she'd first seen him standing there.

Steffie hadn't hesitated. Her happiness at seeing him was real, so real he had felt humbled. Stef's mother, on the other hand, was tough to read. Damn tough. And that was frustrating the hell out of him. It wasn't a feeling he particularly relished, not after two long years of waiting for this moment.

"Don't take this wrong," he said, "but it looks like nothing has changed much with you, either." He cleared his throat. "Could have been worse, though. Spaghetti from a jar is awfully messy when it explodes."

Color rose in her face, and her eyes turned tawny with temper. "If you mean that I'm not a slave to household routine, you're right."

She kicked a piece of glass out of her way and stalked to the broom closet. Her movements were jerky, her cheeks getting pinker and pinker as she picked up the pan, threw it and the part of the ruined cake still clinging to the sides into the sink, and then set about sweeping cake and glass into a dustpan.

"Pardon me," she said when he neglected to move his big feet.

"Sorry," he drawled, stepping back a few paces. She was wearing slacks and a shirt, something silky and loose-fitting, rippling over her skin with each movement of her shoulders and arms.

Muttering something he didn't catch, she dumped the pan full of debris into the trash basket, then threw the broom and dustpan into the broom closet and slammed it shut.

"Now," she said, crossing her arms. "I'm ready. Go ahead."

He was still thinking about the creamy skin and soft secret places under her shirt, so it took him a moment to notice the dark turbulence of her eyes.

"Uh, give me a hint, okay?" His heart was thudding, and his throat was dry. For the life of him he couldn't figure out what she was thinking behind that small storm. Or, more importantly, feeling. About him. About them.

"It's very obvious to me that you've come here to tie up loose ends. Sell your house, sever your partnership with Neil, say goodbye to Steffie. And me."

"Looks like I can't fool a crackerjack newswoman like you, Ms. Crawford."

Her mouth formed a furious pout, and her hands moved to fist on her hips. If she'd stamped her foot, it wouldn't have surprised him. "Publisher. And I'm warning you, Kincade—"

"Cabot. Dylan Kincade's dead."

Her face changed. "I'll miss him, I think."

"Will you?"

She ran her tongue over her lip in that quick way that told him she was more nervous than she seemed. "Yes, I will. I did."

"I missed you, too." Even at forty-one, a man had only so much patience. "And I did come to sell my house and dissolve the partnership agreement I had with Neil, but only because it wasn't fifty-fifty and it should be. As to saying goodbye..."

He stopped, astonished to find out he was scared. More scared even than he'd been that first day in prison. All the confidence he'd built up on the long plane ride to Medford and the drive to Myrtle seemed to have dried up.

"I, uh, I brought something for you, too. A present."

He pulled another box from his pocket. Smaller than Steffie's. A plain white pasteboard box, unwrapped.

Her face twisted. "I'd rather you didn't," she said stiffly. "A nice, straightforward goodbye will do quite nicely."

"Maybe for you," he muttered. Taking her hand, he slapped the box into her palm. "Here, open."

Arden glared into those dark, commanding blue eyes, fighting to keep from throwing her arms around that bull neck of his and hanging on tight. "Don't give me orders."

His eyebrows drew together. "*Please* open the damned box," he said through a tight jaw.

A dozen retorts came to mind, but she couldn't utter a one. Not when her breath was hitching in her throat and her eyes were threatening to tear. She would *not* humiliate herself and beg him to stay.

Pleased to see that her fingers were shaking only slightly, she pulled the top off the box, then froze. Her head came up swiftly, her lips parting in shock. "It's a ring," she murmured, a little dazed, a little disbelieving.

"Looks like it." His grin came slowly, grew lopsided, a little shy. "Do you like it?"

She blinked, giving him his first good look at the lashes he'd imagined tickling his chest again for too many nights to count. "That depends."

"On what?"

"On what comes with it. Who comes with it."

The woman was impossible, he decided. Stubborn, bossy, a real handful for a man who was dreadfully out of practice when it came to women.

Neil had assured him three times at least that she was still in love with him, but Neil was still a kid. What did he know about reading women? He should have taken it slower, given her a chance to get used to him again.

Maybe court her the way his father had suggested. Flowers, champagne, maybe take her away for the weekend to some romantic spot by the Pacific. But, damn, he'd waited so long already, he'd gotten hard the day he'd bought his ticket and stayed hard. Two years of torture was enough for any man.

Furious now, he framed her face with his hands and kissed her hard. "What the hell do you think goes with it?" Before she could answer, he kissed her again. Harder. "A wedding, damn it. Maybe some kids."

She blinked. "Oh."

"Is that all? *Oh?*" He was ready to explode. Or turn tail and run. He stood his ground and decided to keep standing it until she gave in.

No Easy Way Out 243

Her lips curved slowly and her eyes grew very, very soft. "How about a little persuasion, tough guy?"

He was ready to strangle her. Instead, he pressed his mouth to hers in a long, slow, yearning kiss. A tremor ran though him, and he felt something break loose inside.

Lifting his mouth a few inches, he struggled against the violent need to haul her into bed and show her what two years of missing her could do to a man.

"How's that?" he whispered.

"Not bad," she whispered back, her eyes beautifully glazing over and her mouth pouting for more. "For a man who wrote one letter back for every three I sent him."

Heat seared his face. "I'm not much for putting things in words."

"I noticed."

"You're mad."

"You bet your life, I'm mad. Good and mad." She sucked in her breath. "Didn't it ever occur to you that I might have been sitting here worrying about you, wondering how you were coping, maybe needing to know that you were just a little worried about me, too?"

"I worried, especially when Dad told me Steffie's father was trying to win you back. I was sweating bullets until I found out you'd sent him packing."

She blinked. "*Who* told you about Mike?"

His face was getting hot, and his collar was pinching. "Uh, my father, actually. Via Neil."

"You had someone spying on me?"

"More like keeping track. I... They wouldn't let me call. What else could I do?"

"Oh, Dyl—Aaron. You softhearted... jerk."

With a groan he was helpless to prevent, he dragged her against him, his heart thudding against his best Boston stuffed shirt and tie.

"I'm sorry I didn't write more often," he whispered against her temple. Feeling her tremble took some of the edge off his panic. "And I'm sorry I couldn't come to you sooner."

"What was it you told Steffie once? 'Saying you're sorry is a good start, but it's only a start.'"

He kissed her hair and felt drunk on the familiar fragrance. She still fitted perfectly in his arms, and her arms were creeping around his neck, one small hand still fiercely clutching the ring box.

"How about this, then?" he asked, looking into the eyes he loved. "I'm crazy about you. Over-the-moon nuts about you, and damn near as crazy about that bossy daughter of yours." He dropped a kiss on her nose, then nuzzled his forehead against hers. "If you won't marry me, I'll hang around and pester you until you say yes just to get rid of me."

He drew back. "How's that?" His voice was rasped, his gut tight.

Her eyes were soft, her lips parted. He nearly lost it when she suddenly brushed them over his mouth. "Better," she murmured.

"You drive a hard bargain, lady," he muttered.

"Compromise, remember?"

"Yeah, I remember." His voice wasn't quite steady and he had a feeling he'd better sit down damn soon, before his knees gave out on him. He closed his eyes, took a deep breath and squared his shoulders.

"Okay," he muttered. "This is my last offer." He took another breath, then said very softly, "I need you, Arden Crawford, on any terms you decide to set. If you want compromise, I'll give you compromise. If you want fancy words, I'll try to give you those. Anything you want."

He paused. She waited. He scowled, ran his big hand through his hair. Scowled again, then sighed. He had a feeling he'd better get used to giving in to this woman.

"Damn it, I love you. Is that what you wanted to hear?"

Her smile was very gentle, very loving. The most beautiful welcome-home smile he'd ever seen.

"Perfect," she murmured. "Absolutely, totally, wonderfully perfect. I couldn't have put it better myself."

And then she was suddenly too busy being kissed to say any more for a long, long time.

Epilogue

The party was in full swing when Arden found Aaron at her elbow again. He smelled like soap and ice cream. Chocolate chocolate chip. He'd bought four gallons for the kids, one for himself.

"C'mon," he whispered close to her ear. "Neil's going to play chaperon to these hellions for a while so you and I can take a walk."

Arden was absolutely certain she hadn't stopped smiling since he'd slipped the magnificent square cut diamond onto her finger.

Neil hadn't noticed the ring, but he'd seen the glow in her eyes and guessed. His congratulations were heartfelt, and just a bit relieved, especially when he found out he wasn't losing a partner, just gaining a larger share of the partnership.

Steffie had noticed the ring as soon as she'd appeared upstairs again and had smugly assured her mother and soon-to-be stepfather that she was not a bit surprised. And furthermore, when were they going to get busy on making a baby?

Arden was kept busy wondering that same thing every time Aaron looked at her and she saw the sexual frustration in his blue eyes.

Hand in hand they slipped down the front steps, as furtive as eloping teenagers. Aaron didn't wait until they reached the bottom before lowering his head to kiss her.

Now, as they strolled along the quiet streets, Arden noticed a new contentment about him, as though he'd finally come to terms with his past and learned to deal with the guilt that she suspected would always be with him.

"I love fall in the mountains," she murmured, breathing in the crisp, wood-scented air.

"I love you," he said, watching her closely, just as he'd been doing all evening.

"I know," she murmured. "You've told me that a lot tonight."

His mouth quirked. "I've been saving up."

"I'm glad."

When they reached a more sparsely populated section of Spruce Street, he drew her to a stop under a towering oak. "There are some things I need to explain."

"All right."

"First, I need to hold you." He drew her into the loose circle of his arms and rested his cheek against her temple.

He'd discarded his coat and tie, opened his collar and rolled up his sleeves. He seemed more like the man she'd fallen in love with, and yet different. It was that difference that had her keeping a part of herself separate.

He drew back slowly, his eyes troubled. An obvious reticence deepened the creases alongside his hard mouth and crinkled his eyes.

"I know you were hurt that I didn't come back here when I was granted parole last summer," he said slowly, as though feeling his way. "I had intended to, but when the parole board started making things difficult, it was like..." He shrugged, then took a moment to collect his thoughts.

Resting against him, her arms around his waist and her cheek against his chest, she waited, sensing that the things he needed to say were coming from some very vulnerable place inside him. Perhaps one he'd never opened before.

"It was all mixed up inside me," he said in a low, rough tone. "The things I did wrong, the alienation from my family, the life I'd had here. You."

He kissed her, his mouth hungry for hers. But the steely control was still there. In many ways it would always be there. But not in every way. Not anymore.

"Part of me was Dylan, part of me was Aaron," he went on, more quickly now, as though he were on firmer ground. "I had to figure out who I was and what I really wanted before I came to you. So I served my parole in Boston, did my best to mend my fences with my sisters and a few old friends, and worked my tail off helping Father in the OR."

And he had wanted her so much he'd had to resort to lacing his hot chocolate with brandy damn near every night before he could fall asleep.

"I imagine you learned a lot," she murmured, letting him know that she knew and accepted how important his work was to him. Would always be.

"More than I thought I would." He sighed. "God, my old man's good with a knife." The pride shining in his eyes warmed her. The wounds hadn't completely healed, but they were well on their way.

"He wanted you to stay, didn't he?"

He nodded. "I said no. I belong here, where the other half of my family lives."

Her heart started thumping harder. "And where your patients have been impatiently waiting to welcome you home."

His mouth thinned. "I hope so. But I know I have a lot of fences to mend here."

"Maybe not as many as you think," she whispered, nudging him with an elbow. "Look."

He frowned, his eyes taking on the old guarded look as he followed the direction of her gaze. The old garage he expected to see on the corner had been torn down, leaving a vacant lot between this street and the next.

Beyond the empty lot was the big, ugly old house that housed his office and Neil's. Yellow ribbons, most faded to near white and many little more than tattered shreds, hung from every branch on every tree in the big front yard. By the looks of them, they'd been there a long time, waiting to welcome him back.

He had to work hard to keep from breaking down and bawling, something that would have had him running for cover faster than anything else. Except losing the woman in his arms.

"Was that your idea?" he asked, gazing down at the face he adored.

"Mine and Stef's and just about everyone else in town. We love you." Her cheeks dimpled. "Doc."

His chest heaved. This time he was the one gnawing on his lip and fighting back tears. Her own eyes began to fill.

"There's just one thing I'm not sure of," she murmured softly.

His eyes grew worried. "What's that, honey?"

She pretended to think, loving the look of pure masculine impatience crossing his face.

"It's like this," she said when she sensed he reached the end of his always short fuse. "I just got used to having a man named Dylan in my bed. Now, he's gone, and there's another man who says he wants to make love to me." She peeked at him from suddenly lowered lashes. "You, um, did say that, didn't you?"

His deep-throated growl of frustration had her insides warming. "But I'm a one-man woman, and I'm not sure how I'm going to like having this guy Aaron as a lover. Or a husband."

His arms tightened, and his head lowered. "Tell you what, honey," he whispered close to her mouth. "You just trust old Doc Cabot. He'll take care of you."

Arden smiled against his hungry mouth and wondered if Nettie, too, was nestled into the arms of the man she loved, then knew with absolute certainty that she was. And that she was smiling.

* * * * *

And now for something completely different from Silhouette....

SPELLBOUND ROMANCE

Unique and innovative stories that take you into the world of paranormal happenings. Look for our special "Spellbound" flash—and get ready for a truly exciting reading experience!

In February, look for
One Unbelievable Man (SR #993)
by Pat Montana.

Was he man or myth? Cass Kohlmann's mysterious traveling companion, Michael O'Shea, had her all confused. He'd suddenly appeared, claiming she was his destiny—determined to win her heart. But could levelheaded Cass learn to believe in fairy tales...before her fantasy man disappeared forever?

Don't miss the charming, sexy and utterly mysterious Michael O'Shea in
ONE UNBELIEVABLE MAN.
Watch for him in February—only from

Silhouette
ROMANCE™

SPELL2

SPRING fancy '94

They're sexy, single...
and about to get snagged!

Passion is in full bloom as love catches
the fancy of three brash bachelors. You won't
want to miss these stories by three of
Silhouette's hottest authors:

**CAIT LONDON
DIXIE BROWNING
PEPPER ADAMS**

Spring fever is in the air this March—
and there's no avoiding it!

Only from Silhouette®

where passion lives.

HE'S AN
AMERICAN HERO

January 1994 rings in the New Year—and a new lineup of sensational American Heroes. You can't seem to get enough of these men, and we're proud to feature one each month, created by some of your favorite authors.

January: CUTS BOTH WAYS by Dee Holmes: Erin Kenyon hired old acquaintance Ashe Seager to investigate the crash that claimed her husband's life, only to learn old memories never die.

February: A WANTED MAN by Kathleen Creighton: Mike Lanagan's exposé on corruption earned him accolades...and the threat of death. Running for his life, he found sanctuary in the arms of Lucy Brown—but for how long?

March: COOPER by Linda Turner: Cooper Rawlings wanted nothing to do with the daughter of the man who'd shot his brother. But when someone threatened Susannah Patterson's life, he found himself riding to the rescue....

AMERICAN HEROES: Men who give all they've got for their country, their work—the women they love.

Only from

INTIMATE MOMENTS®
Silhouette®

IMHERO7

INTIMATE MOMENTS®
Silhouette®

THE WILD WEST
by Linda Turner

Out in The Wild West, life is rough, tough and dangerous, but the Rawlings family can handle anything that comes their way—well, *almost* anything!

American Hero Cooper Rawlings didn't know what hit him when he met Susannah Patterson, daughter of the man who'd shot his brother in the back. He *should* have hated her on sight. But he didn't. Instead he found himself saddling up and riding to her rescue when someone began sabotaging her ranch and threatening her life. Suddenly lassoing this beautiful but stubborn little lady into his arms was the only thing he could think about.

Don't miss COOPER (IM #553), available in March. And look for the rest of the clan's stories—Flynn and Kat's—as Linda Turner's exciting saga continues in

THE WILD WEST

Coming to you throughout 1994...only from Silhouette Intimate Moments.

If you missed the first book in THE WILD WEST series, GABLE'S LADY (IM #523), order your copy now by sending your name, address, zip or postal code, along with a check or money order (please do not send cash) for $3.50, plus 75¢ postage and handling ($1.00 in Canada), payable to Silhouette Books, to:

In the U.S.	In Canada
Silhouette Books	Silhouette Books
3010 Walden Ave.	P. O. Box 636
P. O. Box 9077	Fort Erie, Ontario
Buffalo, NY 14269-9077	L2A 5X3

Please specify book title with your order.
Canadian residents add applicable federal and provincial taxes.

WILD2

**It's our 1000th
Silhouette Romance
and we're celebrating!**

Join us for a special collection of love stories by the authors you've loved for years, and new favorites you've just discovered.

**It's a celebration just for you,
with wonderful books by
Diana Palmer, Suzanne Carey,
Tracy Sinclair, Marie Ferrarella,
Debbie Macomber, Laurie Paige,
Annette Broadrick, Elizabeth August
and MORE!**

Silhouette Romance...vibrant, fun and emotionally rich! Take another look at us!

As part of the celebration, readers can receive a FREE gift AND enter our exciting sweepstakes to win a grand prize of $1000! Look for more details in all March Silhouette series titles.

**You'll fall in love all over again
with Silhouette Romance!**

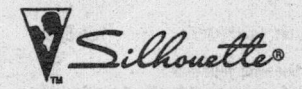

Silhouette®

CEL1000T

**Relive the romance...
Harlequin and Silhouette
are proud to present**

by Request™

A program of collections of three complete novels by the most requested authors with the most requested themes. Be sure to look for one volume each month with three complete novels by top name authors.

In January: **WESTERN LOVING** Susan Fox
JoAnn Ross
Barbara Kaye

Loving a cowboy is easy—taming him isn't!

In February: **LOVER, COME BACK!** Diana Palmer
Lisa Jackson
Patricia Gardner Evans

It was over so long ago—yet now they're calling, "Lover, Come Back!"

In March: **TEMPERATURE RISING** JoAnn Ross
Tess Gerritsen
Jacqueline Diamond

Falling in love—just what the doctor ordered!

Available at your favorite retail outlet.

REQ-G3

HARLEQUIN®   Silhouette

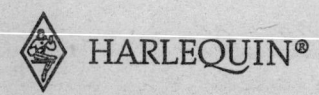

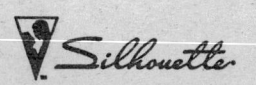